I'll Be Yours

JENNY B. JONES

Cover Design: Jenny Zemanek/Seedlings Design Studio

For information contact:
Jen@jennybjones.com

Follow Social Media:
Instagram: @JennyBJonesAuthor

Facebook:
facebook.com/jennybjones

Twitter:
twitter.com/JenBJones

Sign up for Jenny's Book News
www.jennybjones.com/news

Chapter One

SOMETIMES I STARE out my bedroom window, find the North Star, and wonder if it's shining down elsewhere—on the life I was supposed to live.

A different version.

With different people.

And a different me.

When I was nine, I came to live with the O'Malleys. For my eleventh birthday, they adopted me. Rescued me, really.

They were a family of beautiful, athletic, overachievers.

And me?

Let's just say if life were a nerd parade, I'd be its grand marshal.

"Harper, you just sighed three times in fifteen minutes." My mom passed me a bowl of peas. "Are you feeling okay, honey?"

"Yeah." I handed the offensive vegetables off to the person to my right, pulling my thoughts from the deep, dark edge, then shooting my two brothers a glare at their buffoonish guffaws. "Here, DeShawn. Your favorite."

"Are you sure?" Mom asked again.

"Maybe after the guys leave, we could talk?"

Her pink lips gave me that familiar smile. "Of course."

"What's wrong over there?" my dad asked from the end of a table big enough to feed half of Kentucky and still leave elbow room.

"Nothing." I adjusted the napkin in my lap, gaining the rapt attention of the two dogs on guard beside me. Jay-Z and Kanye were not stupid. If there was any time to expect floor scraps, it was when the football team came to dine. I'm a vegetarian who eats a whole lot of salads and beans, so the mutts gave up on me long ago.

"I know what's wrong with her." My oldest brother, Michael, wore a grin as wicked as a snake rattle.

I felt the earth shift beneath my chair.

Oh, no. Not this. Not now.

Not with them.

"That's enough, Michael. I don't need you to—"

"Harper likes a boy."

Fifteen heads swerved in unison.

I sank lower in my chair. And watched the table explode.

This wasn't just any dining room table. It was Coach O'Malley's table. Almost every Sunday, my mom, dad, two brothers, and I sat down for pot roast or fried chicken. And so did about a fourth of the football team from the University of Southern Kentucky.

Voices fired around me like grenades, and I did what any miserable girl could. I reached for more gravy.

"Who is he?"

"He dat punk kid who wears the trench?"

"I want a name!"

"What's his GPA?"

"He treat his mama right?"

"Where's that fool live?"

"You got pictures?"

"He got a hot sister?"

Even with my burning face and exasperated thoughts, I

couldn't help but smile.

Though the faces of the players changed through the years, their presence in my life, at my dinner table—it was a constant I held close to my heart.

Most times I wouldn't have traded it for anything.

This wasn't one of those moments.

I had finally, *finally* contracted the Love Plague.

And the only remedy was Andrew James Wesley Levin.

A boy so fabulous his parents had to give him three names just to contain all the wonder. He was basically the most amazing junior at Washington High School to ever sit in the trumpet section.

Unfortunately, when it came to guys, I was kind of remedial. We're talking *way* behind.

At the age of ten, while my friends were writing love notes, I was watching *Shark Week*. When I was twelve, my friends all proudly had boyfriends. I just wanted to show off my VIP library card.

But six weeks ago, during an ordinary Monday of my junior year at Washington High, I got it.

The Boy Crazies.

It was as if a fairy had tapped me on my curly head and sprinkled love glitter and man-awareness magic.

Because on that auspicious day in September, not only did Andrew enroll at WHS, but he showed up in my band class.

Boys were scary business to me, but I had resolved to push through the fear this time. I would have a normal crush if it killed me. Not only could I confirm that I liked Andrew, but also I had developed a strategic plan in winning him over. So far I hadn't implemented it, unless you considered stalking him from afar my warm-up.

The doorbell rang, and the melody was a chime of salvation. "I'll get it!" I jumped up and ran toward the foyer. Sensing imminent danger, one of the dogs leaped after me, ready to maim someone with slobber.

I cut through the living room, walking past framed pictures hanging on walls and occupying tables. Pictures of my dad clutching championship trophies. My mom smiling at the finish line of the Boston Marathon. My brother Michael shooting a buzzer-beating three. Ten-year-old Cole in a graceful leap over a hurdle.

Oh, look. There was one of me. Holding a band camp certificate.

The bell sounded again, and mid-impatient ding, I swung the door wide open.

And I did not like what I saw.

I blinked against the sun, the heat, the arrogance.

On my front step stood Ridley Estes.

I took in his dark jeans and his Washington Wildcat T-shirt, observing a tiny hole in his sleeve and the outline of muscles sculpted from years of football. A baseball cap covered the short-cropped black hair that complemented his Latin skin, which looked forever tan. Pasty white girls like myself noticed these sorts of things.

"Hello . . ." His voice trailed off, as if he'd just hung a question mark in the air.

"Harper," I reminded him. "My name is Harper." I gave my best first-chair trumpet stare of intimidation. But it was no use for the one the girls called Ridley with all the reverence and awe usually reserved for pop stars and movie heartthrobs. Wide receiver of my high school football team, a little too rugged to be an Abercrombie model, king of campus, and unexpected guest.

A guy who'd clearly made an illicit deal with the underworld.

I couldn't stand his type. Too cool to be aware of the rest of us mere mortals. Used to everyone *oohing* and *aahing* over him.

"Harper," he said, trying my name out on his lips. "I knew that."

"Oh, no reason to." His crooked grin was a rubber band on the sunburn of my annoyance. "Just because we've been at the same school for four years, we had art together, and last year your locker was over mine." Constantly hitting me in the head while he snuggled up to some honey. "No reason at all."

He cocked his head as his brown eyes studied me. "I'm sensing some anger issues here, *Harper*. You might want to do something about that. Frustration could shrivel up some of those genius brain cells."

Before I could respond, he looked past my shoulder and straightened his six-foot posture.

"Can I help you with something?" I asked. *Like letting some air out of that ego?*

He stared right through me. "Your brother invited me to lunch."

"With the team? I doubt—"

"Ridley!" Michael stood behind me and nudged me out of the way. "Don't mind her. Come on in. Get yourself a seat."

The two filed on into the dining room, and I was left to walk in their shadow.

"Dad, you know Ridley."

My dad's smile slipped as he sent a sharp eye to Michael. "Son, we live and die by NCAA rules in this house," he said quietly. "I don't have to tell you that possible recruits cannot be sitting with me at my dining room table."

"He's not." My brother plopped back in his seat and grabbed

another cob of corn. "He's sitting at *my* dinner table."

Dad mumbled something about a waiver and violations, but nobody else seemed too concerned.

So Ridley was a possible University of Southern Kentucky recruit. I knew he was good, but I hadn't known he was *that* good. Normally my dad liked boys who had decent GPAs and stayed out of trouble. Surely that counted Ridley out.

The campus darling settled into a chair beside my brother.

Forks paused. Water glasses stopped mid-sip.

The stare down began. Happened every time a new person sat at our table, especially one who had his eye on being an Eagle. My football family was protective of us. Plus, they didn't like to share Mom's chocolate pie.

Mom cleared her throat. "Well, I'm glad you can join us." She gave the team the discreet glare that promised dish duty to anyone not behaving. "We always love having the kids' friends around. You know Harper, right?"

"Oh, yeah." Ridley had the nerve to smile. "We go way back."

My mother introduced my younger brother, then quickly named off the team.

Michael sent the senior captain a look that said, "He's cool."

Dominic Vago nodded, then smacked Ridley on the back. "Get you some potatoes. Mama O'Malley makes some mean mashed potatoes."

"Yeah." Tyler Nicholson talked with his mouth around a bite of green beans. "You gotta try her garlic bread too. She makes that herself, dude. It's not frozen or nothing."

"You guys are so sweet." My mom's face flushed pink as my dad wrapped an arm around her chair and gave her a quick kiss on the cheek.

"The lady can cook," Dad said. "These Sunday lunches will add at least another hour to your workout."

Ridley took the platter of roast from the junior wide receiver. "Sounds worth it to me."

"Harper"—Marcus Ross pushed up his glasses with a fat finger—"you were telling us the name of this boy you like."

My eyes automatically flew to Ridley. Then away. Anywhere but him. "No. No, I wasn't."

"Yeah, she's wasn't," said my ten year-old brother. "Michael was."

I shot my oldest brother a look promising creative forms of death and torture. To no avail.

"His name is Andrew Levin."

"No, it's not!" I shook my head like my hair was on fire. "It's not. I don't like anyone. That's just the name of some boy at school. Michael, I don't even know where you got that."

Cole took a bite of potatoes. "Your laptop. The file labeled *diary*."

The blood drained from my face, my arms, my legs. If I looked down, surely there would be a pool of it at my feet.

"Did you read your sister's diary?" Mom's voice carried an edge that let my brother know he would be dealt with later.

"He like you back?" Marcus asked.

Marcus sat at my right, and I had to admit he was one of my favorites. Overweight, short, and totally in the closet. The book-reading closet, that is. Over the past two years, we'd spent many an hour talking Harry Potter, Shakespeare, and the psychology crap his professors made him read.

"He does not like her back," Cole said. "Ow! Quit kicking me, Michael. You told me that's what it said."

I wanted to die. I wanted to flop in the floor like an oxygen-deprived fish in my torment and slip away into the great beyond—far, far away from this inhumane humiliation. My brothers were clearly conspiring to make sure I had zero self-respect left. Might as well announce to the table that I'd never had a date. That I'd never been properly kissed. That the only reason I had boobs was because I bought them at Victoria's Secret.

"He'd be a fool not to chase you, Harper." My dad smiled and gave me his comforting slow wink. Just one drop of the eyelid, one easy grin, and for a few seconds, I felt special. Beautiful.

I just wished it was enough for Andrew Levin.

"We should probably meet this dude." Tyler Nicholson turned to Michael. "You know him?"

"Nah."

"I do." Ridley set down a pitcher of tea and looked right at me.

At this, the whole team broke out into celebration, like the boy had just handed off the game-winning pass.

"Let's hear it." Dominic cut into his roast beef. "Oh, girl, you in trouble now."

"Maybe we should respect her privacy," Marcus said.

"Yes, let's." I stared down every single member of the team.

Fifteen men dropped their attention back to their plates, and knives and forks clanked as they quietly returned to their lunch.

"Then again," laughed Marcus, "she's always up in my business."

The table once again erupted into shouts, and soon the questions flew anew. Only this time for Ridley.

Mr. Arrogance watched me from the opposite end of the table, a pirate's smile curving those lips. "I could talk to him for you, Harper."

"That won't be necessary." As I expected to self-combust within the next minute.

"Just think," Michael said. "If the Eagles offer Ridley a contract, he'll be eating with us every Sunday."

I glared at my brother's newest annoying friend.

I was angry that he had shown up. Even more angry at my brothers.

But determined more than ever to be Andrew Levin's next girlfriend.

Chapter Two

"**H**ARPER, OFFICER LAMAR called."

I watched my one-eared cat Lazarus sashay through the kitchen as I swallowed the most perfect combination of vanilla ice cream and Oreos. "Oh?"

My mom reached around my dad for the Rocky Road to serve up in his special "World's Best Father" dish. It was our Sunday ritual. Big Sunday lunch after church with the team, then a supper of something light and frivolous—banana splits, popcorn, or cereal. I was grateful it was ice cream night.

"Michael, did you need some help with your homework?" I asked. But my mom would not be diverted from the subject.

"He said a man over on Davis Street reported two of his dogs missing. Know anything about that?"

That they were in a better place? "Mom, I'm hurt and offended you would think I had something to do with this." Fifteen animal cruelty rescues to my credit in the last year. Officer Lamar called it stealing. I called it . . . emancipating.

"Any takers on these two?" Dad stepped over the black poodle–mix. "Are you even trying to find them a home?"

"It's hard." I rubbed the top of the spoiled pit bull's head. "Jay-Z and Kanye have to go together."

I volunteered at an animal rescue in town and often fostered strays, including the two we had now. The fact that I was forever picking dog hair off my clothes obviously added to my sexy allure.

We all stood in the kitchen, hovering over bowls, scoops, and sprinkles. My parents and brothers were as tan as Hawaiian natives compared to me. We'd gone to Cozumel in June, and even months later, they still looked completely bronzed and Coppertoned. My tinge of pink had faded before the returning plane had touched down, and I was back to my usual translucent self. They all shared the same hair color, a beautiful chestnut that shimmered with threads of auburn and gold when the light hit it just right. My own blonde locks matched my complexion, so faint it was nearly white. My favorite feature was my blue eyes. Because they looked like the ocean, the summer sky. They looked just like my adoptive dad's.

My dad squirted some whipped cream on Cole's ice cream. "Harper is a reformed girl. She said last week she gave it up, and I believe her." He took the can and plopped some white stuff right on my brother's button nose.

"Oh, by the way, sis, that Mavis lady from the shelter left you a message. She said some man called about a dog that was tied up. She said, and I quote, 'You know what to do.'"

"Must've been a wrong number," I said. This was the third time some old man had called the shelter about a neighbor's dog. We hadn't been able to get the terrier yet, but I had done enough recon to know it was time.

"Pretty funny that Harper's gonna be the first one with a record." Michael gave a snort so obnoxious, I wanted to kick a shin.

"Too bad serial dating bimbos isn't illegal," I said.

"Nothing criminal about my dating practices. It's my gift to the ladies of—"

"No one in this family is going to get arrested." Mom turned those eagle eyes to me. "Ever. The first kid to get a mug shot gets disowned."

"And not inherit Daddy's trophy collection?" I leaned my head against my dad's shoulders. "Tragic."

He pulled me to him and planted a kiss atop my head. "I'm sure Harper heard us loud and clear last week when we talked grounding and car removal. If she said she didn't take those two dogs, then she didn't." He lowered his voice for my ears only. "This animal stealing career of yours is over. Those two spaniels are smelling up my shed. You have twenty-four hours to move them."

Dad's words put the lid on any more quick remarks I had to fire. What did I cherish above innocent cats, malnourished dogs, and the occasional disrespected chicken? My desire to lock heart and lips to one Andrew Levin.

"Speaking of trouble—" Dad's voice went all coachy as he gave his attention to Michael, and I was relieved to be off the hook. "I'm sure Ridley Estes told you we made an offer for him last Wednesday."

Michael shrugged. "I dunno. He might've mentioned it. Who can keep up with that stuff?"

"The NCAA?" Dad had that tick thing going in his jaw. "He can't be hanging around here until he's signed."

"Signing isn't 'til spring."

"Then we get a waiver for now."

"Then do that because he's going to be coming around. He's my friend."

"Since when?" I asked. My brother typically hung out with the other basketball players.

"He's been helping me with my workouts. Dude is cut. Unlike your dork crush."

"Who has more brains than you and Estes put together."

"Ridley is really trying to get it together," Michael said. "He knows he has a lot on the line. Harper, I told him you tutor some of the Eagles. Since he's as good as one of them now, you should offer your tutoring services to him."

"Yeah, I'll get right on that." I didn't have time to take on any more tutoring. I had a job at the shelter, a boyfriend to snare, and one more dog out on a county road that was desperately waiting for a rescue.

"Just watch it." Dad grabbed his keys off the kitchen counter. "I'm putting my neck out there by bringing that kid on. He's a risk. And I don't want that to blow up in my face for any reason." His cell phone vibrated and he gave it a quick check. "I gotta go."

"Now?" Mom put her bowl down. "John, you can't leave now." Sunday night was our only night of the week to be together during the craziness of the football season. It was sacred time. "We were going to watch a movie."

"Yeah, Dad, you bailed on us last weekend too." Cole consoled himself with more hot fudge.

"I'm sorry." Dad shoved his phone into the pocket of his Eagles polo. "One of the boys got in trouble last night, and I need to go talk to him."

I hoped it wasn't one that I tutored. "Who is it?"

Dad gave me a quick kiss on the cheek. "I'll be back in a few hours." And with a ruffle to Cole's hair, he left the four of us standing in the kitchen.

Mom sighed.

Michael rolled his eyes.

I grabbed the container of Blue Bell. "Dibs on the couch. Oh, and Michael, about reading my diary?"

"Yeah?"

"That's going to be amateur hour." I took a bite of ice cream. "Compared to my revenge."

"So tell me about this boy."

My mom posed this question about halfway into a movie about zombies and aliens duking it out for control of the universe. When you lived with two brothers, your suggestions of rom-coms and animal-friendly documentaries got vetoed in favor of mind-numbing cinematic disasters every time.

Mom sat next to me on the couch with her laptop. I took a peek at the article she was reading. "Making Moments Count: When the Team Sees Coach More Than You Do." *Ouch.* But what did she expect? It was the height of football season, and Dad had a solid team this year. It was basically like this every fall. Sharing our dad was all we'd ever known.

The house phone rang, and I started to get up. "I should probably answer that."

"Leave it," Mom said, petting a purring Laz, who was curled up beside her. "What you should do is answer my question." From the kitchen came the garbled sound of a message being left and ignored.

"Andrew is. . ." I tugged on the sleeve of my shirt, pulling it toward my wrist. Fall had hit my town of Maple Grove hard, but I sported long sleeves year-round. "He's just a guy at school. In band."

Mom smiled and nudged me with her shoulder. "What does he look like?"

"A Greek god."

Michael laughed from across the room. "Yeah, minus all the

muscles and the pretty face and good personality."

I grabbed the remote and punched up the volume. Michael's dating bar was set so low, I'm surprised it didn't trip him. So I definitely did not want his input. "He's gorgeous," I said to Mom. "He's very musical. And he has this laugh . . ."

"Have you talked to him much? Does he know you're interested?"

"He doesn't even know she's alive."

"Shut up, Michael!" I threw a pillow and nailed him in the head. "At least he hasn't made out with half the school population, unlike your current girlfriend who—"

My phone blasted, interrupting my rant and my brothers' hearty chuckles. If I had a dollar for every time I'd begged my parents to send my brothers to boarding school . . .

I looked down at my phone and saw it was my BFF, Molly. I also saw that I'd missed ten texts.

Breaking a rule of movie night, I got up and stepped into the hall. "What's up, Mol?"

"Turn your TV on."

"It is on. We're watching *Zombies and*—"

"Harper, *now*. Channel 7."

"Molly, what is it?" I walked back into the living room.

"It's your dad."

I dropped the phone and lunged for the remote. With a few buttons, I turned off the movie and brought up Channel 7.

There on the screen was Chevy Moncrief, the university's athletic director.

". . . confirm there was an accident tonight involving Coach O'Malley."

My mom jumped from the couch. "Where's my phone?"

In my head I began a litany of pleas to God. *Let him be okay.*

Let my dad be okay.

". . . was driving his motorcycle without a helmet . . ."

My dad never rode without his helmet.

"He apparently lost control of the motorcycle on a curve, and it flew out from under him."

My pulse hammered in my head. I was dimly aware of Michael standing beside me, my shoulder pressed to him. My arms pulled Cole to me, holding him close.

"I can confirm that Coach O'Malley is pretty banged up."

Dad was alive. Thank God.

"He's in stable condition and currently being treated at St. Vincent's Hospital. Coach O'Malley's suffered a broken arm, a concussion, quite a few lacerations, and some other minor injuries. He's a very lucky man to be alive."

The blood began to move in my body again. My dad was going to be okay. "Was Coach alone?" a reporter asked.

Chevy Moncrief took a visible breath. "I'm giving you all the information I have at this time. Thank you. That's all."

Mom burst into the living room. "I've got to go to the hospital. Your dad—" She froze mid-stride as her eyes locked on the TV. "Turn it off."

"But—"

"Turn it off!" She ripped the remote from my shaking fingers and the TV went dark. Cole sniffled beside me, and I patted his back.

"What's going on, Mom?" I asked.

"Your dad was in an accident."

Michael nodded toward the TV. "We know."

Mom pulled Cole into her arms and pressed her lips to his head. "He's going to be okay, sweetie. Your dad is okay."

My ice cream did a somersault in my stomach. "We want to

see Dad. I want to talk to him."

"No." Mom looked at Michael and me. "I've got to go. People have been trying to reach me for hours. I need to go see him myself. Then I'll call when I know the situation."

"Is he gonna die?" Cole's voice was small and younger than his ten years.

"No, baby." Mom smoothed back his hair and gave a tight smile. "You listen to your brother and sister. I'll call when I get there and get an update." My phone rang as Michael's buzzed. "Talk to no one," Mom said. "I mean it. You speak to no one but me. I don't want anything we say funneled to the media. Am I clear? And keep that TV off."

The three of us nodded. We stood there for several minutes after Mom left. The ceiling fan overhead whirred in the otherwise silent living room.

I looked at Michael's pale face. "So . . . Mom said we had to stay here."

"Right." He rubbed the back of his neck. "We'd get in major trouble if we went to the hospital."

Cole sniffed. "So which one of you is driving?"

Chapter Three

I DROVE MY Honda Civic like it was the front-runner in the Indianapolis 500.

I navigated a turn a little too sharply, and in the rearview mirror I saw Cole's head bobble to the left.

"Mom seemed mad," I said. *Dad's hurt, and she's angry?*

"She's just upset," Michael said. "She probably feels guilty for not answering her phone."

Pulling into the emergency room lot, I wheeled into the nearest parking spot. The three of us jumped out. I wrapped my arm around Cole's thin shoulders and let Michael lead the way.

The sun sank in the distance, and at eight thirty, the November air carried a sharp chill. The doors swished open, emptying us into a waiting room of people holding their stories of distress. A mother rocking her feverish baby. An old woman sitting alone, trembling in a wheelchair. A wife pressing an ice pack to her husband's head.

Michael walked to the front desk and leaned close to the man behind it. His badge declared his name was Bob. "We're here to see John O'Malley." Michael showed him his license, proving he and Dad shared the same last name.

"No visitors for the coach."

"Please," I whispered. "He's our father."

Bob shook his head. "I'm sorry. Strict orders."

We expected this. For the last five years, my dad had been

coach of one of the top college football teams in the nation. He'd rescued the Eagles from years of neglect and losses. John O'Malley had put USK back on the map. And John O'Malley had made himself famous.

I nudged Cole. He knew what to do.

My brother stepped forward, locked eyes on the man behind the desk, and let his bottom lip quiver. "Please . . . please, sir. My daddy . . . we're so scared." He swiped at his tears. "I just need to see him. To know he's okay. To tell him I love him." Cole's tortured eyes met mine. "I didn't even get to tell him I loved him today." With one last parting look to Bob and a tiny little whimper, Cole lowered his head to the counter and cried into his hands.

I patted Cole's back. "It's okay. If anything happens to dad . . . we still have our memories." I sniffed twice.

Bob heaved a deep breath and glanced behind him. "You swear you're the coach's kids?"

I nodded.

He scribbled a number on a Post-it. "He's already been admitted. Go through those double doors, then take the elevator. Fourth floor."

No one said a word in the elevator. A sign on the wall invited us to a class for breast-feeding moms. The woman on the poster smiled as if there was nothing that could make her happier. On the other wall, a colorful poster asked if my STD had me down.

The doors opened, and the blue-tiled hallway stretched before us.

"Hold up." Cole came to a stop as we passed the bathrooms. "I gotta go."

"Now?" I hissed.

"This is what stress does to me." He clutched his stomach.

"Stress?" Michael lifted a brow. "Or the beef jerky you were eating in the backseat?"

"Give me two minutes."

"I'm going to see Dad," I said to Michael. "You can deal with this one."

I left my brothers standing in the dust of my anxiety and runaway fears. I just wanted to see for myself that my dad was okay. A week didn't go by that I didn't have a nightmare about losing one of the O'Malleys. Or them kicking me out of the family. I wasn't the same shell of a scared girl they'd adopted years ago, but some of the old fears still lurked and taunted.

Room 407.

Outside the door stood two burly men I recognized as security from the university.

"Good evening, gentlemen."

"Hey, Harper," said the one in a USK cap.

The other held up his large hand. "Let me get your mom."

"No need." I stepped past them and opened the door.

And stood in the entry. Behind the pulled curtain.

When I heard my dad's voice, my feet locked to the floor.

"Talk to me, Cristy," he said.

"What do you want me to say?" My mom's tone was thin, strained. "You tell me what happened."

"I just did."

"Again, John."

"Don't do this."

"Start at the beginning."

My heart beat three times until he answered. "I picked her up."

"Josie," Mom added.

Who?

"Yes," Dad said. "I picked Josie up and we went for a ride. I overshot the curve and lost control. The bike went out from under us. And then she—"

"You've been riding your whole life. You don't miss curves."

"I looked away for a second."

"At her?"

Fear was a clammy hand that wrapped itself around my throat, cutting off my air, pulling me down. My dad had been on his bike with a woman. A woman who was not my mother.

"Where was your helmet?" Mom demanded.

"She was wearing it." My dad's voice broke. "I . . . could've killed her. Both of us, Cristy. I never meant for this to happen. The accident . . . this relationship. I don't understand—"

"I don't understand how my husband was sleeping with another woman. How long has this been going on?"

Hot nausea snaked through my gut as reality roared in my ears.

"I've got to get out of here," Dad said. "Then we can talk at home and—"

"How long?" she yelled.

"I'm sorry, Cris. I'm just so sorry."

I stepped into the room and rolled back the curtain, startling both my parents.

"How could you do this to us?" I moved toward my dad. A navy sling covered his left arm, and a brace curled around his neck. One eye was swollen shut, there was some contraption on his leg, and dried blood and cuts covered the face I had grown to love so much.

"Harper—" Dad reached for me, wincing as he sat up.

"We were just leaving." My mom grabbed me by the shoulder and pointed me to the door. "You were explicitly told to stay home."

I wrenched free just as my brothers stepped inside. "Tell me this isn't true. I know you wouldn't cheat on Mom. On us."

He opened his busted lips. Then clamped them shut.

"Say it!" I cried.

"Harper." Dad shook his head, then looked at my mom. "I wish I could."

IT FELT LIKE someone was pulling stitches out of my heart, one jolting thread tug at a time.

Before tonight I was a Daddy's girl. I was the daughter of two parents who still loved each other. Parents who held hands and laughed at each other's corny jokes. Even when I didn't like who I was, I liked who my family was—who we were together. When the nightmares came, the memories resurfaced, and I would rock myself back to sleep with the thought that I was an O'Malley. I was safe, loved, protected.

Now who was I?

What would happen to our family?

What would happen to me?

Upstairs, I lay on my bed, feverishly typing in my diary, Laz curled by my legs. After Mom kicked us out of the hospital room, my brother had driven us home, air conditioner running full blast and windows open to the night air. Like he had wanted to blow away all the evil of the day.

But it had only messed up my hair and given me a runny nose.

I absently rubbed one of Laz's lopsided ears, my thoughts sliding to Josie Blevins.

The other woman.

It was now all over the news. The beloved Coach O'Malley had not been alone on his motorcycle. The story had been picked up by every news outlet, from the local journalists to CNN. The reporters had descended on the story like vultures on roadkill, and I knew they would pick it apart 'til nothing was left but the bones. My dad wasn't just any coach. He had breathed life into the team, restored a college football legacy, made a name for himself. People in the South took their football as seriously as any religion. It was church, it was revered, it was holy. John O'Malley had come in four years ago, revived a dying program, and been exalted as a savior.

But he'd just been dethroned.

I found an online report that said this *Josie* was in critical condition. They hadn't elaborated. But they had posted her staff photo.

She was young, beautiful. Strawberry blonde and thin.

Was she married?

Did she love my dad?

And . . . did my dad love her?

Laz jumped down at the knock at my door. Mom walked in, my two brothers behind her. She looked tired. Older.

The bed groaned as she sat down and pulled me into her arms. I inhaled her familiar perfume of lilacs and vanilla.

"We're going to be okay, guys." Mom looked at each one of us. "Things are bad right now, but we will get through it."

"I don't understand any of this," Cole said.

Her smile was bitter. "I don't either."

"Dad has a girlfriend?" Michael sat down on my carpeted floor, leaning back on his athletic arms.

"The important thing to remember is your dad loves you,"

Mom said. "That hasn't changed."

"That doesn't answer his question," Cole said.

She picked a stray cat hair from her jeans. "They hadn't been seeing each other long."

"Makes me sick," Michael said. "How could he do that to you?"

Mom slowly shrugged. "Your dad and I have some things to work out."

"Are you going to get a divorce?" My stomach caved in a bit more at Cole's question. The uncertainties, the various endings this story could have—it had my breath coming in shallow heaves. Our family was a train flying off its tracks. And I was simply an onlooker, standing helplessly to the side, watching it all happen.

"We're a long way from that." Mom's long hair, usually falling free below her shoulders, was now clamped in a messy ponytail. Normally perfect, her bangs went every which way—including up, like she'd been running her fingers through them in aggravation. "We're going to have to take things day by day. I love your father. But he's . . . he's made some bad decisions. And it's cost him. He has a lot to deal with right now. There will be an investigation into the accident by the police. And there will probably be some repercussions from the university as well."

"For what?" Cole asked.

"Moral code," I whispered. "It's in a coach's contract. That they don't do anything to embarrass the university or make them look bad." How many times had Dad lectured us about character? About doing the right thing no matter how uncool? My father, deacon of the Maple Grove Community Church. Leader of Sunday lunch prayers. Famed for his high standards for the team's behavior and grades.

Now this.

"So he could lose his job?" Michael studied the poster of jazz greats on the wall beside him. "And we could have to move? Again?"

Mom gave my hand a squeeze. "We're not going to think about that right now." To say I did not handle change well was an understatement. We had moved three times in the five years I'd been an O'Malley, and each move had shaken the snow globe of my well-ordered world. "Day by day."

Michael glanced at his phone. "Our friends are calling and texting like crazy."

Molly had left me exactly twelve voice mails and fifty-three texts. Her last few texts had been nothing but emojis, as if she'd run out of words.

"You know the drill," Mom warned.

"No details." Dad had trained us well, and I had his instructions memorized. "We tell them it's a family matter."

"Assume everything you say will get back to a reporter." Mom pointed a manicured finger at Cole. "Understand?"

"Yes, ma'am."

"We'll get through this." Mom stood and held out her arms. We all walked into them for an O'Malley family hug. Only we were missing one. "We pray, we hold our heads up, and we stick together. I love you, guys."

I squeezed my family tight, as if I could hold us all together. "I love you."

While the four of us held on, my dad lay in a hospital bed.

And I knew when he came back, nothing would ever be the same.

I would never be the same.

Chapter Four

TWO DAYS—HOW LONG Mom kept us home and out of school.

Seventy-two hours—how long I went without seeing my dad.

Forever—how long this situation was going to break my heart.

Our house became a compound for hiding out. My brothers, mother, and I went to our respective rooms and pretty much stayed there, only gathering for quiet meals where Mom would update us on Dad's improving condition in the hospital. Mom had little to say, and judging by her lack of ever-present makeup and hair clearly in need of a vigorous shampoo, I guessed she would've been hard-pressed to find the energy to make much conversation even if she had the words. We weren't allowed to go in or out, as our neighborhood could easily be a target for reporters.

I wished I'd had more to show for my two days off of school, but all I'd accomplished was making my plans to retrieve my next endangered dog and organizing my closet first by color, then by favorites, then finally by outfits most likely to appeal to a member of my favorite rock band. Just when I thought the walls were closing in and I was going to die if I didn't get a chocolate milkshake and fries, Mom informed us over Tuesday night's dinner of Cheerios that we'd be returning to school the next day.

I hadn't slept more than five minutes in the last two nights, my same thoughts looping in my head on repeat. By three o'clock Wednesday morning, I had completely given up on sleep again, and instead crept downstairs to sweep and mop the floors, do the dishes, dust the living room, and make muffins for breakfast. Of course, I'd also done my daily homework of checking a local shelter to see if there were any death row doggies I needed to swoop in and save. And to top off the cruelness of the heavy eyelids and grief residue, I had a test in AP econ over material I knew nothing about.

I stepped into the band room second period, only to be tackled by Molly. She hugged me fiercely before pulling me into a practice room and slamming the door shut.

"What the heck, O'Malley?"

I scrubbed a hand over my face and shook my head, tears pooling in my weary eyes. Molly was my best friend, my sister in all things nerd. And more than anything, I wanted to sit down beside her and spill every single detail.

But I couldn't. Because I was a coach's daughter.

"Why haven't you returned any of my calls?" Her black eyebrows lifted high above her red-framed glasses. "I texted a million times."

"I texted you back."

"'My dad is okay and I'm okay' doesn't really tell me much."

"It's all I can say right now."

"You know I'm not going to breathe a word to anyone."

I did know. But accidents happened. Things slipped. Dad had drilled that in us. "There's so much going on. Things are totally jacked up. It's hard." I blinked back more tears, hating every one of them. "It's killing my mom. And Cole."

"I'm here for you, got it? If you need to vent or need a coffee run. Or maybe we can find a neglected, sad animal for you to save. I know that would make you feel better. Would you prefer mange or malnutrition?"

My laugh was small, but it was a welcome relief. "I'm banned from any more clandestine rescue missions. I can't get myself grounded on top of all this crap. Though missing the band dance doesn't seem like such a big deal at the moment. Who cares?"

Molly gasped. "You do! You positively must. I have some news to cheer you up."

"Can you rewind time to Saturday?"

"No. But I can get you a band seat right next to Andrew Levin." My friend's every gesture, her every word was performed with the same enthusiasm as one on a Broadway stage. She threw her hands over her heart. "Guess who tried out for second chair—and got it? Andrew. That's right. Your little cupcake, right this very moment, is gathering his stuff to come sit by your golden first chair." She pursed her ruby red lips together. "Harper, I'm trying to be on board with this crush of yours. But wouldn't you prefer a more exciting James Paxton or Matthew Delamonte?"

"No. It's Andrew." He was basically the most amazing thing to come to this school since a Little Debbie truck crashed into the gym last spring. It had missed me by only a few feet, but there were worse things than standing under a downpour of Swiss Cake Rolls.

"He's not even that cute."

"For my league," I said, "he's quite dreamy."

I believed in the League Theory. It would've been a waste of time to crush on the popular guys, the jocks, the beautiful hipsters. I didn't even look at them, in the same way I didn't look at Gucci or Prada.

"He's just another band geek," Molly said. My best friend was not the next Miss Kentucky, but she was cute and her enviable personality attracted the guys like bacon and waffles.

"*We're* band geeks. You go ahead and go out with your football players and stage managers. Band boys—that's where it's at. They're musical, get decent grades, and have at least average intelligence." And they often needed seatmates on darkened game buses running low on clean air and chaperones.

"Then today's your day. Go forth and conquer Mr. Second Chair."

My sigh could've blown the door off the tiny room. "I'm a wreck. I look like a total mess." I wore jeans, a hoodie, running shoes that had never seen a track, and my wavy blonde hair sat in a knot on top of my head like wobbly, frizzy button.

My best friend held up a small bedazzled bag. "Have no fear. Molly and Maybelline are here."

She had the skin of Beyonce, and the folks at Sephora knew her by name. So I let the girl work her cosmetic voodoo.

Lips got glossed, cheeks blushed, and concealer layered on heavy as wall paint. I felt like a trollop. But the mirror Molly held up showed a fairly normal looking girl.

No signs of a sleepless night. Or a shattered heart.

Molly snapped her compact shut. "My work here is done. I know you're upset, but if you've got your sights set on Andrew, then snagging a date with this boy could be just the thing you need. And life has all but thrown him in your path today."

She flung open the door and gave me a gentle shove into the band room just as the tardy bell rang. I skittered to my seat, my shoes squeaking as I walked across a concrete floor that had seen more than its share of horn spit over the years.

Squeezing between two music stands, I slowly sat in my seat. Right by Andrew Levin.

"Hi," I whispered. I arranged my lips into what I hoped was a smile. I wasn't even trying for a sexy grin. That was completely beyond me even on my best day.

And then the most magical thing happened.

Andrew smiled back.

"Harper, right?"

The fact that he knew my name was all I could want from this moment. Aside from maybe his dropping to a knee and declaring his undying love. While showering me with chocolate. And some Adele concert tickets. But still—a great start.

"Yeah," I said. "Harper." Andrew and I had talked a few times, but nothing more than some hellos and a *Hey, wasn't that history homework hard?* And now he was sitting beside me. I was pretty sure my deodorant had just clocked out.

Andrew rested his trumpet case on the floor and flipped open the lid. "I'm second chair. Tried out for it yesterday after school." He shot me a crooked side grin. "I'm gunning for your chair next."

I thought of offering my *lap* for all his seating needs.

"That's great," I said. "I mean, congratulations. I mean—"

Before I could swim out of my verbal cesspool, Mr. Sanchez, the director, stepped onto his riser. "Listen up." He held up a hand and waited for the room to quiet. Meanwhile, I was smelling the rich air that was Andrew and sweating through my shirt. "Band dance is next Saturday. If you're bringing a date from another school, you gotta sign up. Don't show up drunk, high, or wearing something that would make your granny cry."

"Are you going?"

I started at Andrew for a few glorious moments before I

realized he was posing this question to me. I was paralyzed with the wonder.

"Um . . ." Words. I needed words. "Probably. Or I was." Until my dad took a bulldozer to our lives. "I'm on the decorating committee. I have quite the way with tulle and tablecloths." I reached for my own trumpet to give my hands something to do, wincing when spit leaked from the instrument and dripped onto my shoe. "They have the dance every fall. Mr. Sanchez DJ's. It's the only time you see him without a bow tie. There's food, some dancing, karaoke." I had just successfully strung a handful of complete sentences together. They had nouns and verbs and everything!

He put his music on the stand. "Doesn't sound too bad."

"B flat concert scale." Mr. Sanchez swept his hands in the air for us to raise our horns.

Andrew leaned into my space. "Hey, is your dad—"

Seriously? Could I not escape this? "Yes, Coach O'Malley. But I can't discuss—"

"Who?"

I blinked. "My dad. He's the coach for the Eagles."

"Oh. Cool." Andrew's smile stretched wide. "I'm not really up on my sports. I was gonna ask if your dad was going to the dance. Mr. Sanchez said he was recruiting some fathers to help with the bonfire, and I haven't decided if mine's going."

"Mine's definitely not."

"So this dance. You'll have to tell me more."

My heart leaped in my all-too-flat chest. I tried to think of something sophisticated and nonchalant. "Okey dokey."

Andrew laughed, then pressed his full lips to his trumpet and began to play.

I turned back to the clarinet section and gave Molly a discreet thumbs-up.

Maybe my life wasn't ruined after all.

THE REST OF my school day consisted of me dodging fellow classmates who wanted to tell me what a d-bag my dad was, avoiding stares that ranged from pitiful to predatory, and my checking out at lunch because I couldn't take it anymore. I needed to go to a safe place and just think.

That place was the Walnut Street Animal Rescue.

The cool thing about animals is they don't ask questions. And they don't make mistakes bigger than a gnawed shoe or a new hole in the backyard. Animals are givers, trustworthy. Well, minus that beagle who once peed in my backpack.

At one o'clock, I whipped into my parking spot and pulled my tired body out of the car. The rescue was a large metal building that sat crooked on a road jutting from downtown. When you stepped inside, you were assaulted with barks and howls, and it was music to my ears. And a constant reminder to me that there was lots of work to be done. The place always smelled of cleaning chemicals and fuzzy paws.

Walking into the rescue, I threw up a halting hand. "I don't want to talk about it."

"Fabulous!" Mavis Blackstreet smacked her nicotine gum and plucked an overstuffed tabby off her front counter. "I was afraid I'd have to listen to your sob story and pretend to care."

"Just here to walk some dogs."

"You oughta be in school." Her bouffy white hair looked like the icing on a cupcake that had been dropped one too many times. As usual she wore polyester pants the color of an unloved crayon. Tortured Tomato. Pickled Purple. Mossy Mistake. Her arm bore the tattoos of men she had loved and lost amid what she called her "military phase." I assumed this phase happened sometime around the colonial period because Mavis was just flat-out old.

"I'm taking the rest of the day off from school." From her desk, I found the clipboard containing the day's walking schedule. "My mom signed me out."

"That's the problem with you kids." She pointed a salon-created nail in my direction. "You got them helicopter parents who just hover and fix everything. This country's going to hell in a handbasket, and do you know why?"

Normally it was because of the Republicans and the rising cost of cable TV. "No, what's today's excuse?"

"Because you little wimps aren't ever allowed to fall on your face and pick yourselves up. Bunch of babies, that's what you are. Your generation's president will get elected and quit two months later."

"You'll be dead then anyway."

"Go walk your dogs and get out of my office," Mavis said. "Disrespectful brat."

Mavis was the only person on the planet I could talk to like that. It was a job requirement. The first time I'd sassed her, I'd had a moment of panic, a flashback to being a little girl and waiting for the hand to slap across my face.

But Mavis had just thrown her white head back and laughed. "That's a girl," she'd said. The freedom to push back—it was exhilarating.

A door separated the front public space from the animals, and I punched in the three-digit code to gain entrance, hearing the cacophony of dogs.

"Hey," Mavis barked.

The door lock gave a pop, and I pulled the handle. "Yes?"

"Those dogs back there." She worked her piece of gum real good. "They got stories to tell, and I reckon so do you." She paused so long, I thought maybe she was considering having a senior moment. "But you saved most of them, and you're gonna be fine yourself."

I'd worked with this woman for two years. And underneath that old, leathery heart was pure gold. She couldn't get along with an adult to save her Velcro shoes, but nobody loved those animals more than her. "Thanks, Mavis."

"Yeah." She went back to her computer. "Now get out."

Skippy and Oreo were only too happy for me to put them on a leash and take them outside. We walked to the nearby square, where the large collie mix and Maltese sniffed flowers, wagged tales at pedestrians, and finally flopped over to bathe in the sunshine.

I sat on a park bench, the dogs comatose at my feet. In front of us a statue of the founder of the town, Betsy Callaghan, and her horse Blue, stood in a fountain. Squirts of water spiked from small concrete maple leaves, as if they were spitting on their pioneering mother.

Maple Grove was a small but bustling college town, and it often served as a pit stop for tourists on their way to Bowling Green. The downtown area struggled, as it was hard to compete with the big-box stores ten miles down the road, but the antique shops and mom-and-pop diners welcomed older crowds who knew the value of a homemade piecrust or a vintage teakettle. The mayor had finally caught on to the idea of food trucks, so restaurants on wheels crammed into alleyways to sell their street tacos and crepes. On Friday nights, local bands played on makeshift stages in the center of it all while families picnicked, sitting on tattered quilts as the breeze carried the music away. Besides the top-notch sports teams, the college was an increasingly popular pick for students looking for a small town environment with lake access, lots of biking trails, and nature all around. For me, it was just home.

"Penny for your thoughts."

I startled at the voice and lifted my head.

Marcus Ross walked up the sidewalk, wearing one of those looks of pity I'd seen all day. I didn't know if it was for him or me.

"Let me guess: you're going to dip your giant football-playing hands in the fountain and pull up some loose change?" I scooted over to give him room on the bench.

"I'm a poor college student who's not above stealing from Betsy and Blue."

He sat down beside me, taking up more than his share of the seat. It hadn't been that long ago that such close proximity would've had me finding an excuse to stand up, gain some space. But Marcus and I had hung out enough that he was on my safe list. He knew it was a club with small membership.

Marcus gave both dogs a scratch beneath their chins. "What's going on, Harper?"

"I wish I knew." I wish I had some explanation that made it all make sense.

"Your dad's the last person—" His words came to a halt, and the tough athlete wiped at his eyes. "He was my hero, you know? My daddy sure wasn't any role model. But when I met Coach O'Malley, saw how he treated us, how he loved his family, I thought, that's the man I want to be." He smiled and nudged me with his elbow. "'Cept not white."

"I didn't see it coming," I said.

"This could be the end of his program, you know?"

"Yeah, I do." And I knew what it meant for all of us if my dad got let go. I would have to move. My dad's coaching staff would all be fired when a new head coach picked his own staff. The team would lose their ranking. Recruits wouldn't want to join. And that wasn't even the worst of it.

It was a cataclysmic mess.

"How's the team?" I asked.

"Tore up. I've never seen so many grown boys cry since we all watched *The Notebook*. They don't care what Coach did. They just want him to stay."

"And you?"

The white mop of a dog flopped over, and Marcus rubbed his pink belly. "I love Coach, but . . . I feel betrayed."

"That makes two of us." I picked up the dogs' leashes, ready to leave. "This family was my only source of normal."

"What do you think's gonna happen—with your parents?"

I didn't know. Every older adopted kid knew the horror stories. Kids who were sent back when they left the cute years and turned thirteen. Kids who got unofficially rehomed when the parents divorced. If Mom and Dad split up, where would I go? Stay with my mom? Live part-time with my dad?

Or would they still want me at all?

The logical sixteen-year-old side of my brain said they'd no more give me up than they would Michael or Cole. But the nine-year-old inside worried she'd be tossed aside once again.

"What do you know about Josie Blevins?" I was afraid of Marcus's answer, no matter if his words could fill the fountain or no more than a thimble.

"Not much. She's a trainer. Worked on my ankle this summer. Had a fiancé, but I hear he's left town. I guess she's pretty banged up."

"What hospital is she in?" Because I'd checked, and she wasn't at St. Vincent's, where my dad had gone.

"St. Stephen's." He shook his head. "Oh, no. No, you leave that lady alone."

"I will."

"No good can come from you talking to her."

"Fine."

"You gonna get in trouble, you know that? Promise me you'll stay away from her."

"Okay."

"Shoot." Marcus pushed up his drooping glasses. "That's the same look you wore the day you said you weren't going to kidnap that bloodhound tied up south of town. You promised you'd leave that dog alone."

"He's very happy with his new family."

Marcus sighed. "One day one of your strays is gonna turn on you."

"Every stray's worth saving."

"Josie Blevins is not one of your rescues. She's a feature story on ESPN waiting to happen. Steer clear, Harper."

I knew he was right.

But what could checking on her hurt?

Chapter Five

THERE IS NOTHING like coming home to reporters set up in front of your driveway.

We lived in a gated community, but somehow a few had still gotten in. Unfamiliar vans circled the block, while I spotted at least one stranger with a camera peeking through the neighbor's rosebush. I hoped he got a thorn lodged in his flabby keister.

Michael and I made it home at the same time. We were greeted by Mom, bearing a tray of homemade cookies. "Come in and put your bags down. I have some goodies for you."

We followed her into the kitchen, where Cole, wearing a chocolate mustache, already sat.

"I made everyone's favorites. We have Harper's chocolate chip cookies, Cole's peanut butter, and Michael's favorite caramel brownies." When my mom got stressed, she did two things. She baked and ran. "I also have two pies in the oven. Thought about taking those over to Mr. and Mrs. Pringle down the road."

"I wouldn't," Michael said. "They're sitting in lawn chairs watching for news trucks."

I bit into a warm cookie as Mom poured milk. "How many miles did you run today?" I asked.

"Ten." She handed me a frosty glass. "Why?"

Cole took a sip. "When's Dad coming home? I want to see him."

Mom sat down on a leather bar stool. "The hospital released him this afternoon. Or more likely, your dad forced them to." She consulted her running watch, a marvel of a thing that could tell distance, laps, calories. But it couldn't tell us how much longer my family would remain cracked and broken. "He called a bit ago. He'll probably be by in an hour or so."

I wanted to ask about his girlfriend's status, but I knew I couldn't in front of my little brother.

"I don't want to go to football practice," Cole said. "I want to see him."

Mom folded a napkin in half, then fourths. "He, um . . . we should talk about this, okay?"

I went to the sink, squirting dish soap into the hot water.

"Harper, sit down." Mom gestured to an empty bar stool. "Kids, your dad and I need some time apart. We felt it best if he moved out for a while."

"But I don't want him to!" Cole grabbed Mom's hand and shook it, as if he could dislodge the idea from her mind. "For how long?" Each word punched with rising panic. "Just a few days?"

"We don't know, sweetie. As long as it takes, I guess."

Crumbs outlined Cole's upper lip while tears streaked his ruddy face. "If that lady dies, will Dad go to jail?"

"No," Mom said. "It was an accident. A horrible one."

"Do we have to see him?" I wasn't ready. I needed time to think.

"Yes. I know you're angry, Harper, and believe me, so am I. But he's your father. And he needs you."

Angry? Was that what I was? "What about you?" I asked.

Mom fingered the charms on her silver necklace. All our names were engraved on discs, even Dad's. "I need time to think without your dad around." She reached for Cole's hand. "We're a tough family, right?"

I wondered if my mom would lock herself in her room again tonight and totally fall apart.

A car door shut outside, and all heads turned toward the kitchen window. "I guess your dad's early."

"I don't want to see him right now." I grabbed my milk and a handful of cookies, then stomped up the stairs, slamming my bedroom door with a house-jarring flourish. I hoped it made my dad's cheating teeth rattle.

Flouncing on the bed, I pulled out my phone and scrolled through some emails and texts. Some from friends. Some from people I didn't even know, asking for information or quotes for their story. One revealed there would be another press conference at the university tonight at seven. What else was there to say?

I clicked on a text from Mavis.

Man called about dog again. Terrier not going to make it long. Assess situation, but don't do anything dumb. My liability don't cover stupid.

A photo of the saddest looking dog stared back at me. It was a dog in serious need of medical attention and a steady diet of food and love. How could people be so cruel?

Animals and human beings—you couldn't just toss them out and ignore them. This dog needed me.

When the knock finally sounded at my door, I wasn't the least bit surprised.

I knew my dad wouldn't leave without seeing me.

"Harper? Can I come in?" He peeked his head in before limping inside. He looked like a man who'd been in a wreck, all right. Cuts, bruises, a swollen eye, his arm still tethered with that sling. He was painful to look at, and I knew the polite thing to do was to inquire about his condition—but I was a long way from doling out niceties.

I said nothing, but continued to check my texts.

The bed sagged as he sat down beside me. Lazarus shot out from underneath my blankets and fled out the door.

Even my cat didn't want to deal with Dad.

"I know I've let you down, babe." He scratched at the thick stubble on his cheeks. "I let myself down. I made some huge mistakes, and I regret them with everything I am."

"You regret them because you got caught." I pulled my eyes from my phone and to his face. His bruised and battered face mirrored the condition of my heart. "You cheated on Mom." I had thought he was different. Better. "Why, Dad?" My voice broke, tears choking out the syllables. "How could you just . . . walk away from us?"

"Harper—" He reached out, and I moved away as if he were coming at me with a fist instead of a gentle touch. "I know you don't like me very much right now." He swallowed, let out a breath. "I can't stand myself."

"Mom said she needed some time away from you." The heat filtered through the vent in my ceiling, yet I was chilled to the core. "I do too."

"Okay," he said. "If that's what you want. But I'm not staying away forever. I love you."

Words. They were the three words I hadn't heard until I'd come to this family. Now they were sour notes in my ears. "You have a funny way of showing it."

He chewed on his bloated lip. "I'm renting a house near the campus. I came to get some stuff. I'll pick up the rest when you guys are gone tomorrow. I need you to be there for Cole, okay? He's upset and confused."

"Who isn't?"

Dad's nostrils flared as he breathed deep. "There's something else, and I wanted you to hear it from me first. Tonight they're going to announce that the athletic director has put me on paid leave. Indefinitely. I know all sorts of things have been on the news, but it's going to get worse before it gets better."

"And you want me to keep my mouth shut. I got it."

"Just be careful who you talk to. The press are circling like vultures, and they'll come after you or anyone you know to get information."

If this had been Mavis, I'd have snapped, *Yeah? Because you really set the bar for discretion.* But it was my father, so I kept my mouth closed.

"There's going to be an investigation by the college. To determine if I violated my contract. ESPN, Fox Sports, they're all over it. I hate this for you guys. I wish . . . I wish things could be different."

I traced the pattern of my white quilt with my finger. "Do you love her?"

Dad paused too long. "It's complicated."

"I think you need to go."

"Babe, I know you're hurting, but I'm sorry. I'm so sorry."

All I could do was nod. My throat thickened and my eyes burned. In that moment I couldn't stand him or the disaster he had brought to us.

"I know you want time, but please don't shut me out. I—"

"John, it's time to go." Mom stood in the doorway, her arms crossed over her chest. "The kids have had enough."

Dad rose and ran his hand over my hair. Like old times.

But things were different. I didn't know this man.

"I love you, sweet girl. I love all of you. You guys mean so much to—"

"John." Mom's one word, fired like a bullet, pierced the fog of tension that hung over us.

Dad stood beside my bed for a few seconds that seemed all too still and unbearable, like when the world turns green and quiet before the tornado touches down and tears down everything in its path.

Then he finally walked away, his head dipped low. "Goodbye."

I AWOKE WITH a start, my strangled cry piercing the air, my sweat soaking through my Hogwarts T-shirt.

Pushing my damp hair away from my cheek, I looked around my room. I was home. I was safe. Wasn't I? Somehow the house didn't feel as secure without Dad here. Yet another thing to blame him for. Before I'd gone to bed, I'd triple-checked the locks on all the doors and windows.

We were safely locked down, and yet my nightmare had still returned.

When I'd closed my eyes, I'd gone right back to that filthy apartment. Heard the yelling. The anger. Felt that uncertainty of never knowing when the slapping and hitting would start. When the food would stop. I'd gone back to when my insistence on long sleeves had begun.

I flicked on my lamp. The way I saw it, at one in the morning, a girl had two options: stay in bed and count her woes while eating chocolate chip cookies from the stash in her bedside drawer, or sneak out and go rescue herself a dog.

Mom had shut herself in her downstairs bedroom hours ago. But I knew she couldn't be asleep.

My dad's words replayed in my ear.

"This animal stealing career of yours is over."

Who was he to tell me what to do? Like his judgment could be trusted.

I was done listening to that man.

The night air waved over my face, and I inhaled it as I pushed up my window. The stars glittered above, just doing their thing, as if the universe hadn't completely shifted, as if the earth hadn't flipped.

After changing into black yoga pants and a black hoodie, and throwing my hair into a ponytail, I turned off our security system with my phone and stuffed the device in my bra. Lord knows my boobs didn't need all that room in there. I could've used the back door, but it was too close to my parents' bedroom. So out the window I'd go.

In sixty seconds, I had detached the screen and climbed over the sill, setting my feet onto the barely slanted roof of the covered porch below. My feet dug into the shingles, and I gingerly walked down, stopping at the edge. This was not my first time to escape the second story, but tonight it all felt different. My *everything* felt different.

Hanging onto the ledge, I threw my legs down and . . .

The patio table wasn't there.

The one I had specifically moved that afternoon.

My fingers burned, cramped.

Crap!

My feet dangled, my hands grew slick.

How would my mom feel finding my body in a broken heap in the morning?

I couldn't hold on much longer.
Felt myself slipping.
With no help in sight.
And then I heard that deep voice.
"Going somewhere, Miss O'Malley?"

Chapter Six

M Y BODY JOLTED with shock at the voice, and my grip loosened.

Slipping.

Falling.

Stars exploded in my head as I collided into one strong chest. Connected to two waiting arms.

My body collapsed into him, and he held on tight.

I lifted my head.

And even in the dark, I could make out his form, his face.

Ridley Estes.

"You." I wiggled to be released, but his grip locked around me.

"I think the words you're looking for are *thank you*."

"What are you doing here, Ridley?"

"Saving a girl from dashing her brains out on the patio."

"Besides that." I snaked out of his arms, landed on my two feet, then stumbled on a rock. The corners of his lips lifted as his arms reached out to steady me again.

"Why are you at my house?"

His hands slid down my arms as he released me, his voice a low whisper. "I tried the front door, but no one answered."

"That usually means the people inside don't want to be bothered." I couldn't deal with this tonight. I seriously couldn't.

"I've been trying to call your dad," Ridley said. "I've emailed him a million times. He won't respond."

"I'm sure he's busy." I tried to step around him, but Ridley blocked my way.

"I've got to talk to him." That ever-present cockiness evaporated. "The athletic director rescinded your dad's offer letter today. Said I had been too big of a risk all along. My whole future depends on this. You have to get me a meeting with your dad. Your brother said he won't talk to him for me."

"Neither will I."

He stilled. Took a deep breath. I could see the hints of his features in the glow of the distant solar lights that outlined the backyard. His desperation was a scent that mingled with my mom's nearby rosebushes.

"I can't do anything for you. And I've got to go."

"Please, Heather."

"Seriously?" I hissed. "It's Harper. My name is *Harper*."

"I knew that."

I shoved past Ridley and just started walking.

I didn't get two steps before he flanked my side. "Just a short meeting with him. A phone call. An email. A text. Anything."

"My dad's currently suspended. He can't do anything for you, and he's not even here. Not to mention, this is not my problem."

"Oh." He stopped. "It's a shame I'm going to have to go tell your mom that you're sneaking out. Is she asleep? I'd hate to wake her up. With all she has going on, she probably needs her rest."

The wet grass soaked into my shoes as I pivoted and faced him. "You're a first-class jerk."

"Meeting some guy, huh?"

This boy was hilarious. "As a matter of fact I am."

He shook his dark head. "Scandalous. I didn't know you had it in you."

"Yeah, because you clearly know me so well."

"Guess I'll go try the doorbell again. If that doesn't work, I'll bang on some—"

"Fine," I said through gritted teeth. "I will pass the message on to my dad. Just keep my mother out of this."

Even in the dark, I could see his posture slightly relax. "Where are you going and why was the front door not an option?"

"Study group." I lifted my chin, grateful he couldn't see the flush climb my face. I was a horrible liar.

"Is that the best you can do?"

I sighed. "Apparently so."

"I need one more thing from you."

"I'm not your type."

And then he laughed. "That's cute."

"Feel free to get off my property any time."

"I . . ." His gaze dropped and he dug the toe of one boot into the grass. "I know you're all good at school and stuff. I need . . ."

"Shock therapy?"

"A tutor."

"You? You care about your grades?"

"I'm behind on credits. I haven't had a lot of time for school."

"Education can be really inconvenient."

"The only way to make the classes up and graduate on time was to take a college course. English comp. But I'm struggling. I need help. Your brother said—"

"Is this your way of asking me to do your homework?"

"No." He almost looked offended. "Geez, do you expect the

worst in everyone?"

I blinked away the sudden tears.

"Look, Harper, this is a big deal. If I don't pass, I don't play football anywhere, much less USK. I can pay you."

"I have nothing to gain from this."

"You're not the only one whose life got jacked up Sunday."

I had no reason to do anything but walk away. This boy and his problems meant less than nothing to me. But it was his voice. That thread of desperation buried beneath the words, barely perceptible to the human ear.

I knew that sound.

That feeling.

And it held me still before him.

"I'm sorry my dad has ruined your life too. I'm sorry for a lot of things," I said. "And I'll try to get you in contact with him, but he probably can't do anything for you as long as he's suspended. As for helping you with your classes, I just can't." I began to walk away. "You should probably leave before I reactivate the security system."

"You didn't tell me where you're going," he called. "When I send the picture of you crawling out of your window to the local news, I want to get the story somewhat correct."

I stopped and swiveled on my heel. "If you *must* know, there's a blind, malnourished terrier tied to a tree in Cedarville, and I'm going to . . . visit."

Ridley tilted his head and gave a smile that probably scored him many a date. "You stealing this dog?"

"I prefer the term *relocate*."

His eyes traveled over my dark outfit, right down to the extra large bag hanging around my waist. "This isn't your first rescue, is it?"

"I don't think it's in my best interest to incriminate myself further."

"I like your fanny pack."

He did sarcasm so well. "It's a rescue kit."

His grin could've blotted out the sun. "Come on. Let's go get your dog. I'll drive."

"Wait." I pulled my eyes from that chiseled face. "*We're* not going anywhere. You're going home, and I'm going to—"

"Trespass on private property."

"I work alone."

"You're not going by yourself."

I planted a hand on my hip. "Is that right?"

"Gentleman's code would not allow me to let a girl go out in the dark of night by herself to some stranger's house."

"Did you learn that from *Maxim?*"

"*Grand Theft Auto.* Now, let's go find my Jeep. It's parked down the hill on the other side of your neighborhood."

His hand guided at my back, and I immediately swatted it away.

Why hadn't I just stayed in bed with my cookies?

"Here are your choices, Sticky Fingers. Either I take you or I wake up your family and tell them I found you hanging from the roof."

My head throbbed from all the injustices in my life.

If my mom learned about my sneaking out, I would not get to go to the band dance. And I would not get to dance with Andrew. And we would not make out. And he would never know I could rock his trumpet-tooting world. And who needed something good in her life? This girl.

"Fine."

Ridley wasn't kidding when he said he'd parked down the

hill. After a half-mile walk, he led me to his Jeep, parked in a neighboring subdivision that didn't have a gate and attendant like mine. The fact that he'd gotten in on foot didn't exactly make me feel all safe and cozy.

Ridley held open the door, and his hand briefly touched mine as he helped me step inside.

"Buckle up, now," he said. "We have a dog to save."

I couldn't help but appreciate the manly scent of the vehicle as Ridley walked to his side and hopped in. His car smelled like leather and cologne, and judging from the Happy Meal bag crumbled on the floor, maybe a note of deep battered fries. His fingers turned the key, bringing the engine to life, and some Spanish music poured out of his speakers. He quickly turned it off.

"Don't change it on my account," I said. "I'm fluent."

He answered by turning on some rap about girls' butts.

"Wanna tell me where we're going?" he asked.

I gave him the directions, and he didn't say a word about the fact that he'd be driving at least thirty minutes out of town.

For ten miles neither of us spoke. It wasn't until we passed the city limits sign that Ridley turned down the radio and gave me a quick glance. "So . . . your dad."

"I don't want to talk about it."

"Did he say when he might be reinstated?"

At USK? As a member of my family?

"My dad and I aren't speaking."

Ridley braked at a red light. "Could you ask him for me?"

"Why don't you just watch ESPN like the rest of the world?" My dad had gone from being nationally famous for his wins to nationally renowned for a whole different kind of scoring.

Long fingers drummed on the leather steering wheel. "I'm

disappointed, too, you know." He gave me a long stare. "I've watched him for years. Even before he came to USK. Read articles on the great Coach O'Malley. He seemed . . . like an awesome dad. Not just an amazing coach, but a good man."

I had nothing to say to that.

"Maybe the accident wasn't what it seemed," Ridley said.

I was sorry to shoot down his hopes. "It was."

The light turned green, and he put his attention back to driving. "So this Levin guy."

"Don't want to talk about him either."

"You're boring me, O'Malley."

"Want to talk about my literary heroes from nineteenth-century Europe?"

He flicked on his blinker. "I was more in the mood for subatomic particle physics."

I smiled in the darkened car until I saw where he was turning. "This isn't the way."

"I know a shortcut."

"If you plan to do me bodily harm, I request you wait until we get the dog. I don't have time for death and torture."

"Sticky Fingers"—Ridley leaned far over the console—"if these hands were on you, dying would be the last thing you'd be thinking about."

Chapter Seven

"COULD YOU HAVE picked a worse part of town to steal a dog?"

Ridley stopped the Jeep in front of a white house, where snaggled siding looked to be at war with its disintegrating roof.

"Pull in the drive," I whispered, as if my voice could wake up the neighborhood. "Keep the headlights on. I'll need the light."

He rested his hand on my seat and regarded me with doubt. "Do you want to get caught?"

"The house is abandoned. Nobody's lived here in months."

"Fine. Your funeral." He threw the car into drive. "When you get caught, do not list me as an accomplice."

"Like I'd admit to hanging out with you. Just pull in the drive. Dog's in the back."

The Jeep crept onto the dirt path that wrapped around the house. My skin tingled with the nerves I always got. The rush of adrenaline. The feeling that someone was watching me. The risk of getting caught and having to explain to my parents the grittier details of my life of crime.

"She's right there." I pointed to a small barn. A light shone down on it, illuminating the crooked tree where the dog was tied.

The Jeep stopped, and I reached for my special leash before hopping out. Ridley reached for his door handle.

"Remember, I work alone."

He peered out into the darkened yard. "I'm not usually one to back away from a fun misdemeanor, but this doesn't feel right, O'Malley."

"It's best if you stay here, keep the car ready to go."

His left cheek dimpled with his slow smile. "So I'm the get-away driver."

In movies, it was always the dumb guys who drove. "Ridley, I think you're just the boy for the job."

With the song of the crickets and frogs in the neighboring field, I walked away, making my way to the lump I knew was the dog.

"You're a good girl, aren't you?" Feet moving light and slow, I eased toward her. I'd visited her a few times before, and the dog, though leery, knew me by now. "I'm here to take care of you, get you out of here just like I promised. You're gonna be so happy in your new home." The dog's ears twitched, but she had yet to raise her head. "Are you hungry? I bought you a snack."

I stood a few feet away and held out my hand. The terrier lifted her head as if it pained her, as if her head weighed more than her slight body. She sniffed the air for a full minute before I took another step. Five minutes passed before I kneeled by her side, holding out a small handful of baked chicken.

The dog's left eye was matted shut, wounds dotted her hind-quarters, and one ear looked as if something had tried to gnaw it off.

"It's okay, girl. Eat the chicken. I know you're hungry."

Animals were so much easier to gauge than people. Boys I didn't really get. Parents were not my specialty. But cats and dogs, they were easy. We communicated on the same plane, especially these lost ones. My gut told me this dog would just as soon bite her own paw off as attack me. And my animal instinct had yet to fail me.

She sniffed at the chicken for a scant few seconds before gobbling it up. "Lots more where that came from."

Forgoing my leash, I reached into my pack and pulled out a small pair of scissors. I could just cut the tether it was already on—

"Get off my property!"

A door slammed, and I whirled around to see a shirtless man stomping onto his rotting back porch. He waved a shotgun in the air.

And fired.

"Harper!" Ridley sped toward me as another shot pierced the dark sky.

The dog cowered, and I reached for her rope with the knife from my pack.

"Are you insane?" Ridley grabbed my hand and pulled, his arm wrapped around me like a shield. "Get to the Jeep. Go!"

"Move away from my dog. Get off my land!" A bullet pinged the building beside us, splintering the wood.

I struggled in Ridley's grip. "I have to get the dog."

But Ridley wasn't listening. My heart pounding, I let him drag me to the running vehicle, as the old man yelled obscenities and threats.

Ridley covered me as I jumped in, then he ran to his side, slamming and locking his door. He threw the car in reverse. Dirt and rocks flew.

"Holy crap." The tires tore against the gravel. "Can't you just call animal control like a normal person?"

"Stop the car."

"No way."

"I can't leave that dog!" And then to my utter shame, the

tears started. Not just for the animal, but for *everything*. My lack of sleep, my dad, my family. I hated crying in front of people! I held my breath, desperate for him not to hear my pitiful sobbing, but it was no use. With a strangled sound from my lips, I dropped my head to my lap and buried my face in my hands.

"Harper?"

I couldn't speak. My body shook with angry tears, as I tried to push the overwhelming defeat away.

I should think of happy things. Rainbows. Kitty cats. A Shakespearean sonnet. Two for one night at the Taco Palace.

"Stop crying," Ridley said. "This is exactly what my sister would do, and I'm not falling for it."

I felt the car move onto the paved road, and then everything slowed as Ridley pulled over onto the shoulder.

He jerked the car into park. "Are you even breathing in there? If you pass out, I'm tossing your body out."

"You probably would." I lifted my head to find a gentle smile on his face.

His fingers flexed on the gearshift, and he softened his plea. "Please don't cry."

I reached into my bag and pulled out a tissue to swab my nose. "Just shut up." I was a holy mess.

"Look at me, Harper."

I couldn't. Because my eyes were watering like Niagara, and I knew I had mascara running down my cheeks like runny finger paint.

"It's too dangerous," Ridley said. "Your parents would kill me if they knew I let you go back there."

"You've totally ruined this."

"I ruined this? You saw that freak brandishing the firearm, right?"

"You just *had* to come with me. This was all planned out." I blew into the tissue, wishing I could unsee the eyes of the terrier. "I would've gotten the dog."

"And that would've been a lovely sentiment on your tombstone."

Raindrops sprinkled on the windshield like a final seal on one horrible night.

"You don't understand." I blew indelicately into the tissue. "He beats her. She just lays there in her own filth. You can see her rib cage. Even in the dark, you can tell she's starving. She's dying, and she wants out. And she wants a home."

"She could bite," Ridley said. "Maybe she's tied up for a reason."

"She does not bite."

His laugh was devoid of humor. "You've been here before."

"I'm a very fair pet stealer."

"For the love of—"

"I have to try again. Everything is spinning out of control, but this is one thing I'm not giving up. I have nearly a hundred percent success rate, and that dog is mine." I opened the Jeep door. "Wait here and—"

"Heck no." Ridley's arm whip-locked onto mine. "Just stop." His eyes looked beyond me, through my passenger window, as if searching the night for the secret to dealing with an animal-loving nut job. I slipped my fingers from beneath his.

He muttered a few curse words in Spanish under his breath. "I'll go back."

"Oh, thank you! I know—"

"We do this my way. Are we clear on that?"

I hesitantly nodded.

"You are not to be trusted, O'Malley." He started the Jeep,

redirecting us back toward the house.

Nearing the property, Ridley cut the lights, drove down the driveway and right to the dog.

"I'm going to get out." He unlatched the seat belt stretched across his chest. "You climb into my seat. Be ready to tear out of here. Can you handle that?"

"You're going to need this." I handed him my utility knife. "The dog is tied. Not on a leash." My hands trembled slightly, but I gave him a wobbly smile. "Be careful, okay?" It was one thing to risk my own welfare, but I'd never had to consider the responsibility of someone else.

Ridley ran toward the dog like it was a bomb ready to detonate. No leash, no treats. No Kevlar jacket.

My eyes on the situation, I climbed over the console and into his seat. It was still warm from his body, and my chilled form snuggled in deeper.

"Hurry, hurry, hurry." It was a litany, a wish, a prayer in the dark of the car.

Ridley slowed as he came up on the animal. He bent down to unleash her from the rope. His lips moved, and I wondered what he said.

I jerked in my seat as the first shot rang out. I watched in frozen terror as Ridley ducked, scooped up the dog, and took off in a dead run. The terrier tucked under his arm, he cut a hard left, then a sharp right.

The old man leaped from his porch, his gun no longer pointed at the sky, but right toward Ridley.

Shots exploded in the air like a scene from a war movie.

Ridley kept running in a zigzag pattern. A game play.

This had been a mistake. A huge one. What was I doing, asking Ridley to do this? I wanted to take it back. I wanted him to make it. *Please, God, let him make it.*

I revved up the engine and threw open his door. Pulling closer, I yelled, "Get in!"

Ridley hurled his body inside, his breath coming in gasps. He hugged the dog in his football player's arms.

"Duck down and gun it."

The tires squealed as I put it in reverse, before Ridley even shut his door. We roared down the driveway, onto the street, then squalled down Garrison Avenue toward freedom.

No more shots fired.

No more slouching in the leather seat of the car.

"That was stupid." Panting, Ridley looked down at the trembling dog in his lap. "That was the stupidest thing I've ever been a part of."

I began to laugh. Nerves, fear, all of it tangled together until I couldn't contain it. We'd almost died. Over a dog.

"You think this is funny? Geez, this thing smells."

The puppy cowered further into Ridley's arms, and with one hand on the wheel, I reached into my rescue bag and procured more chicken.

"It's okay, girl. You're gonna be all right now. That brave Ridley saved you." I smiled at my champion, but he just shook his head and muttered more words in Spanish. I was pretty sure he either called me a beautiful tropical flower or a raving lunatic. Sometimes I got my nouns mixed up.

"Why?" I asked. "Why did you risk that?" It was more than just wanting to protect the coach's daughter.

Ridley lightly rubbed a finger over the terrier's good ear. "Because I knew I could do it."

"Because you know how to dodge bullets?"

"Because I know a drunk when I see one." He worked the

collar off the dog, revealing angry lesions in need of a vet's care. "I might struggle with poetry analysis or quadratic equations, but I know someone that drunk can't hit a moving target."

"Thank you." I couldn't say it enough. He was underplaying what he'd done, because even an intoxicated old man could get lucky with a gun. At the very least Ridley could've been injured, affecting his ability to play football.

Ridley ignored my gushing appreciation. "This dog's a mess. Is this gonna get fleas in my Jeep?"

"I'm sure all your ladies won't notice." I glanced to the backseat. "But for their safety, I'd recommend they keep their clothes on."

He smiled. "What are you going to do with her?"

"She'll stay at my house tonight. Then I'll take her to the animal rescue in town. She'll get medical care, get cleaned up, then nursed back to health."

"Why would the shelter take your stolen dog?"

"Because I work there."

"Like the coach's daughter needs a job."

"I volunteer."

"That's what I thought."

His tone pinched. Grated. Of course Ridley thought I was some privileged, spoiled rich kid.

"What you did tonight . . ." My pulse had yet to calm down. "That might've been a little out of my league."

"Nothing in your fanny pack to handle that?"

I reached out and scratched the terrier's chin, letting her sniff my hand. "Ridley?"

He leaned his head back and closed his eyes, his chest still rising in rapid huffs, the dog cradled in his strong arms like a child. "What?"

"I'll tutor you."

He stilled. "Is that right?"

"On one condition."

He opened an eye. "I almost took a bullet in my near-perfect backside. You're not really in a position to make conditions here, O'Malley." The rain pattered harder, and I turned on the wipers.

"I need some help." Oh, the humility. "Guy help."

He shifted his body my way. "I suddenly find myself intrigued."

I might as well spill it all. "I . . . I have no clue how to get a guy. None."

"We're not that difficult."

I pulled my eyes back to the road. "I got no game."

He laughed, a rich rumble from his rain-dampened chest.

"Flirting—I don't get it. Witty banter? Cannot do it. And I have no idea how to read your Man Signals. Last year on a field trip to the museum, I thought Dalton Simpson was winking at me on the bus. So I winked back. *Saucy* winked back. Turns out he just had tummy issues, and two minutes later, the bus pulled into a McDonald's so he could take care of business."

Ridley faced the window and seemed to be contemplating the path of a raindrop.

"Andrew Levin now sits beside me in band. I have this gift of an opportunity three times a week, and I can't screw it up. Nobody has ever made my heart"—I flapped a hand in front of my chest—"do this fluttery thing. I get around him, and I just want to throw myself right at him."

"You could try that."

"Really?"

Ridley tossed his head back and laughed. "I really have my work cut out for me." His words were so true, yet they still smarted. "So you'll help me with my classes, and I'll teach you all about the ways of guys. Do I have that right?"

"You'll tell me what to do, what to say?"

"Your Cyrano de Bergerac."

I made a left turn, then eyed my partner in crime. "Did you just reference classic literature?"

He shrugged. "SparkNotes."

This had all the makings of a disastrous ending. It hinted of humiliation and total pride shredding. Yet I was desperate.

He held out a hand like a used car salesman closing a deal. "We swap tutoring, plus you get me a meeting with your dad or the athletic director." His dark head gestured to the dog. "I think I've proven myself tonight."

I slipped my hand in his and gave it a shake. His fingers, warm and strong, surrounded mine.

"This should be interesting," Ridley said.

"I don't care about interesting." I returned my attention to the road. "I just need it to be successful."

Chapter Eight

NOTHING IS EVER as it should be.

I thought a simple phone call to the athletic director, Chevy Moncrief, would be all that was needed to arrange a meeting for Ridley. Yet Mr. Moncrief had yet to answer any of my calls or messages today. Some people just did not respond well to harassment.

That stupid handshake agreement.

Now because of a weak moment last night, when I was drunk on puppy rescue relief, I had agreed to a farcical plan and had to deliver on my promise to Ridley.

It would be worth it when I had my first date with Andrew. When he kissed me. When he was no longer just Andrew Levin, but Andrew Levin, *my boyfriend.*

The University of Southern Kentucky athletic complex appeared in my sights, a behemoth of a building teeming with equipment, athletes, and sweat. I turned on my blinker and braked to let three college students jog the crosswalk before I pulled into the parking lot. Which was jam-packed with vehicles. Television station vans crowded the entire first two rows. CNN. Fox News. Local networks. A small group of students sat in lawn chairs in one parking spot, holding neon signs that said, "Third Year Freshmen For O'Malley." I circled the lot, finally finding a spot for my Civic in the overflow across the street.

The automatic doors of the lobby paused before opening, as

if trying to decide if I was friend or enemy. I walked into the newly redecorated space, and it spilled over with men in logo-emblazoned shirts. Reporters. Local, network, cable, radio, newspaper, magazine. Every news outlet was represented here, and you could smell their yearning for a good story, for more information. The university had been silent since Monday, and everyone knew the final chapter in this tale had yet to be written.

"Can I help you?" The frazzled receptionist behind the granite-topped front desk gave a weak attempt at an interested smile.

"I'd like to see Chevy Moncrief, please."

"Do you have any appointment?"

It was a rhetorical question, as we both knew I did not. "No, but I think he'll want to see me. I'm Harper O'Malley. Could you please just tell him I'm here?"

Her overgrown eyebrows lifted at the mention of my last name. "I'm sorry, miss, but Mr. Moncrief isn't available. He's in a meeting."

I doubted it. I had timed this perfectly, leaving ten minutes after school and allotting twenty minutes for the drive. It was now four o'clock, Moncrief's daily workout time—when his personal trainer visited his office, which was complete with a small gym. Dad had said Moncrief's mostly-controlled OCD meant nothing interfered with his workout session.

Until today.

"Mr. Moncrief is a friend of our family," I said. "It's important I speak to him. Today."

With a stiff smile, the receptionist picked up her shiny black phone and punched three numbers. "This is Cynthia. Is Mr. Moncrief available? Coach O'Malley's daughter is here to see him." Cynthia, of the heavy bronze eye shadow and tea-stained Eagle polo, studied me as she listened to the voice on the other end. "Uh-huh. Yes. Okay, thank you." She hung up and shook her head. "I'm sorry. Mr. Moncrief can't see you this afternoon. He's booked solid. But I can take your number and—"

"That won't be necessary."

Her shoulders relaxed ever so slightly.

I turned to the assembled crowd of tired, bored reporters. "I'm just going to step over there and speak to some of those nice men. This whole ordeal has been really hard on me, and maybe I'd feel better if I just had someone to talk to, someone to hear . . . the rest of the story."

"Let me try Mr. Moncrief one more time."

What a helpful lady. "I'm feeling perkier all ready."

Five minutes later, I rode up the elevator that emptied me out onto the top floor. I walked to the north wing, where another receptionist intercepted me. "I'll show you to Mr. Moncrief's office."

I had been here a handful of times and certainly knew my way around. Moncrief's office was immaculate, without clutter or trace of dust. No stacks of papers. He had hired a feng shui decorator, so everything in the room was in alignment, in perfect accord with symmetry and nature. It was supposed to give an effect of peace and tranquility, but I bet he wasn't feeling that symmetrical today.

"Harper, hello." Mr. Moncrief put down his twenty-pound hand weights. He wore shorts and a school T-shirt instead of his usual dark suit. "I was just starting my session with Miguel here." His beefy trainer stood cross-armed, his face wrinkled in a scowl directed at the intruder. "It's biceps and triceps day."

Though I wanted to make a snide comment on the ridiculousness of caring about your arm muscle in a time like this, the shadows beneath Chevy's puffy eyes told me that he, too, had spent some sleepless nights over my dad's personal implosion. Eight weeks into the season, the Eagles had been poised to dominate the SEC but were now without a coach.

"I just need fifteen minutes."

He glanced at his expensive gold watch. "It's not possible today, dear. Get with Martha out front, and she'll set up a time next week."

"I noticed that 94 FM talk radio guy downstairs. The one that gives you and Dad so much trouble. He seemed . . . kind of lonely. I guess on my way out I could talk to him. Cheer him up. Give him some company. Some inside scoop might perk him up." I adjusted my purse strap on my shoulder. "Thanks anyway."

"Wait." Chevy Moncrief's voice halted me before I hit the door. "Miguel, give us some privacy." He waited until we had the room to ourselves before nodding toward the seat in front of a desk so clean I could see my own reflection in it. "Please sit down. I assume you're here to talk about your father, but—"

"Actually, I want to discuss Ridley Estes."

Twin lines appeared between his brows as he thought for a moment. "Ah, yes, wide receiver from Washington High."

For some reason it bothered me on Ridley's behalf that Mr. Moncrief had to pause to recall his recruit.

"Ridley was your dad's project. And also someone I shouldn't be discussing with you."

"I'm tutoring him. He's a friend of the family." That was stretching it. "He's devastated to be cut."

"Signing day isn't 'til February, so technically it's not possible to cut someone we hadn't even signed."

"He had a verbal commitment that says differently."

"From your father."

"Who represents the Eagles. So the university offered for him. Set up the expectation that Ridley would turn down any other offers and sign with you this winter."

Mr. Moncrief steepled his fingers and leaned his elbows on the desk. "Harper, this young man was one red flag after another. Prior to your dad coming on as coach, we had five consecutive years of having more than one player arrested or in some sort of legal or personal mess. We're a new team."

Until their coach became the personal mess.

"Your friend is in jeopardy of not graduating, and at eighteen, he has a record. You know he was arrested just two nights ago, don't you?"

The Romeo Football Wonder had not disclosed those details. I curled my fingers into my hands. "Ridley would like a meeting with you. Thirty minutes, tops."

"Not necessary," Mr. Moncrief said. "As you saw from the shark frenzy downstairs, I don't have time."

"But—"

"I haven't seen my wife in three days. Yesterday was my mother's eighty-fifth birthday. Do you know where I was? In meetings 'til midnight. Here. Tonight I'll miss my youngest's recorder concert, which actually works in my favor—"

"The recorder is an underused instrument that generates music appreciation and is simply misunderstood." I cleared my throat and shifted in my seat. "Which is not relevant to the topic at hand, I suppose." Music nerd detour.

"The point is," Chevy said, "we're in crisis mode here. This athletic department is under siege. It's both a war and a circus, and who's the ringleader and general?"

"You."

"That's correct." He leaned back into his chair, his head

relaxing against the leather. "I can't help you or this young man."

I lowered my gaze to my lap, watching the light flick through the small diamond ring on my right hand. My parents have given it to me for my sweet sixteenth. It wasn't my actual birthstone, but the stone for my month of adoption. "I tutored your son last year."

"I recall."

"He had an F in senior English. Do you know what he had when he accepted his diploma, the one he was in jeopardy of not getting?"

"I believe it was a high C."

"And the last two years, I've helped fifteen of your players."

"I'm aware of that. You do a wonderful job."

"They talk to me about more than the books, you know?" I speared him with my best Coach O'Malley Eagle stare. "Just because you haven't had a player get bad press in the last few years doesn't mean there hasn't been trouble." One of the perks of keeping a diary and recording every detail of my life was that I always had a record I could pull up at the touch of a button. "There was Jerrod's cheating scandal. Interesting how his professor let that one go. Or that time when Martin crashed his SUV into the bridge. He told me how glad he was someone on the coaching staff picked up his five drunk underage passengers before the police arrived. The hotel room that got trashed last year. The player who—"

"Okay, I get it."

"I not only help those guys graduate, I become their friends. And I listen to their every problem, every secret, every piece of team gossip that never reaches the ears of their adoring public. I keep those secrets, and I'll continue to do so. All I ask is that you give Ridley Estes thirty minutes. You've taken away his dream for the future, and the least you could do is speak to him about it in person."

Chevy Moncrief came to his Nike feet. "One meeting. That's it."

"Thank you, sir." The meeting would probably change nothing, but I had done my part. "I'll let you get back to your workout."

"You're quite the negotiator, Miss O'Malley." He led me to the door and held it open. "Your father would be proud."

I turned then. Looked right into the fatigued eyes of the man who had hired my father, been his boss, become his friend. "Did you know?"

I didn't have to clarify. He understood exactly what I meant.

Mr. Moncrief slowly shook his bald head. "No. I had no idea."

I saw the hurt flicker there, knew the same blade of betrayal had sliced us all.

"Your father is a good person, Harper. He just made a terrible mistake." I breathed deep as his hand fell on my shoulder in a gentle squeeze. "He's still the man we all know and love."

But was he? I wasn't so certain.

I thanked Chevy, then punched the button for the second floor in the elevator. This was where most of the support staff had their desks, and I had one in particular I wanted to see.

The doors opened, and I stepped out into a maze of cubicles. Televisions hung overhead, some playing game footage, some on ESPN, some tuned into the news. I tried to walk confidently, like I was supposed to be there, and I passed by three desks where men wearing polos pressed phones to their ears and typed away on computers. I sailed past two more rows before I found my target.

Josie Blevins's desk was immaculate. It housed her computer, a calendar, and a photo of her and a cute guy I assumed was her fiancé. Or had been. A furtive glance told me no one was paying attention to my snooping, so I crouched low enough to be hidden by the cubicle walls and get a closer inspection. The large desk calendar had the names of players penciled in for treatment. She had a doctor's appointment last Tuesday, probably to check on the condition of her black heart. This Thursday was lunch with the girls. Guess she wouldn't be making that. Unless that had been code for snogging with a married man.

I slowly eased open her top drawer and found nothing but three pens and an old mint. My hands closed around the handle of the next drawer, and when I pulled it toward me, there on top of some files was a framed photo. Of my dad at the last championship game with his arms around two people. One was a player. The other—Josie Blevins.

"What do you think you're doing?"

I jumped up, shoving the drawer shut with a bang. "I was just—" I knew this face. "Marcus." Relief was a Gatorade shower over my head. "You scared me to death."

"I would hope so." He crossed his arms over his chest, his face mirroring the strict granny who had raised him. "Are you crazy?" It was quite the talent to whisper through gritted teeth. "You can't go through people's desks."

"This isn't just any people." I stepped away from Josie's belongings. "It's my dad's girlfriend's."

He grabbed my arm and pulled me toward the nearest exit. "You got some twisted sense of private property. Stealing puppies, rifling through people's belongings."

"It's for the greater good."

He mashed the elevator button until it lit up. "Yeah, well, your greater good's gonna get you thrown in the big house one day. And when you waste your one phone call on me, I am not going to bail you out. No, I'm not."

The doors opened to an empty elevator, and he lightly pulled me in. Had anyone else manhandled me like this, I would've screamed my head off. Or huddled in the corner. "You'd never let me rot in jail."

"I watch a lot of court television, girl. It does not end well for people like you."

I pressed my lips together on a laugh. "I'm sorry."

"No. You're not."

We both swayed as the elevator chugged and began its descent. "Googling Josie didn't get me much info. I just wanted to see if I could find out anything else."

"What did you expect to find?" Marcus asked. "Red hearts and hot date destinations on her calendar?"

Maybe. Kind of. "I don't know. I hadn't really thought that far. I came here to see Chevy Moncrief."

"Moncrief?" Marcus frowned. "Why?"

"We had a meeting about a Washington High recruit of my dad's." I quickly explained how Ridley had been dropped.

"What position is he?" Marcus asked.

"Wide receiver."

"Moncrief has his eye on some hotshot senior from Kansas. I'm guessing that's who he wanted all along."

"Ridley's a pretty big deal."

Marcus's skin glistened, like he'd just come from the showers after practice. "Kansas boy has stats that have NFL teams keeping tabs."

And he probably didn't have a record of arrest. "Any updates on my dad today?"

He pushed up his crooked glasses. "It's not good. Right now they're trying to determine who originally hired the gal Coach was messing around with. If your dad did, it's not going to end well." Putting his mistress on payroll would get my dad terminated for sure.

"Any word on when the decision's expected?"

"Maybe next week."

In a matter of days, I could discover if my dad still had a job. And if I had to move yet again.

"And what about *her*? What about Josie?" I asked. "Any news?"

He lifted his chin and studied the doors. "I don't think I need to tell you."

"I'll go to that French film festival with you next month."

"Okay, so I heard she's still in the hospital, but she's been moved out of ICU."

I didn't know how I felt about that. Of course I didn't want her horribly injured, but selfishly, I knew that as long as Josie was in a coma, she definitely wasn't with my dad.

"No more snooping, Harper. Your dad's case is pretty fragile, and you don't want to be messing it up. There are reporters everywhere. I had one buy my lunch at Subway just today. Said he was a fan, but two bites into my footlong, he started asking questions. I had to leave that beautiful sandwich behind. You know how sad that made me?"

"Do you really want to trade heartbreak stories here?"

"The point is, there are reporters everywhere, and they wouldn't stop at using a kid. If you overstep some boundaries, someone will be there to capture it on film. Trust me."

"Fine." We walked into the lobby, and I saw the press still

swarming like a beehive that had been rattled. "I won't go to the hospital to see Josie Blevins."

"Or to her house."

He knew me so well. "Or to her house."

"Good girl. Hey, I got something that'll cheer you up." Marcus's cheeks lifted in a grin as we stepped outside into the sunshine. "I won two tickets to see *Phantom of the Opera* at the art center tonight. I don't know why, but none of the guys want to go. How about it?"

It was so tempting. "I'd love to, but I have tutoring."

"Who's the poor flunky falling behind this time?"

I gave my friend a winsome smile. "That would be me."

Chapter Nine

I WAS FEEDING on a steady diet of anger.

Watching Ridley from the twenty-yard line of the Washington High football field did nothing but add kerosene to the flames.

Though the sun was sinking below the clouds, the heat provided a worthy opponent for the players. As the head coach barked some parting words, the boys ran to the coolers, sweat dripping. Some peeled off shirts, Ridley being one of them.

My gosh.

He certainly presented a striking picture. If one was into that sort of thing.

Shoulders angled with chiseled, sinewy muscle. Abs corded by endless sit-ups and using his body as a weapon on the field. Ridley took a cup of water and poured it over his head, the water sluicing over his chiseled cheekbones and down his reddened neck and beyond. It was no wonder girls frequently sat on the bleachers and watched the guys practice. The finale was quite worth it.

"Hit the showers," the coach called.

Ridley grabbed a towel and a bottle of water, then ambled toward the field house.

I stepped into his path like a cornerback ready to intercept a pass.

Don't look at his chest. Don't look at his chest. "You didn't tell me you were recently arrested."

He quickly pulled me away from the nearby players with something less than chivalry and care. "What are you doing here?"

"I put myself on the line for you today. Went to the university, which I was loathe to do. Because that's a friendly place to be right now if your name's O'Malley, not to mention it's crawling with reporters. Threatened my way into Chevy Moncrief's office, then secured you a meeting. Only to learn that my efforts were a complete waste of time because you have a rap sheet straight out of Compton."

He pressed the towel to his neck. "Hardly."

"I think you could've bothered to mention that your face is probably hanging on a Most Wanted poster down at the post office. I don't know if you've noticed it, but I'm all out of patience for men and lies."

"I didn't lie to you." Ridley's eyes narrowed, and he took a step closer. "I don't have to explain myself to you any more than you needed to explain why we spent last night stealing a dog. You think that won't earn you a mug shot?"

"That was totally justifiable—"

"And so was mine."

"Oh, what, you were at a keg party and had to defend your drunk girlfriend-of-the-week's honor? Did someone take a swig out of a Keystone can that had your name on it? Or maybe you went to talk to one of your new college professors—with your fist?"

"You know nothing about me." He towered over me, sweat slipping from his temples. "Nothing."

"I know you have a reputation that is exactly what the Eagles don't want. *You* knew that, and you screwed up last week. Am I right?"

Fury radiated from him like a homecoming bonfire. There was anger in him. I knew it without hearing it whispered in the hallways of school, without getting a report from the director of athletics. That simmering fury had a scent, a glow, an energy. I'd cowered from it my whole life.

Yet I stood there, as tall as I could in my five-foot-four body, shoulders back, chin lifted. And I stared this angry boy right back and dared him to unleash.

Because just like the animals I recovered, instinct told me which ones bared their teeth out of fear but no intent to follow through. And which ones aimed to draw blood.

"Fine." I lowered my voice. "Tell me about it then."

Ridley's chest rose and fell in three ragged breaths before he spoke. "It's none of your business."

"I took up for you with the AD today. Threatened to go public with every dirty little secret I knew about his team if he didn't give you half an hour. I think it is my business."

Ridley made a thorough study of the ground before slowly lifting his head, a grin dimpling his cheek. "Made some threats, did you?"

"At least three." I had to admit, I was kind of proud of it myself.

"She dodges bullets, blackmails, and knows when to pull a knife." Now the smile encompassed his whole face, the other dimple making a prominent appearance. "Harper O'Malley is not one to be underestimated."

"The town's probably gonna ask me to be their superhero."

He laughed, a sound so rich and melodic, it surely had angels fanning themselves and shouting glory. "Thank you. For getting me the appointment."

And just like that, we both stood down. His fangs retracted. My claws sheathed.

"You were telling me what you were arrested for."

"Jaywalking."

Right. "How are you still on the football team?"

He blotted his face with his towel, a shadow eclipsing that fading smile. "Today's my last day. Coach is telling the team when I leave. I'm benched, okay?"

"This is kind of a big deal." Not to mention regional playoffs started next week. "You need to be on the field if you want a chance at college ball."

"Thanks for that update. Look, I need a shower, and I gotta check on some things at my house. If memory serves me right, you're helping me with my essay on heroism for comp, and I'm . . ." His brow furrowed as he chewed his lip in reflection. "What is it I'm teaching you?"

"How to win Andrew Levin's heart until the end of time."

"Can't wait."

"My house in an hour?" I had to stop at the shelter, then our plan would be afoot.

He turned and ambled toward his Jeep. "Be ready, Harper." He looked over his shoulder and grinned. "I'm *very* good at what I do."

Chapter Ten

"ACCORDING TO MAVIS, you've called on the hour all day long," Molly said as I walked into the shelter to check on the terrier. My best friend held a small white puppy in one arm and hugged me with the other. "I'd say it's made our boss extra irritable, but it could also be attributed to the beans she had at lunch or because it's a day that ends in *y*."

"Has the vet seen her yet?" Mavis had given me a key last year, so this morning I had arrived early and put the dog in the area they now reserved for my acquisitions.

"Got here an hour ago."

I put my feet into motion to head to the back, but Molly's hand stopped me. "Not so fast." Her smile went soft. "How are you holding up?"

My white sleeve had inched up my arm, and I tugged it down. "I'm fine."

"Any updates on your dad?"

"Not really."

"If you want to talk—"

"I don't." Hurt flashed in Molly's brown eyes. "But thank you. I just need some time to sort this all out. When I'm ready to talk, I promise I will."

My actress friend gave an unconvincing nod. "Per the instructions you left this morning, they're calling the dog Trudy." Molly motioned for me to follow her. "She's gotten the royal treatment today. They've treated her for mange, fleas, and some of those infected wounds."

Dr. Sherman, the vet who volunteered on Thursdays, smiled as we entered the isolation room. "We're still waiting on some blood work for a few other mysteries," she said.

My eyes filled at the sight of the dog lying on the exam table, her eyelids heavy like we were keeping her from a nap. I pet her now-clean head, my fingers gliding over her shorn fur. Looking at this animal, I felt a sense of peace for the first time in days. This was my purpose, what I was put on earth to do. Not every rescue had a happy ending, but the point was, I'd tried. And my saved pets got new lives and spirits, and they brought joy and laughter to their forever homes. The world was a better place because of these rescues.

The vet, my particular favorite, gently touched the bandage circling Trudy's raw neck. "She's in pretty bad shape. Did you have any trouble getting her?"

Memories of a getaway car and dodging bullets came to mind. "None at all."

"Trudy will be okay, Harper." Dr. Sherman brushed her hand over the dog's back. "She's just going to need some recovery time. Nothing you haven't seen before. I think she might regain sight in one of her eyes."

I inspected the dog closely. "But look at her expression. She's not okay yet." The dog didn't respond to my hand, just stared at her blanket and pretended I wasn't there.

"Healing takes time," Molly said. "Right?"

Dr. Sherman scribbled a few things down on her notepad. "She's been hurt inside and out. It could take her a long time to be whole again. To trust people. To trust herself."

She returned Trudy to her kennel, carrying her like a delicate baby. While Molly followed the vet out, I spent some one-on-one time with the dog, talking to her, trying to get her to eat. I pulled up a stool and sat next to her, though she mostly ignored me. I knew without a doubt this dog was mine. Normally I didn't have a problem letting them go, but Trudy would be an O'Malley.

We had a lot in common really. And I was in need of a friend. I described my house, explaining how she could sleep on my bed, play with Laz. I told her about my day, about Andrew, asked her if she had her eye on anyone in the shelter. There was a handsome chocolate lab right outside that door who was quite the looker.

"How'd the rescue go?" Mavis asked later as I walked back out front.

"Maybe I'll tell you about it one day when you're older."

She wheezed out a rusty cough. "I could fire you, you know."

"Or dock my pay?"

The bell above the door chimed, and a woman walked in. She wore heels, a vacant air of superiority, and an overstuffed pencil skirt that hadn't received the message its owner was no longer a size six.

"Can we help you?" Mavis asked.

"I'm Angela Smith." The women smiled and set her designer purse on the counter. "I'm interested in adopting a dog. Small one. Something white and cute. Do you have anything pedigreed?"

"We have varying breeds." Mavis's voice was dry as the fall leaves outside. "But none of the dogs seem to remember to bring their papers."

"Of course." Our visitor laughed lightly. "Perhaps I could

look around?"

I was quite good at reading people, but Mavis never needed deciphering. She was an open book, and right now her page said *go away.* "Harper here will show you to the back."

I held up my car keys. "I was just on my way out."

Mavis smiled. "Guess you can exit the back door after you show this nice woman our dogs."

I made quick work of giving Mrs. Smith the abbreviated tour. I pointed out a few of the smaller dogs that might've been what she was looking for. She peered into the kennels and gave the occasional response of "cute" and "aw." But other than that, I could tell she wasn't finding herself the fancy dog she had in mind to stick in her purse like another accessory.

Fifteen minutes later, she straightened from her inspection of a one-eared shih tzu. "You don't have many small dogs, do you?"

"No. We don't typically need to rescue those. They're pretty popular at the shelters, so we try to get the ones that have less of a chance."

"So you save lives?" Again, that barely interested smile.

"Yes, ma'am. Sometimes we even go to the pound and take the animals scheduled to be euthanized that day. We give these dogs a second chance. They seem to know that, because our adopters tell us we produce some of the best pets."

"Well, I guess I can check back in from time to time. See what you have."

We walked to the back door. A nicer person would've taken her through the front where she'd parked, but Mrs. Smith hadn't earned that courtesy. Her dismissal of our ragamuffin collection of animals tore into me like it was personal. As if she had not merely rejected a dog, but me.

"What about the dogs in there?" She pointed to the room on

our left.

"The infirm room. It's for the ones we need to separate for medical purposes."

She walked inside without invitation, her eyes taking it all in. Trudy looked up from her curled position in her kennel. With her shaved fur, oozing eye, and a tail that had been surgically cut, she was a sight of pure ugly. But not to me. Like Mavis said, this dog was a story, and every one of her wounds told of the ugliness of mankind, and the resiliency of one who had overcome. Or soon would.

Mrs. Smith frowned. "What's wrong with this dog?"

"Mistreated. We hope she'll be ready to go in a few weeks. Trudy's in a pretty bad way and still isn't out of the woods." And she was mine.

"Definitely does not appear to be the breed I was looking for."

"Nope. She's just a mix of this and that."

Mrs. Smith nodded her highlighted brown head. "Poor dear."

And then Trudy stood up, as if entranced by Mrs. Smith's snooty voice.

"Hey, girl," I said softly. "You're going to be all right, aren't you?"

Trudy glanced at me, but then returned her attention to Mrs. Smith.

"Look at that, she's wagging that stub of a tail at me," the woman said.

Clearly Trudy did not qualify for pre-AP classes.

"If you'll come this way, please." I moved toward the doorway, expecting Mrs. Smith to follow. But she just stood there, watching that sad dog. And Trudy watched her right back.

"Mrs. Smith?"

"What?" She straightened. "Right. I must be going. Thank you very much for the tour. Maybe I'll check the city pound."

"Good idea."

I let Mrs. Smith out the back door, relieved to see the back of her. I returned to Trudy and opened her kennel, reaching my hand inside to pet her clean fur. "Just hang on, girl. I'm not going to leave you."

WITH THE DOG on my mind, I drove home, my heart a few pounds heavier.

"Pizza night!" Cole raced by me on in-line skates as I stepped into the house.

Mom was a big believer in the meals hitting all the food groups and including as much green stuff as possible, but since The Disaster, her dietary requirements had become a little less organic farmer and more McDonald's combo meal. Nobody was complaining.

"Hey, sweetie." Mom kissed my cheek as I stepped into the kitchen. "Grab a plate."

"Mom, I want to bring home another dog. A keeper."

"No."

"I'll find homes for the other two. She's an adorable terrier mix. She came into the shelter this morning. If you could see her—"

"I won't change my mind. Now eat."

I would wear Mom down later. Now clearly was not the time, and as every smart teen knew, getting what you wanted was often about strategic timing. "Do you have enough pizza for one more? I'm tutoring."

"Who? Cole Daniel O'Malley, take those skates off this instant."

"Ridley Estes." I grabbed a few extra slices. "We'll be in my room."

"Young man, I am not telling you one more—" Mom grabbed Cole by his shirttail and turned her rounded eyes on me. "You're having a boy in your room? Says who?"

"It's all business." Boys of the romantic variety would not be allowed upstairs with the door shut. Sadly, I'd never had any reason to complain about this rule. "I'm not his type at all. He's the captain of the football team. Model good looks. Mr. Popular. Girls faint in the halls when he walks by."

"You're better than any boy that ever walked the halls of Washington High." Mom stuck a few Cokes under my arm. "Can I talk to you about something?" Her voice lowered, and she walked me to the dining room. "I'm a little worried about you, Harper."

"Because I have a boy over?"

"Because . . . because you've been hit with a lot lately."

"We all have." I had a feeling I knew where this was going.

"I found a counselor I think you're really going to like."

"No."

"Just give it a shot. For me."

"They're all terrible."

"Because they expect you to talk?"

I'd spent a few years in counseling when I went into foster care, and I'd pretty much refused to speak. Especially after my bio-mom went to prison. Session after session of some therapist trying to coax a conversation out of me while I sat in a chair, words failing. They gave me paper to draw on, clay to shape into people, and even a computer to type out my feelings. Yet I'd remained silent, not talking until the O'Malleys drove me home.

"Why aren't Michael and Cole going?" I asked.

"They are. Just not this week." Mom paused, like she was carefully editing her next sentence. "Hon, Becky Dallas's parole hearing is in six weeks."

I closed my eyes against another wave of sorrow. My bio-mom came up for parole every two years. And every year my dad made sure he was at the hearing in Mississippi to speak on my behalf, telling the judge what had caused Becky to lose custody, what had sealed the deal on the O'Malleys adopting me years ago. I wondered if he'd make it this time.

"I think it would help to talk about it." Mom handed me a business card with the words *Vital Roots* in raised, green letters. "I'll even trust you to drive yourself there. Tomorrow morning at seven thirty."

"I'll miss band practice." I'd miss Andrew. "I appreciate the thought, Mom, but I don't want to go."

"I wasn't asking, Harper." With light fingers, Mom brushed the bangs from my eyes. "I'm telling you."

The doorbell rang, interrupting further argument.

I stomped through the living room and opened the door to find Ridley.

Holding a toddler.

"Family emergency." His face was one big apology. "This is my sister Emmie." He hitched her higher on his hip. "She'll be quiet. Won't even know she's there." He stepped inside carrying this curly-headed cherub and an overstuffed backpack. "I have her snacks and a movie."

This was a different guy standing before me. Gone was the cockiness. In its place was someone a little frazzled, a little uncertain. He rested his chin on her head, and I wondered if he knew he'd just pressed his lips to her hair. It looked automatic, a gesture done a hundred times, more out of habit than thought.

"Ridley, it's okay." I waved at Emmie and promptly got a giggle in return. "Come on in."

"Pizza!" The little girl wiggled in his arms, making jerky points to the floor.

Ten minutes later, the three of us sat on my bedroom floor, an entire pizza box beside us. Ridley and I talked about his paper, and by asking some guiding questions, I helped him start an outline. He fed Emmie cut-up pieces of pizza while mopping her mouth and plying her with toys from his bag. This was no part-time brother; he was a pro. What if I'd had a big brother to take care of me in the early years? Would he have protected me? Loved me when my mother couldn't?

"Nice room." Ridley's eyes scanned over every wall, nook, and cranny.

My bedroom was a large space, painted in a soft blue that reminded me of our favorite beach in Alabama. My queen-sized bed was a far cry from the pallet my bio-mom had made me sleep on, and if you didn't mind a little animal hair, my quilt covering the bed was one of my favorite things. Grandma O'Malley had stitched the ivory masterpiece by hand, my present on the day of my adoption.

"So you have your thesis, supporting statements," I said, getting back to business. "You just need to do the research. Keep track of your sources. We can work on that next time." I was starting to believe there was nothing slow about this boy. Maybe it had all just been a lack of motivation. "Next topic, your arrest. I believe you were going to finish that story."

"No." He chewed his slice of pepperoni and swallowed. "I wasn't."

"Was there alcohol involved?"

"Not on my part."

"Did you throw the first punch?"

He slid his plate away from him, as if he'd just lost his desire to eat. "Sometimes you do what you have to do." His dark brown eyes were intent on mine. "I don't care what you've heard. I'm not some idiot who starts a fight just because it's my idea of fun."

"So you were defending someone?"

"I tried. But you're starting to bore me with this, so—" Ridley grabbed his sister and pulled her onto his lap before she stepped on her plate. "Let's talk about you."

A little tingle skittered over my skin, and I swore I would reuse that line on Andrew. *Let's talk about you.* So simple, yet . . . so hot.

"You mean me and Andrew."

He intertwined his fingers and gave them an audible crack. "Where shall we begin?"

Since I knew nothing, the possibilities were endless. "The basics."

"I have some worksheets on how to make out in a movie theater. Or maybe my quiz on backseat shenanigans?"

"Are you making fun of my tutoring methods?"

"No. I thought your graphic organizer was a nice touch."

I pushed to my feet. "Let's forget it." It was all too embarrassing.

"Hey, come on." Ridley reached for my hand and pulled me back. "Sit."

I reluctantly obeyed, but I could feel the heat rising up my neck, knew my cheeks were probably splotched with humiliation.

"Explain what's gone wrong on your other dates," Ridley said. "Tell me about your previous boyfriends."

I pulled my sleeves over my hands, watching my fingers disappear. "There haven't been any boyfriends."

"None?"

"No dates."

"Zero?"

"Can we move past that point?"

"Kissing?"

"I've been kissed."

"As in, you received one? Or you were involved in the process?"

"Are you going to get to the content or not?"

Ridley started to say something, then closed his mouth, seeming to think better of it. I could all but hear his mind assessing the information, finding me lacking, then rewriting his game plan. "Here's where we begin—you just need to talk to this guy. Can you do that?"

It was so easy for someone like him. It was like brushing his teeth or running a lap. For me it was like rebuilding a car engine blindfolded or landing a 747. "I've tried. I have no idea what to say."

"Rule one of conversation is to ask the person about themselves. So you ask him some questions."

"Yesterday I asked him what he uses to polish his brass."

"That just sounds dirty." He laughed. "I like it." He set his sister beside him on the floor, trying one more time to get her to watch *Dora the Explorer* on his laptop. "Tell me some things about Levin."

"He's tall, slender, has these eyes that—"

"Something I can use, O'Malley."

"He's in a band."

"A trumpet band?"

"If you think I don't hear that sarcasm, you are mistaken." I knew from asking around that Andrew played mediocre guitar in a band that sang hard rock covers.

"So you ask him when his band plays next. How they got together. Discuss the stuff they play. And then do you know what to do next?" Ridley nudged me with his shoulder, and I smelled the soap from his post-practice shower. "This is the bonus question."

"I tattoo his name on my butt and become his groupie?"

He smiled. "You go to his show."

"I can't." That would require words. And sentences. And a level of bravery I didn't possess.

"You can. And you will. By tomorrow night, have your plan finalized." His slow wink would've made a weaker girl swoon.

"What are some other things guys like to talk about?"

"Ask him what—" The phone on the floor next to Ridley's leg buzzed. "Hang on. Hello?" He held the phone with one hand and reached for Emmie with the other. Whatever he heard on the other end, he didn't like. "I'll be there in ten."

Phone call ended, Ridley gathered his sister and her belongings, jerking the zipper of the backpack shut. "I've got to go."

"Five minutes of love lessons? That's it?"

"We'll double it tomorrow." His sister fussed in his strong arms, and her cry began to escalate. He took the stairs two at a time, and I followed them out to his Jeep.

"Is there something wrong?"

"Nothing I can't handle. Sorry to cut it short." Emmie thrashed her head against the car seat as he snapped her in. Ridley finally turned to me, his eyes focusing on mine as he paused. "You have homework tomorrow. Talk to your band nerd and get it done."

"Hey, Ridley?"

"Yeah?"

"Wherever you're going now—don't get arrested."

Chapter Eleven

I WAS A big believer in taking my time if the moment called for it. To just slow down and stop and smell the roses. Or the Dumpster next to my parking spot at Vital Roots, where my mom had told me to come for a Friday morning counseling session. I had gone ten below the speed limit to get there, then circled the block a few times when a favorite song came on the radio and simply *demanded* my accompaniment. This sufficient amount of lollygagging ensured I was at least twenty minutes late.

My gag reflex fully engaged, I walked up the cracked sidewalk and through the doors of the lobby. I hated counseling. Hated it. I'd done a few years of it, and I knew all the tricks and gimmicks. Talking about my personal life wasn't comfortable even in the best of situations. And a total stranger with a PhD and lots of nosy questions was even worse. I'd already pulled up the website while wasting more time sitting in the car, and my counselor looked to be about sixty and gray-headed. She probably ate a lot of granola while wearing comfortable shoes.

The lobby was decorated in spa colors, and I walked by three cushy beige couches before landing in front of the receptionist's desk. Light piano music played overhead.

"Hi, I'm Harper O'Malley. I'm here to see Patricia Philpot."

The receptionist smiled and consulted her computer. "Welcome, Harper. Your mom's already filled out your paperwork, so you're ready to go. Mrs. Philpot had a family emergency, so you'll actually be seeing Devon McTavish today. Devon told me to send you on back. Room number three on your right."

In the hush of the space, my boots sounded loud as I walked over the worn wooden planks of the hallway floor. I took in a gust of breath and knocked on the partially opened door number three.

"Come in!" called a voice.

I stepped inside, surprised that the Devon waiting for me wasn't a guy.

"Hello. Harper, right?" A tall, willowy lady stood up from her chair and held out a hand covered in stone rings. "I'm Devon. Come on in here. Take a seat." Her long black hair swinging, she gestured to the floral love seat.

I hesitantly sat, sinking into the cushions. "Sorry I'm late, Ms. McTavish." I was nothing if not polite when being rude.

"Please, it's Devon. You've been to counseling before, right?"

I nodded.

Devon sat in her big chair, pulling one leg beneath her while tying up her massive amount of hair in a knot on top of her head. Behind her ear was a black, swirly tattoo of the word *peace*. "So you know that no matter what time you arrive, we end on schedule."

"I understand."

"Oh, I know you do." Devon smiled. The lady couldn't be older than thirty. "You would know that the later you arrive, the less time we'll have. So next time, you get here five minutes early. Because you might want to have a short session, but the parental unit paying the bill has a totally different opinion." She slipped on a pair of black-frame glasses. "Let's get started, shall we?"

This gal was not what I was used to. She was about thirty years younger than I expected, looked like a supermodel, and totally just called me out. "Yes, ma'am."

"So I've talked to your mom a bit." Devon pulled a legal pad from the table beside her. "I know you've been through a lot."

"I'm a teenager. We all think we've been through a lot."

She watched me, wearing that sympathetic counselor look that said, *You can trust me*, and giving me just enough silence to make me anxious to fill it. But I wasn't going to. I knew this game.

I studied the framed prints on the wall beyond her, a series of seashells with quotes under them like, "Dive in with all your heart."

"Why don't you tell me about yourself," she said.

I hated this question. "I go to Washington High School, I'm in the band, I like animals, I watch a lot of Masterpiece Theater, and I make a mean chocolate chip cookie."

"Cookies, huh? Do you bake often?"

Lately, yes. "Just here and there."

Devon laughed. "You'll have to tell me your secret. I tend to burn everything I touch in the kitchen."

She couldn't handle some Toll House cookies, but people trusted her with children's mental health?

Devon ran her pointer finger across a line in her notebook as she read. She then lifted her head, her eyes peering from above her glasses. "Here's the deal, Harper. You have years of experience in therapy."

Something every teen girl wanted on her life résumé.

"You're a smart girl, and I imagine by now you know how this all goes."

"I think I have the gist of it. We spend the first session talking about mundane things so you can get to know me, make me feel more at ease, and review for any possible revelations."

She tapped her pencil on her notebook. "That's about it. Would you like to skip all that and just get to it?"

I reached for the pillow beside me on the love seat and clutched it to my stomach. "I'd like to not be here, if we're being honest."

The counselor grinned. "Honesty is exactly what I'm going for." Her elbow found the arm of the chair, and she rested her chin in her hand and leaned toward me. "I want you to take a moment and think about the moment that everything changed." Her voice was as serene as the background music in a yoga class.

"It's been all over the news. What you read is pretty much how it went. My dad had an affair, had a wreck, and got caught."

"I'm not talking about your father."

Oh. "I don't think I understand."

"Tell me about your mother. Your biological mother."

Words flew from my mind like startled ravens, leaving me with nothing but empty space. "I . . . I don't know."

"You don't know?"

"I mean, I don't know what you want me to say."

"Tell me about your mother."

"My mother is Cristy O'Malley." Now I made direct eye contact with Devon. Because it was important we get the titles right. "Becky Dallas is my birth mom, and no longer my parent."

She scribbled in her notebook. "Okay, tell me about that."

Most days I'd rather chew a mouthful of razor blades than discuss Becky Dallas, but not cooperating with the counselor would only buy me more sessions. "My bio-mom couldn't take care of me, so I was placed in foster care at age nine. Then I was eventually adopted by the O'Malleys."

Devon leaned back in her chair, her arms crossed over her chest. "That's a very tidy version of the story."

"I call it my Hallmark version."

"How about you give me the HBO documentary version?"

"The one that stars Taylor Swift as me?"

She grinned. "Exactly. How does her story go?"

My fingers plucked at the fringe on the pillow. "It was a long time ago. Bad choices were made, but we've all moved on."

"That's much too simple to be accurate."

"Shouldn't we be talking about my dad or my unhealthy habit of binge-watching Bollywood romances?"

"Frenzies of Bollywood movies." She pretended to jot that down and nodded gravely. "Definitely something to come back to. There might be some medication for that. Like popcorn." The humor left her kind expression, and I knew she was back to business. "It's my understanding your birth mother has a parole hearing."

"True."

"And what do you think about that?"

I shrugged. "It happens about every two years. I'm used to it."

"And if your mother were to be released from prison this time?"

"I . . . I would be okay with that."

"Interesting."

I hated it when they said that. It meant, *This is an issue. This is something I want to take a scalpel to and dissect until you're lying on the floor, bleeding out from the heart.*

"Do you ever think about her being free?" the counselor

asked.

I thought about shrugging it off. But instead I went with the truth. "Yes."

"Does the thought scare you?"

I chewed on my lower lip and inspected the hands in my lap.

"It's okay to be afraid," Devon said. "It can manifest itself in lots of ways. Anxiety. Depression." She paused and watched me. "Difficulty in relationships. Unresolved bitterness. Fear of the future. Even nightmares. Does any of this sound familiar?"

I ignored a rogue tear and met the counselor's stare. "I think our time is up."

Chapter Twelve

I HAD FAILED.

To put it in football lingo, I'd totally fumbled.

By the time I got to school and downed a Dr Pepper to wash away the bad taste therapy left in my mouth, there'd been only ten minutes left of band. That left little time to engage in extensive and witty banter with Andrew. In fact, the sum total of my conversation with him was something along the lines of, "How's it going?" To which he'd romantically responded, "Good, dude."

Was it too presumptuous to interpret "dude" as "my angel-faced love muffin"?

"Molly, I need some help." I got my lunch tray and picked up a juice. "My homework today is to talk to Andrew and find out when his band plays next."

"Homework?" She stopped at the cashier and plugged in her student ID to pay. "Did I miss that assignment in pre-cal?"

I handed the cafeteria lady some cash, thanked her, and walked toward our table in the caf. "It doesn't matter. The point is, time is ticking before the dance." I recalled my instructions from Ridley. "I need to make conversation with Andrew and show him I'm interested in things he's interested in."

She put her tray down on our table. "Where does he usually sit at lunch?"

"Outside. Commons."

"Then let's go."

The warm days of the Indian summer had surrendered to the chillier temps of fall, or as my dad would say, true football weather. A brisk breeze sailed through my wavy bob as we walked outside the side exit of the caf and into the grassy area of picnic tables. The remaining leaves shimmied in flavors of red, gold, and harvest brown, and though I didn't go crazy for sports like my family did, I loved this time of year. From mid-September to early December, the air carried the distinct scent of football season. And nobody did football like Washington High. Warm days and increasingly cool nights. Games that required layers. Huddling up close with mittened hands around watery concession stand cocoa and a band booster bowl of Frito pie for supper. Extra cheese. Extra Fritos.

We weren't a super-large school, but we had a coaching staff the local universities frequently tried to recruit, a team of men who turned boys into champions. And it wasn't just football. WHS had bred high-caliber athletes for decades, causing outsiders to wonder if there really was magic in the air we breathed in Maple Grove. If so, I was clearly wearing invisible nose plugs.

Tonight was an away game, my very favorite kind. With the bus ride, it would provide even more time to talk to Andrew. Or to work on sending him my telepathic loves notes since I couldn't seem to find my voice when he was near.

I spotted Andrew and his friend Zach at a table near the basketball goals. "There's not a table nearby." I was embarrassed to be standing there, hand blocking the noon light from my eyes, surveying the lunchtime masses like I was trolling for guys. Which was exactly what I was doing.

"There may not be a table open," Molly said. "But I see

something even better. There's just enough room for us to sit down with your boy."

"Wait—no." But it was too late. Molly walked to Andrew's table like a woman on a mission. Like she was a bullet, and they were her bull's-eye.

"Mind if we sit with you?"

At Molly's question, both guys looked up from their matching slices of pizza. Her southern accent and throaty voice made it sound alluring instead of intrusive.

"Um, sure." Andrew scooted over and Molly jerked her head for me to sit down.

"Thanks," I managed. I slid into the bench, my thighs pressed against Andrew's. Though it was chilly, I'd worn a pink skirt, and I was grateful I had shaved my legs. A girl just never knew. I would never want stubble to get in the way of me and true love.

"So . . . pizza. I love pizza," I said. I could almost hear Ridley in my head, laughing. What was it he had told me to do? Get Andrew talking about himself. Okay, I could do this.

Attempt number two.

"Andrew, tell me about yourself." I repeated Ridley's words exactly, but they didn't sound sexy coming from me. They sounded . . . weird and nosy. Like I was trying to decide how much energy I wanted to devote to a possible stalking.

"What do you want to know?" Andrew angled his body toward mine, his face alight with interest.

Oh, my gosh. It had worked. That stuff seriously worked.

What did I want to know? When we could go out. When I could call him my boyfriend. When it was socially acceptable to scribble his name all over my notebooks.

"Tell me about your band," I said, gaining a smile of approval from Molly.

Andrew looked totally into our conversation now. "The Mushroom Cloud Raincoats."

Even his band name was adorable. "How did you come up with that?" Andrew answered, but I didn't hear a word he said. I just watched him, as if in a dream. He was talking to me. And he acted like he wanted to. I wasn't used to this reaction from guys. Unless they needed my homework. Or wanted free tickets to a game. I didn't even mind that his shoulder touched mine, that he was in my bubble. Welcome to my bubble, Andrew! I rather liked it. I could do this.

"And then we got our first booking, and the rest is history."

"Harper loves music." Molly took a delicate bite of her salad, and I couldn't help but be envious of the natural grace she possessed. Every move she made was like a dollop of confectionary charm. Why had none of that rubbed off on me? I looked down and noticed I had a piece of romaine on my shirt.

"I play the piano a bit too," I said. "The classics mostly."

"Chopin?" Andrew asked. "Bach?"

I swallowed a sip of juice. "Boy bands."

Zach leaned forward, his elbows on the metal table. "Hey, aren't you Coach O'Malley's daughter?"

And like a dart to a balloon, my happy bubble burst.

"Yes."

"That's crazy what's going on."

"Yep." Suddenly there wasn't enough ranch dressing for my salad. For my life. "So Andrew, your band—"

"Seriously." Zach was not going to let this go. "The news said he's being harassed and stuff. Ticket holders are mad that he's ruined the season. Has anyone come after you?"

I felt pretty harassed right now. "No." I scratched my neck, my skin suddenly itching like I had eaten some bad shellfish. The hives were starting. I knew my skin would be splotchy with red.

"Do you even know this Josie chick?" Zach was a bird dog, shaking this line of conversation like a dead squirrel. "The internet has pics of your dad visiting her at the hospital today." He dug in his pocket for his phone. "They're grainy, but it's totally him."

"We should go." I picked up my tray, a yogurt wobbling and dropping to the ground like a grenade. "I have to study for a test." *And check my phone for these photos.* I didn't even care that I was littering. I just had to get out of there. Away from Zach.

"Harper, wait!"

Only ten minutes and then lunch would be over. I could go to the band room and practice my solo for tonight. I could camp out in the library and study or talk to the Dungeons & Dragons guys. I could—

"Hey." Andrew ran in front of me, pushing his long hair from his worried face. His hands graced my shoulders, and I immediately stepped back at the touch.

So stupid! This was the object of my obsessive affection, and I'd wanted to see those musician's hands on me for weeks. Why was I so freaking weird?

"Hey, I'm really sorry about that." Andrew frowned toward the tables where Molly now appeared to be lighting into Zach. "My friend's an idiot. He didn't mean to stir things up. The guy has no filter."

"It's okay." I had no skill with repartee. I was no Molly, so I just went with honest. "It's hard to have your life out there for everyone to read about in the papers or see on TV. We've always been in a fishbowl, but never like this." And everything was still raw, like a sore that wouldn't heal.

"I can't imagine what you're going through. I didn't know about it until Zach told me." His friend was a total tool. "How are you doing?"

"I'm fine." Mostly. Occasionally. "Andrew?"

"Yeah?"

Ask him about himself. Ask him about his interests. Ask him when his band plays next. "Do you want to go to the band dance with me?"

"What?" His face froze, like the last seconds of a soap opera before it cuts to a commercial break.

No, no, no! It wasn't supposed to go like this. I was supposed to say clever things! Learn more about him! Flirt and toss my hair!

It was ruined.

It wasn't true that I had no game. I had horrendously awful game.

My words flew in a scrambled rush. "Never mind. Forget I asked."

He merely stood there and frowned.

Cursing my past, my future, and this present moment, I did a perfect marching band pivot.

And marched away from Andrew Levin.

I WANTED TO die.

I wanted to evaporate into the popcorn-scented air until the only thing left of me was my stupid bowl hat and red fluffy plume.

At five thirty, I climbed off the band bus, grabbed my trumpet, and focused every bit of energy I had left on not sitting in the parking lot of Randolph High School and bawling my eyes out.

Do you want to go to the band dance with me?

Where had that even come from? How could I go from romantically paralyzed one minute to full-on aggressive the next? I blamed reality TV. Dating shows. The weirdo counselor dredging up all that junk from my past. And that stupid friend of Andrew's. All his questions. A smothering feeling had come over me, like someone had pulled a sleeping bag over my entire body, trapping my arms and legs—frantic with no way out.

I had totally spazzed. My brain had moved at warp speed, searching for a conversation distraction, and I had certainly found it. And to make matters worse, I found the photos Andrew's friend had alluded to. Yep, it was there on the internet, all right. My dad coming out of the very hospital that was taking care of Josie Blevins.

"Where's Andrew?" Molly's head rotated like a periscope. "I didn't see him on the bus."

"Probably getting a restraining order."

"Harper, you asked a boy out. Big deal. If he can't handle it, then forget him. He should've thrown himself at your feet in gratefulness."

"He was probably too busy trying not to throw up on my feet." Andrew had not been on the band bus to Randolph, home of the Roosters, one of the saddest mascots ever. Was Andrew so desperate to avoid me he had stayed home?

"O'Malley, front and center!" Mr. Sanchez called into his stupid bullhorn. "I wanna hear that solo pronto."

While the rest of the band continued chatting about the lives they had not completely screwed up, I stood next to Mr. Sanchez and somehow played my part of our selection from *Wicked*.

"O'Malley, where's your head?" He put his hands on his ample hips. "You repeated that last stanza twice. You missed the high B again. Are you ready for this or not?"

"Yes." My hands shook as I held my beloved horn. "I can do this."

"Are you feeling all right?"

"Today I accidentally asked a boy out."

"See if Mrs. Sanchez has some Pepto-Bismol for that." His stubby fingers tapped some notes on his iPad. "Take it from the top."

We soon lined up to fill our seats on the end of the visitor side bleachers. Tears pressed at my burning eyes. It wasn't that I was ashamed I had put myself out there. That was quite modern of me. No, it was Andrew's face. His slackened jaw. The eyes that went wide as cymbals. In my dreams, he wouldn't have reacted that way. Of course, in my dreams, he would've been the one doing the asking. Maybe I was delusional, and Andrew *was* completely out of my league.

I had just placed my black shoe on the ramp leading to the bleachers when I heard my name. "Harper!"

Just when I thought it couldn't get worse.

Dad.

He stood next to Mom and Cole. He wore a gray hoodie, dark jeans, and a cap that hid part of his face. He looked like a regular father, and not the coach who had become a national disgrace. I could hardly bring myself to make eye contact because all I saw were those photos of Dad and his girlfriend. I wanted to say something so bad. Did Mom know he'd been to see her?

"Your mom said you had a solo." Dad started to rest his arm across my shoulders, but seemed to think better of it. "I wanted to see you play."

What was he even doing here? And with Mom? Cole stood between them. Mom smiled at me, but she couldn't hide the shadows beneath her eyes, the strain at her mouth, the hands clutched in front of her.

"Thanks for coming," I said woodenly. "I better go find my seat."

"You'll do wonderful." Mom gave me a side hug and straightened the collar of my jacket. The tension radiating from her was so obvious, I felt like I could reach out and grab it like a fluttering moth. "Knock 'em dead, kiddo."

Oh, I'd already pretty much killed it tonight. "Thanks. See you later."

"Harper, wait."

My dad stepped in front of my path. "I've missed you."

"Yeah." There I was again, a regular wordsmith. I could almost see Dad's unspoken thoughts hovering over his head, but I wasn't ready to hear them. And the home of the Roosters wasn't the place.

"Your brothers are coming over tomorrow. I'm grilling. Making your favorite burgers."

"Is Mom coming?"

He chewed his lip. "No."

"Is your girlfriend going to be there?"

I'd never seen him so still. "No. Just us. Come on, Harper. I know you said you needed some time, but you can't keep shutting me out. I just want to spend time with you. And we need to talk."

The band had climbed to the top of the bleachers, and I saw Molly lean over and wave me on.

"I need to go." My head was a mess. Like the dregs of an ice-cream sundae, the brown watery goo left in the bottom of the bowl.

"See you tomorrow evening?"

I didn't even respond. Walking away, I made my way up the steps, my feet like lead. My heart was somewhere in the vicinity of my gut. I'd just reached the top and set my trumpet down, when I saw the first flash of the camera. Then heard the reporter call out.

"Coach O'Malley! A moment of your time, sir!"

"Coach O'Malley! Over here!"

"It is O'Malley!"

From my vantage point high above the stadium, I could see it all.

One reporter turned into three. Then five.

Soon Dad was swarmed.

He lifted a hand, like a seasoned Hollywood star blocking the paparazzi's lenses.

"No comment," I heard him say.

The parents in the stands noticed the ruckus, and some stood to get a better look.

I watched Mom move Cole to the side, pulling him into the shadows.

Dad limped away. His life once again center stage.

And my solo forgotten.

Chapter Thirteen

O N SATURDAY, I woke up with a humiliation hangover.

I spent the day moping about, mostly checking Andrew's social media for statuses like, *Can teenagers get restraining orders?* or *Does anyone know how to detox from delusional girls?* I was relieved that by evening, he hadn't posted a thing. But maybe there was a message in his silence. The dating world was seriously the most messed up place ever. I wanted to defect to a different planet where boys were not allowed.

By five o'clock, I sat in the back of my brother's Mustang listening to him and Cole rehashing last night's game. Being the guys they were, they avoided all talk of the reporters swarming Dad. It was all yardages, passes, kicks, and hey, did you see when that cheerleader nearly lost her skirt? I didn't care about any of it.

Because I had asked Andrew out. You'd think hearing "no" in response would be the worst outcome. But actually, it was hearing . . . nothing. I had funneled all my wounded pride and anger into my halftime solo performance, and I had rocked that stadium.

But it had been a hollow victory.

Now my brothers and I were interstate-bound to visit dad for this stupid barbecue. While some of my best memories were cookouts with dad, I still quaked inside at the thought of sitting in his rental house for a few hours, chatting it up as if nothing had happened. As if he hadn't screwed us all over, and the whole state didn't want his head on a platter.

As if he might not ever come back home.

"You're speeding, Michael."

My brother shot me a glare in the rearview. "You've been a hag all day. What's your deal?"

"Nothing." My deal was that I didn't understand boys. My life. The world in general.

"Well, whatever it is, suck it up." Michael gave a quick incline of his head toward Cole. It was a warning to be on my best behavior for the sake of our little brother.

Dad's rental was an unremarkable brick ranch in a gated golf course development five minutes away from the university. Michael pulled into the sloped driveway and jumped out. The scent of charcoaled meat wafted on the breeze. If there wasn't some sort of vegetarian entree with my name on it, me and my crap attitude were walking home.

Dad opened the door and held out his good arm. "Hey!" I guess it was an open invitation to step into his embrace.

Michael and Cole moved hesitantly into Dad's hug.

"Missed you guys." Dad's eyes met mine, assessing the situation. "Harper, you look great, sweetie."

I traced a figure eight on the driveway with my toe. "Thanks."

My dad's left arm hung at an L in his sling, and his face still looked like he'd cleaned the asphalt with his forehead. There were a few scrapes that would probably leave permanent scars. Forever reminders of bad memories. I knew about those.

"Come on back. Got the grill going on the deck."

Like dutiful children, we followed Dad through the house. The living room was cozy with a matching nail-trimmed leather couch and love seat. A large flat-screen hung over the oak mantel like prized art. The small dining room we passed contained a circular glass table and four black Parsons chairs. The kitchen, a room my dad barely knew how to use, gleamed with stainless steel and granite, and a smaller table and chairs were nestled in a corner breakfast nook.

"You've really gotten comfortable here," I said, noticing the geometric art on the kitchen's gray walls.

Dad put his hand in his back pocket and looked around with a bland smile. "It came this way. Fully furnished."

I nodded. "How convenient."

The part of my heart that was as charred as the coals in his grill had hoped to find him in a sparse, empty home. Sleeping on an air mattress, eating ramen and Lucky Charms every night as he cried over his pitiful missteps.

The kitchen opened up to a large deck that overlooked his emerald green yard. From the deck you could see the ninth hole, and a man hefting a bag of clubs waved in our direction.

"Let me check these burgers. Harper, you want cheese on your veggie burger, right? Pepper jack?"

"Cheddar." I didn't want cheddar. I wanted to be difficult. Just to say, *Do you really know me, Dad?*

"I'm sorry I missed the halftime show." The grill hissed as Dad flipped a hamburger patty. "Your mom sent me video though. You were incredible. I'm so proud."

I zipped up my hot pink hoodie and rubbed my arms against the evening chill. "Thank you."

"I texted you last night. Even left a voicemail. Did you get that?"

"I'm not sure," I lied.

"Well." Dad watched me through the smoke, his eyes searching, studying. Perhaps looking for a way in. "I asked if you were up for breakfast at the Main Street Grill next Saturday. Just the two of us, like old times."

Once a month, Dad took me to the diner at a ridiculously early hour before he headed to the stadium. He always let me get a double helping of their magical hash browns, and I always gave him the bacon that had no business touching my plate.

"I'm pretty busy," I said.

I was spared inventing more creative excuses when Cole broke into a story about setting a new time for the half mile in track practice. Then Michael one-upped it with some story about how he'd basically saved the world with his latest three-point shot technique, and I just tried to not stick my head in the bag of chips on the table.

The three of them were so alike. All tall, slender, a natural muscular tone. Hair that belonged in a shampoo commercial, noses that were slightly too angular. And athletic. It was a bond that I didn't share with the DNA-connected O'Malleys. I never would.

In the early years I had tried so hard to fit into this family, desperate for them to like me. On my tenth birthday, I asked for a book on football and stayed up all night devouring the pages. I cried when I finished the last chapter because I knew that by the book's end, I still didn't like the game. Still loved fantasy novels, puppies, and music more.

In seventh grade, I ran track, always coming in last despite my coach's yelling and my parents' sideline cheering. I prayed to grow taller, funnier, cooler. But I guess God was too busy throwing Amazing Dust on my family and tossing me the Nerd Juice boxes.

We ate outside against a backdrop of stilted conversation, the distant whack of a golf ball, and the occasional buzzing insect. A fire pit crackled and glowed near the table, but I couldn't seem to get warm.

Dad chewed his last bite of hamburger as he dipped two of his famous homemade fries into a swirl of ketchup. "Kids, I know this has been hard. Confusing."

So much for small talk.

"I've said it before, but I wanted to tell you again how sorry I am for what I've put you through. I love your mother. I love the three of you."

"So you and Mom aren't gonna get a divorce?" Cole asked, mustard hiding in the corner of his upper lip. "You're coming back, aren't you, Dad?"

Dad rewrapped a damp napkin around his sweating tea glass. "Your mom and I have lots of talking to do."

"What about Thanksgiving?" Cole sniffed. "You'll be back by then, right?"

"I'm not sure, buddy," Dad said. "I'm going to stay here for a while."

"People are pretty mad," Michael said. I knew my older brother was torn up too. But he never let us see how deep the pain drilled down.

"They are very mad," Dad said. "They have every reason to be. Fracturing the team like this affects people's jobs, my coaching staff's families, recruiting options, and money for the university."

"And scholarships," I said. "Like Ridley Estes's. He had his whole future planned out, and now they've gone back on your verbal offer."

Dad leaned back and pinched the bridge of his nose. "It's a mess."

Spilled grape juice on the carpet? A mess. Spaghetti sauce on your T-shirt? Mess. But Ridley losing his chance to play on a full ride at the best university in the South? Life altering.

"Isn't there something you can do?" I threw my napkin onto my plate. "Can't you talk to someone?"

"There was a scout from Tennessee Tech at the game just last night," Michael said. "Ridley has recruiters swooping around him like vultures. He'll land somewhere."

"How can you be sure?" I asked.

"Last year he caught seventy-eight passes for 1,703 yards," Dad said. "This year he's primed to top that. He's a hot commodity. Or would be if he'd keep his nose clean."

I swallowed a cold fry. "It's a shame when a guy's personal life gets in the way."

We stayed through Dad's love offering of s'mores over his fire pit. I'd hoped to leave early, but Dad had made a career in strategy, and he knew I couldn't resist chocolate and the gooey goodness of melted marshmallow. Finally, after I inhaled three of those and sat through the boys challenging Dad to a few rounds of Horse in the driveway in the glow of headlights, it was time to go.

"You guys drive carefully." Dad watched each of us buckle up. "I'll call you tomorrow."

I gave him a stiff hug before shutting myself in the back.

"Dang it," I said as Michael started the car. "Forgot my phone." And I needed it for all those boys who weren't calling me. "Will you go get it, Cole?"

"Nope."

I mumbled some of Ridley's Spanish curses the whole way to the door. This weekend would be the end of me.

"Forget something?" Dad stood in the doorway as I came

back in. Like he'd been watching us go.

"Phone." I crossed the distance to the kitchen in a speed that should've gotten me some points for athleticism, then retrieved the device from the granite bar.

When I sailed back to the living room, Dad has planted himself right in my path, his good arm settled on his hip. "Hold up there, sis."

"Found it." I held my phone out and barely slowed.

"Harper, stop."

Spine rigid, I halted. Stared at the pewter veins running amuck in the white tile.

"Becky Dallas's parole hearing is next month," he said. "Because of publicity, my current attorney advised me not to go to the hearing," Dad said. "I'm only telling you because I was worried you'd hear it from your mom first or—"

"So you're not going? I guess you need to lay low and—"

"Of course I'm going." Dad walked to me, his head tilted as if he couldn't believe he'd heard me correctly. "I could be in the midst of my own court battle, but I'd still get to that parole hearing. We could live across the country, and I'd still be in that courtroom to remind that judge of what happened to my daughter."

I swallowed against the lump in my throat and nodded. "Thank you."

"I hate that I've hurt you so much that you doubt me. Doubt my commitment to you."

Hurt seemed too small a word. "What about Mom?"

"That's a given I've hurt her. And I'm dealing with that, but I'm talking about you. You won't answer my texts, you refuse my calls."

"I'm really busy right now. It's marching season, I have tutoring, the animal rescue is—"

"You're avoiding me."

A pain flickered behind my temples, the intensity building with every second I was in this house, this conversation. But Dad's lack of honesty had hurt me, and it was pathetic to offer him lies in return. So I told the truth. "Yes, I'm avoiding you. I'd asked for space."

"I'm your father."

Those words ricocheted in the room and pinged off my heart. "You said that same thing to me the day you and Mom adopted me." I sniffed and blinked. "This family . . . you've been my world. My safe place. For the first time in my life, I was safe. And the whole time, I kept waiting for the bottom to drop out. It was too good to be true. I *knew* it was too perfect."

"No matter what happens, I'm your father. This family is still your safe place. You're ours, Harper. How many times did we have to tell you that those first few years? No one can take you away from us."

All these years I'd been a tightrope walker, and somehow with Dad's affair, my net was gone. "You can't promise me you and Mom are going to work it out, can you?"

He ran a hand over his stubbly face. "No. But—"

I shook my head, the angry thoughts rattling from side to side. "I hate that you've done this." I swiped at my nose with the back of my hand. "Why did you have to mess this up? Were we not enough?" And then the question that had lurked in the dark recesses of my mind from the day I was born. "Was *I* not enough?"

"Good gosh, Harper. Don't say that. We worked so hard— *you* worked so hard—to find your place with us. No matter what I've done, how can you doubt how much we love you? You're a permanent part of this family, and nothing will ever change that."

"Why are there pictures of you on the internet with that Josie person?"

The vein near Dad's ear twitched. The one that popped whenever Michael came in two hours after curfew or I bought too many books on his credit card. "Maybe they're old. She was my employee, so there are probably lots of photos out there that include the two of us."

"You're wearing your sling, and your face looks like it went through a meat grinder. They're not old."

He suddenly looked like he was regretting initiating our little heart-to-heart. "It's not what it seems."

"It seems like you've recently seen your girlfriend. Want to tell me again how sorry you are for what you've done to Mom and your kids?"

"I don't expect you to understand."

"But I do understand. And that's the most frightening part. I think I see the situation perfectly clear, Dad."

"Josie needed someone to pick her up from the hospital. She had no one. She's lost a fiancé, her parents are zero help, and her friends have left her high and dry. I got her into this mess, the least I could do was—"

"Call her a taxi? Ask one of the other coaches to give her a ride?"

"I'm telling you, no matter what you see in those photos, Josie and I are through."

"You used to be my hero." I sidestepped my father and reached for the door.

"And now?" came my dad's voice. "Now who am I?"

"The man who chose his girlfriend over his family." I turned and looked at my father. "Someone whose words I don't believe."

Chapter Fourteen

SUNDAY MORNING'S RAINSTORM woke me up at four thirty. Menacing shadows lunged and loomed on the walls, and I pulled the covers over my head to block out the noise.

I was right back in that dingy duplex on Mockingbird Street. Seven years old, and the tornado sirens wailing their call to all of Templeton, Mississippi, to take shelter. My shoebox-sized bedroom was on the second floor, and even at that young age, I knew from drills at school that I was supposed to get to the ground level.

But I couldn't.

My mother had gone out for the night, and I didn't have to try the door to know it was locked. They often say the tornado comes in the quiet, but outside the wind howled, the thunder crashed, and rain fell like metal pellets. I prayed for God to save me. Protect my mom. Make the tornado go away. For somebody to come and rescue me.

But no one ever came.

The tornado hit the edge of town, ripping into homes with a brutal savagery that tore into roofs, walls, and lives.

And it stopped two miles from my house, deciding it was bored with Templeton and had chewed and spit out all it desired.

Storms still kept me awake. On thunder-filled nights, the O'Malleys used to find me in the floor of their bedroom with my pillow, teddy bear, and blanket. My counselor once told me eventually storms would no longer bring me terror. And one day I'd see it as a beautiful musical score by nature. I think that woman drank a lot.

Now, after perusing the internet for more photos of Dad and finding nothing new, my phone told me it was only five a.m., but I slipped out of bed, dressed, and made my way downstairs. My earbuds in, I listened to some classic One Direction while unloading the dishwasher and whipping up cinnamon rolls for breakfast.

Hours later, the storm grew lazy. As it wound down to a sprinkle, my family and I stepped out of the car and onto the sidewalk leading to the doors of the Maple Grove Community Church for the first time since the scandal. Church had been new to me when I came to live with the O'Malleys. Previously Sundays had been dedicated to doing my bio-mom's laundry and staying out of her way. By about my fifth visit to the O'Malleys' church, I knew something had a hold of me. I think God speaks to us all differently, and I heard him first in the music. The church choir had been something straight out of a Tyler Perry movie, full of gospel and soul and movement, with a full band backing them up. A powerful current had climbed up my arm and traveled the expanse of my skin, and I'd lifted my hands to heaven as if I was trying to catch the music notes in the air. I knew I'd met God that day. He'd been in the atmosphere, in the vibrato of the soloist's voice, and in the tripping, bluesy call of the piano keys. Church quickly became a safe harbor. But since Dad's event, it was like God was calling my phone, and I was letting it go straight to voice mail. I just wasn't interested.

"I think that sun's going to pop out yet," Mom said, adjusting Cole's shirt collar as we walked.

"Mrs. O'Malley! Mrs. O'Malley!"

We all turned toward the man hopping out of a Ford sedan.

"Keep walking, kids." Mom's heels clipped against the pavement. "Heads up and keep moving."

"Do you know him?" Cole asked.

"Mrs. O'Malley!" The man caught up to us, his large belly quivering with his hustle. "Can you confirm that the university is going to fire Coach O'Malley?"

Mom said nothing, and her hand at my back pushed me forward.

"Do you have any comment about the recent photos of your husband with his former employee, Josie Blevins?"

At that Mom stopped. She spun around on the reporter so fast, he tottered backward, and for one hopeful second, I thought he might hit the sidewalk.

Mom poked her finger right in his bloated face. "Since you know who I am, let me remind you who these three individuals are—they're my children. And they shouldn't have to be subjected to someone so low as to make catcalls ten feet away from the Lord's house." She stepped so close she was surely breathing his same air. "This is sacred ground you're standing on, and I don't mean because we're at church. I mean because *I'm* standing on this ground. And who am I? I'm a mother. And these are *my* children. And if you get near them again, I will go full-on Mama Bear, throw down my handbag, and rip out your throat until it comes out your big mouth. *Are we clear?*"

Wide-eyed, the man nodded.

"Oh, I don't think I heard you." Mom reached for her purse strap.

"Yes, ma'am! Yes, Mrs. O'Malley."

"Good." She exhaled loudly and found a cool smile. "You

have a blessed day now. Come on, kids."

As the man scurried away, Mom did a 180-degree glare around the parking lot, circling like a vengeful satellite in case any other reporters had the same idea.

"Whoa," Cole said as we continued our trek to the sanctuary. "I thought we weren't supposed to talk to those guys."

"I've been wanting to do that for years." Mom waved to a friend across the lawn. "Felt kinda good."

"So can we yell at reporters too?" Michael asked.

Mom opened the big glass door. "Not on your life."

Cole escaped downstairs to youth, but Mom, Michael, and I walked into the sanctuary amid curious stares and whispers behind hands. My mom was brave to return here. Twice she'd been out in the last week, and some Eagle-worshipping redneck had set her straight on what kind of life-ruining joke of a coach she'd married. The odds of us moving were greater than the odds of a zit on picture day.

We sat in the back, and I couldn't help but be relieved when an hour and a half passed, and the minister bid us a good week.

"Good message by the pastor," Mom said as she pulled her SUV into the garage at straight-up noon. The sermon had been on forgiveness, and I had tuned most of it out. A few sentiments squeezed their way through the cracks of my hardened heart. Like when the pastor said we all mess up. That we're to forgive pretty much to infinity. That when you point a finger at someone, you have three more pointing right back at yourself. He made it all sound so simple. But it just wasn't. I hadn't told my beliefs to God yet, but He was free to read it in my diaries.

"Glad we went." Cole climbed out of the backseat. "I hit the donut jackpot in youth."

Michael gave his brother an air high five. "The good Lord

giveth and the good Lord taketh."

"Yep." Cole grinned. "And I tooketh three glazed and an éclair."

We were barely inside the house when the doorbell rang.

"Don't open it without checking," Mom called as Cole's long, skinny legs carried him to the foyer.

The security at the gate had finally gotten good at weeding out most reporters, but occasionally one got through.

"It's Tyler and Marcus!" Cole called.

"From the team?" I asked.

"Yeah. Might be a few more too."

Marcus and three other university football players stepped into the house, their hulking bodies filling the space.

"Hi, guys." Mom's smile was hesitant, apologetic even.

"We were all sitting around in the dorm," Marcus said. "And it just didn't feel right. It being a Sunday afternoon and us not being together."

"We missed you, Mama O'Malley," said Desmond Phillips, right guard.

Mom blinked quickly and delicately cleared her throat. "Oh, boys. I . . . I don't have lunch today. I didn't think you'd—"

"No need, Mrs. O'Malley." Marcus put two fingers to his mouth and gave a shrill whistle. "This time we brought it to you."

It was like a parade of the Eagles' finest coming through that door. One by one they filed in, hands full of bags from Chauncey's Chicken House downtown. Even a salad for me. Each football player hugged my mom, gave me fist bumps, then shook my brothers' hands.

Marcus took off his Eagles hat and the rest of the team followed. "I'm gonna say grace." He paused and his dark eyes swept the room. Normally my dad did the honors, and it was lost on no one. But Dad wasn't there. It was just the houseful of us. Black, white, Hispanic, young, and middle-aged. A family united in its hurt and in its loss.

"Let us pray."

Marcus grabbed my hand as he thanked God for my family, calling us out by name, asking for help for the team, and blessings on the extra-crispy food. He gave my fingers a squeeze, and I squeezed his right back.

"Amen."

Mom brought out paper plates, her nose noticeably red. But her smile lit up like Cole's on Christmas morning, and happiness surged deep within me and melted a little of that ice.

"You gone out with that punk kid yet?" Desmond asked, handing me a biscuit.

"No." Humiliation was my drink of choice this weekend, so I just tipped it back and guzzled even more. "I asked him to a dance, and he turned me down." Ten heads swiveled in my direction, chicken suspended before open mouths. "Actually he didn't even answer."

Hand grenades exploding in the house couldn't have been louder than the reaction of the team.

"Gimme dat kid's address."

"I'm gonna punt him into Georgia."

"I'd like to throw that freak over the goalpost."

"That fool ain't fit to kiss the soles of your little bitty girl shoes."

"He gonna talk to my friends Righty and Lefty!"

Beside me Marcus laughed and pulled me against his sweater-vest for a catch-and-release hug. "Say the word, and we will find him now."

Dominic Vago pushed up his sleeves. "Yeah, we can call that dessert."

I laughed at that, letting some of the tension roll off my shoulders, buoyed by these amazing college boys. I could get a team of campus kings to love me, but boys my own age? I was invisible as air.

"Dessert will be the cookies from my kitchen," Mom said. "Made by Harper herself."

Tyler shook his head. "Boy don't know what he's missing. Those your monster cookies?"

I smiled at the snaggletoothed twenty-year-old across the room. "They are."

"You got enough?" he asked.

Mom knew the answer to that. "She baked two hundred."

Dominic scratched his goateed chin. "That might do."

The doorbell chimed again, and as Mom and Cole went to get the fruits of my chronic anxiety, I ran to let the new visitor in.

"Ridley," I said, opening the door. "You're ten minutes late."

He lifted a hand by way of greeting and removed his black sunglasses.

Ouch. "Up all night doing homework by the light of the keg?"

"Yeah," he mumbled. "Don't forget the drugs and wild chicks."

"I'm sure *you* didn't."

His lips moved into what could only be a sneer as he stepped into the living room, squinting at the chaos and noise. "What's going on?"

Instead of answering, I just studied his face. His red-rimmed eyes watched the team with a look of such longing, it was like staring at one of my rescue animals when a visitor at the shelter stopped by their cage, only to walk on by. This was what Ridley wanted more than anything—to be part of this team. To be one of the guys. I had a feeling it wasn't just the jersey and scholarship he longed for, but the camaraderie and connection. Even though he wore the sash of Mr. Popularity, could it be that there was some part of him still searching for somewhere to belong?

Ridley finally pulled his eyes from the team, as if remembering why he was there. "Got your text about asking Wonder Boy out."

Heat infused my cheeks as that moment replayed in my mind again. Maybe ten years from now I would be able to think on it and laugh. Or at least not want to strangle every member of the male species. "Yeah. Andrew was so overcome with gratefulness, he forgot to answer."

He shrugged. "It happens."

"Ever happened to you?"

His lips curved. "Don't be ridiculous."

I couldn't help but laugh. "Want something to eat?"

"Nah, ate at—" He pressed his lips together, as if canceling out his words. "I ate earlier. Besides, I owe you a lesson. Grab your purse."

"Where are we going?"

He jangled his keys. "Class field trip."

THE BLACK JEEP slipped into a parking spot downtown in front of the statue of Betsy Callaghan and Blue. The pilgrim woman held a rifle and pointed it east, the direction we now walked. The old-timers said that Betsy came over on a covered wagon as an Irish immigrant by way of Tennessee. She had a lazy husband,

Lochlan, who made her cook, clean, tend the horses, navigate, and drive the wagon. When they got to the Appalachian Mountains, Lochlan got stung by a bee, puffed up like a rotten fish, and died right in his seat. When Betsy finally noticed, without slowing the wagon, she gave his shoulder a shove and over the side he went. Betsy kept on traveling, not stopping 'til she landed in what is now our town. She eventually found a man to build her a cabin beside her favorite grove of maples, trading her cooking for his manual labor. The well-fed Ezekiel asked Betsy to marry him, but she wouldn't say yes until Ezekiel agreed to help her with her dream to build a town. The two of them put their heads together, and buildings started taking shape— including the first saloon Betsy named Lochlan's Loss. I always thought Betsy would be proud to know the college sitting five miles from her favorite maple grove was one of the first to allow women.

"I can't be gone too long," I told Ridley, as I stepped onto the puddled sidewalk. "I'm due at the animal rescue by three."

"This way." He held an umbrella over my head and pressed his other hand to the small of my back, guiding me on the cracked sidewalk. "Why do you do that?"

I didn't slow at his question. "Do what?"

"Tense up when people touch you. I've watched you with the team, so I know it's not just me."

"No, it's just you."

"It's gotta be some weird hang-up you have. Because normally when I touch a girl—"

"She flings off her bra and morals?"

"And those are just the off days." His grin was sweet as cake icing as he held open the door to the coffee shop and ushered me in.

Liquid Courage was the name of the shop, and maybe that's exactly what I needed. The place buzzed with patrons, mostly sitting in pairs at cafe tables, chatting over steaming mugs of heavenly smelling caffeine. I inhaled deep and let the scent fill my senses. When I opened my eyes, Ridley was watching me, a small smile playing about his lips.

"You're cute when you do that."

"Do what?" I asked.

"Smile." He watched my lips for a moment too long. "You were smiling just then."

"I smile all the time."

"No, you don't. But when you do . . . it's nice."

"Right, nice . . . cute." I chuckled and stared at the chalk-scribbled specials.

"I knew you'd do that." He regarded me with sleep-deprived eyes. "Lesson number three—"

"What were one and two?"

"Lesson three is you never reject a guy's compliment."

"What if it's creepy?"

"Am I wasting my time here?"

"No." I stepped up to the cashier. "I'm listening."

We each ordered our beverage of choice, and before I could dig out my wallet, Ridley handed the college girl behind the counter enough to cover our drinks and a very nice tip.

"Here." I handed him some cash.

"Keep it."

"I want to buy my own."

"Harper, lesson number four. If the guy tells you you're not paying, let it go."

"But this isn't a date."

He handed me a straw and an ample number of napkins.

"Sorry, habit." He took half the napkins back. "I'm with my sisters a lot."

We moved to stand in the waiting area as the strains of an indie band played overhead. "There's more than Emmie?"

"Faith is eight."

"There's quite an age difference between you and Emmie. Did your parents—"

"It's just my mom."

"So your dad—"

"Never met mine. Here're our drinks." Ridley grabbed our cups and carried them to a seat way in the back, tucked in a dark corner beneath a poster of a famous local bluegrass musician.

He put our drinks on the table, then pulled out my chair.

"You're weirdly polite," I said.

He let out an audible breath. "We gotta work on your compliments."

Judging by his order of a triple-shot Americano, I assumed somebody'd had a long night.

"Did you finish your essay?" I sipped my hot chocolate.

He removed the lid from his coffee, as if merely sipping wouldn't deliver the caffeine fast enough. "We're here to talk about you."

"But it's due Monday and—"

"I did the paper, O'Malley. It's in your in-box for proofing. Now quit deflecting. Did you catch what I did when we were in line?"

"Looked at the cashier's boobs?"

"The other thing." He waved at a fellow WHS jock fives tables away. "I complimented you. Everyone likes compliments, am I right?"

"I don't really. They make me feel—"

"Every *normal* person likes them. Even guys. Find something to compliment him on."

"Okay. How about, 'Hey, Andrew, you're *awesome* at being a douche bag. Thanks for bolting after I asked you out.'"

Ridley didn't bother to hide his amusement. "Did you even try to ask one of his friends about it?"

"And bring more attention to my shame? No, I don't believe I did."

"Well, I did." He leaned his chin in his propped hand, and for the first time I noticed a charm dangling from a thin silver chain around his neck. It was the number thirteen. "He didn't go to the game, right?"

"So?"

"So he got sick."

"How do you know this?"

"Social media. Ever heard of it?"

"Yeah, and I checked it."

"Apparently not well. Did you just look at his or did you snoop on his friends' and get your answer like I did?"

"You don't even know his friends. You couldn't pick them out of a lineup."

"A lineup of nerds? Not necessary. I asked a friend of mine, who asked a friend of his, and through about ten degrees of separation, we infiltrated band geek world and got my intel."

"Andrew was sick? But why hasn't he called me? Texted? Sent a homing pigeon? Anything?"

"He got sick, Harper. I don't know. Maybe he got a look at his reflection in that ridiculous outfit you guys call uniforms."

"The plumes on our hats are a very sexy addition."

"It looks like you're wearing a peacock butt. But I take it Andrew was out of commission all weekend. So for the sake of my efforts, let's assume he's still a candidate for the man of your incredibly boring dreams."

Dare I hope? What kind of "sick" were we talking about? A fake cold? An emergency room visit involving a need for a girl to hold cold compresses to his head and whisper sweet words in his fevered ear?

"Look, either way, I have to fulfill my end of the bargain, so pay attention. Think of casual ways you can compliment this guy." Ridley's eyes traveled down my form. "Like, hey, I like that shirt. It looks . . . really good on you."

Fake flattery or not, his words spiked my system with happy. Behold, the power of a guy paying attention to a girl.

"Lesson number seven—"

"I think you missed—"

"Don't put yourself down to this dude. When I gave you a compliment in line, you completely rejected it."

But he'd said I was cute. Absolutely ridiculous. He'd dated the teen equivalent of Victoria's Secret Angels, and I knew I was nowhere near that realm of pretty. Granted I wasn't ugly and in need of a backpack over my head, but nobody was voting me Prettiest for the yearbook anytime soon.

"If a guy gives you a compliment and you shoot it down, he feels stupid. When we say stuff like that, it's our way of getting closer to you. To impress you. Let you know we notice things about you."

"You said I was cute." I had to laugh at the very idea. "What was I supposed to say to that?"

Ridley planted his elbows and leaned over the table. Eyes the color of molten chocolate pierced into mine. "How about *thank you?*"

Stars above, he had a beautiful face. And the way he looked

at me, I knew it was how he looked at all females. But still, I saw why the girls all but tripped over themselves to be in his very presence. But he was out of my league, so total immunity here. No fear of falling for *that*.

"Harper?"

His voice could heat an iced latte. "Yes?"

Ridley reached out, and his hand covered mine.

"What are you doing?" I whispered. It felt like the morning's lightning had reignited right where our skin now met.

"Do you remember what I told you?"

I nodded, my heart doing a clumsy pirouette.

"Andrew Levin just walked in."

I tried to jerk my hand out of his grip, but Ridley held tight and gave the smallest shake of the head. "Lesson number nine— sometimes guys need a little prodding. And the one thing they can't stand is to see a girl they like with another guy. Jealousy is a bitter pill." His thumb made a lazy swipe across my knuckles. "But sometimes it's exactly the medicine we need." He turned toward Andrew, then looked back at me.

"How did you know he'd be here?"

"Do I need to explain the internet again?"

Andrew stood at the register to order, but his eyes zoomed right toward me. Hope gushed like the fountain on the square.

"He's coming over here." I wanted to both hide in the bathroom and jump on the tabletop. "What do I do?"

Ridley stood up, reached out his hand, and tucked a strand of wayward hair behind my ear. "Steps one through ten."

Chapter Fifteen

S ITTING AT THAT corner table alone, all the rules flew away like startled birds as Andrew Levin meandered through the cafe, headed my direction.

Oh, geez.

Oh, geez.

What did I say? What did I do?

The old me would have broken eye contact, grabbed my purse, and made a break for the bathroom, the exit, the next town.

But no. I could do this. I was ready.

I could be a girl in Deep Like with a boy. I could talk and smile and do what normal girls did. I could do this freaking crush right. He was the first boy I'd felt the tingle for, and I knew, if I fought for it, he could be the one.

"Harper, hey." Andrew looked over his shoulder and gave a quick check of the door Ridley had just exited. "How are you?"

"Good. Fine. Caffeinated." Three seconds in, and my conversation was a sinking torpedo. "I mean, how are you?"

He smiled sheepishly. "Been a bit under the weather. Um, do you need to go? That Ridley guy—"

"Is a friend. I help him with homework."

"Oh." His smiled broadened. "So, funny story, all four of us in my band got this two-day bug, and Friday I thought I was over it, but apparently I wasn't. And it might've been one of my fevered delusions, but I thought I remembered you asking me to the dance." The way he nervously clutched his coffee absolutely charmed me. "And if you did, then I owe you a huge apology. And if you didn't"—twin spots of pink bloomed on his cheeks—"then this is a really awkward moment."

Hope spiraled 'til I was giddy-drunk with it. "I did do that. Ask you out, I mean."

"Would that offer still be open to the jerk who didn't get a chance to answer?"

"I don't see a jerk here."

"That's not a no, is it?"

I laughed and looked at the clock on the wall behind him. "The deal expires in ten minutes. It's a really lucky thing you came in here when you did."

Andrew's eyes went a little blank, and he said nothing. "Um . . . what?"

"I'm kidding." Maybe he was still a little off from being sick. Because my line had been worth at least a coy smile. "And yes, my question still stands."

"Then I accept."

I pressed repeat on those words at least five times in my head. I wanted to go to each table and say, *Hey, I asked a boy out and he said yes. I did that. Me, Harper O'Malley.*

He gestured to the seat that was probably still warm from Ridley. "Are you going to be here for a while?"

"Actually I'm not. I have a shift at the Walnut Street Animal Rescue and have to . . . oh, no."

"What?"

"It's nothing." I could just call my mom. "I forgot I don't have my car here." *Be bold! Be brave!* "Would you want to maybe, um . . ." Why was this so hard? "Take me to the shelter?

It's just a few miles away. If it's an imposition or if you have somewhere to—"

"I'd be glad to take you."

I needed to start carrying brown paper bags to hyperventilate into if this went much further. "Thank you."

He graciously helped me with my chair and walked behind me as we left Liquid Courage. No hand at my back, no umbrella over my head as we raced in the rain to his truck, but we were soaked and laughing by the time we got in. And that made it even better.

One minute and three right turns later, Andrew's truck pulled up to the rescue.

"So you work here?"

"Yeah." The metal building looked in sad need of some landscaping and paint, but it was one of my favorite places on earth. When I was here, I didn't have to guess at rules or worry about anyone getting too close to my space. I knew animals. And they seemed to know me. They listened when I talked, and they needed me, just as I was.

"Are they open?" Andrew put the truck in park. "Looks pretty empty."

I fished the key out of my purse and gave what I hoped was a playful smile. "Just open to VIPs." *You can do this, Harper.* "Do you have any pets?"

"No, I'm really not a cat or dog person."

I think I quit breathing for a few beats of my heart.

I will not hold this temporary lapse of judgment against him.

"We move a lot with my dad's job, so it's just easier," he said. "My parents did let me have a fish once."

Well, that was just depressing. Surely over time I could show him how amazing animals were. Ones with fur. "So on Sundays

I walk some of the dogs and just play with the animals." I imagined myself on a staircase, and it was time to take another step. "Want to help me?"

If Andrew's band ever put out an album, that gorgeous smile had to go on the cover. I wanted to take a picture of his face right now and Instagram it all over the place with the caption, "Andrew just looked at me like *this*."

"Sure, I'll help." Andrew shut off the truck, and I let us inside the building. We were instantly greeted by a din of barks and even a few meows.

"It's pretty noisy in here." I flipped on the lobby lights and led him back to the heart of the shelter.

"Whoa, are we walking all of these dogs?"

"No, volunteers come in shifts." On the wall hung a clipboard, and I consulted it to see what my assignment was, then turned my full attention to the cages. "Hello, Midge." I scratched an orange tabby through her cage. "I see your BFF Bootsie got a home. Your day's coming, girl." We were a dog rescue, but occasionally we made exceptions. Sometimes when I'd go to the city pound to rescue dogs from their death row, I came back with . . . extras. One time that included a ferret. Mavis had not seen the adorable potential in what she deemed "a really skinny rat."

I pulled a treat from my purse and pushed it to the cat, then went to find the dog Ridley and I had saved. "This is Trudy. She's had a rough life. I'm trying to talk my mom into letting me keep her when she's released by the vet, but it's not going well." I opened the door to her cage and slowly reached in and rubbed my hand over her soft little head. "We're going to change Mom's mind though, aren't we, girl?"

"What happened to her?" Andrew asked.

"Her owner beat and starved her. Left her tied to a tree where animals could attack her."

"How'd she end up here?"

I smiled, thinking of the night Ridley had found me climbing out my window. "Two crazy people rescued her."

"You can't save them all."

"No," I said. "But I like to try." What if no one had wanted to save me seven years ago? Where would I be now? "Do you like to dance?"

If Andrew noticed my topic-change completely lacked finesse, he was kind enough not to let on. "I'm not bad. Went to a lot of dances at my old school."

Was a lot more than one?

I didn't really dance. My style probably fell somewhere between a convulsion and a fit.

I pulled myself away from the dog and leashed the three scheduled for walks. "This is Carly, Jax, and Sonny." The amount of tail wagging as we stepped outside could've powered a wind farm. The dogs pulled, ready to take the lead. "They've each been at the rescue at least a year."

"Let me take one." Andrew reached for my hand and grabbed a leash. Was it just me, or had he held onto me just a moment longer than needed? "So no luck talking your mom into taking Trudy home?" He frowned as Jax jumped up and pawed his jeans.

The rain had dwindled to a mist, and I figured my hair probably looked like the French poodle in kennel number seven. "We have a lot going on right now."

"Hey, the Mushroom Cloud Raincoats are playing a benefit show next Monday night. Performing with some other bands. You should come hear us."

"I'd love to." Score one for me. I couldn't wait to report my success to Ridley and to record Andrew's every word in my diary.

"I'm really sorry about your parents," Andrew said as he turned down Davis Street. "My folks and I are pretty tight. I can't imagine what it's like to watch them break up. It's gotta be hard seeing your business all over the news."

"It is." That understatement was right up there with *I get a little moody with PMS.* "My dad says he still loves my mom. So I'm hopeful they'll work it out."

"You think he and that lady are over?"

Andrew had obviously caught up on the story. It was hard to live here and not hear all the sordid details. "I think so. I want to believe they are."

"Do you know where she lives?"

We took another left toward downtown. "No idea. Why?"

"Down, boy. This way. Hey, this way. This guy needs some obedience school."

I ignored Andrew's annoyance. "Why do you ask about Josie?"

He shortened the length of Jax's leash to pull him from the center of the road. "Because I think she might be my neighbor."

Any crumb of news I could glean on Josie made me both curious and repulsed. "You know her?"

"No. I've never really met her."

"Then how do you know it's her?"

"Because I saw some guy bring her a bunch of groceries to-day." His next words filled my head before Andrew could give them life. "Harper, it was your dad."

Chapter Sixteen

"D ID YOU JUST pour yourself a cup of coffee?"
On Monday morning, Mom frowned at my mug of Columbian blend as she sat on a kitchen bar stool.

"I just need a little energy." I took a sip of the vile stuff and winced. How did people drink this? Hot motor oil would probably taste the same. Was this how Ridley felt after a night of booze, cheap girls, and rousing bouts of fisticuffs?

"Are you sleeping well, Harper?" Mom buttered her toast, then unscrewed the lid of peanut butter. "I'm worried about you."

"I could say the same for you."

Her lips thinned. "I'm the parent here. It's not your job to worry about me."

"That's stupid." I set my motor oil on the counter with a loud *thunk*. "I am worried."

"Honey—" She picked up a crumb with the tip of her finger. "Did you do your brother's laundry last night?"

"Yes." Mom was always so on top of chores, but I'd noticed their dirty clothes turning into a small mountain in the laundry room. "I thought I'd help."

"I woke up to three clean bathrooms. Know anything about that?"

"Maybe. So?"

"Do you remember when you first came to stay with us?"

Why did everyone keep bringing that up? "What does that have to do with anything?"

"I'm seeing behaviors . . . familiar patterns. And I'm concerned. Your dad and I both are."

The dad who was probably still seeing that Josie lady? That dad?

All night I wrestled with whether to tell my mom what Andrew had said.

I still didn't know.

"I think if you had someone to talk to about all that's going on, someone you trusted, you'd be—"

"Devon McTavish was pushy. And she asked predictable questions. I don't want to go back to her."

Mom cut her toast in two and pushed her plate to the side. "You need to give her another chance."

"How about you find someone for yourself?"

Her eyes widened, and she waited a full five seconds before speaking again. "Chevy Moncrief called the other day. He told me you went to the university to speak to him."

I took a bolstering drink of the awful brew. "Yes."

"You're not to go there again. You have no reason to be on campus."

"I went to help Ridley—"

"It's crawling with reporters who will stop at nothing to get a quote from our family. And you certainly do not go snooping around in offices."

"Who said I was snooping in offices?"

"I know people in that building, Harper. They saw you skulking around and told me about it."

Shame did a prickly slow walk on spider's legs up my spine. "I got lost?"

If glares could ground a girl, I'd be on lockdown 'til I was thirty. "Stay away from anything having to do with Josie Blevins. Are we clear?"

"Yes, ma'am." Did she catch how weak my agreement sounded? "But don't you want to know—"

"No." Mom's voice snapped like a wet towel. "I do not want to know anything about that woman. And I certainly cannot imagine why you would feel the need to go rummaging through her office. I'm very concerned."

"What if he's still seeing her?"

"Let's get back to the original issue. If I hear one more word of your being on campus for anything other than tutoring purposes, or if I catch even a hint of your going anywhere near Josie Blevins or her property, I will take away your car and all social privileges. Furthermore, I've made another appointment for you at Vital Roots tomorrow at four." Mom placed her plate in the sink, the ceramic hitting with a *clunk*. "Go get ready for school."

And just like that I was dismissed.

With leaden feet, I walked back upstairs.

Certain my family was irreparably broken.

JOY AND SORROW wrestled for control of my thoughts as I stepped out of my Civic and walked to the courtyard of Washington High School. Sitting on top of a picnic table waiting for me was Molly, her hair in two ponytails that jutted from her head like broken antlers.

"Details." She took off her sunglasses to reveal blue eye shadow bright enough to glow in the dark.

"The fake lashes are an interesting addition. I like them."

"Thanks." She batted the fringy things. "Pretty sure I got glue in my eye, but what's a little loss of vision when you look this good?"

I slipped off my backpack and climbed onto the table beside her. By 7:45 the campus was a buzz of activity, from the fellow nerds playing chess underneath the large oak, to the couple at the bike rack, making out like the world was ending and they were saying desperate good-byes. With their tongues.

"Start talking," she said. "That quick text you sent last night was not nearly enough information. So you spoke to Andrew?"

"Yeah, ran into him at the coffee shop downtown. He came over, told me why he hadn't given me an answer, and then he went with me to the shelter."

"Mmm. The shelter. Did you kiss to the yelps of schnauzers and abandoned bassets?"

"No." Though that did sound quite romantic. "Just talked."

"Talked." She scrunched her nose like it was a great letdown. "Probably just as well. No makeout session is worth getting sick. He might've still been germy."

For all of Molly's wild girl ways, she was a closet germophobe. Only she and I knew she carried hand sanitizer in her purse, backpack, car, and clarinet case. In the flu months, her hands were one raw sore from all the alcohol.

"Saw on the news that Josie Blevins got released from the hospital," Molly said.

"Yeah."

"Even though she's a ho-bag, I'm glad she's okay. If she'd been permanently disabled, that would hang over your dad for the rest of his career."

Did he have a career? A marriage? A family? Or was he giving it all up for this younger thing?

Molly slipped her shades back onto her nose. "Look at that. Now that's a boy I'd endure some whooping cough and sinus drainage for."

Ridley ambled toward us, his backpack slung over one shoulder, his dark hair glinting in the morning light. The pink polo he wore should've looked girly on him, but against his dark skin and fitted over that muscular chest, it was the manliest color. His silver chain peeked from the V where he'd ignored the top two buttons.

"Hello, ladies."

Molly's mouth formed an O as he stopped at our table. "Hey," she whispered. "Hey."

Did he make every girl a bumbling mess? He obviously ate testosterone for breakfast and hotness for a midmorning snack because the boy radiated his own brand of aloof charisma just by walking upright.

"How did your date go last night?" Ridley asked. He didn't bother taking off his own sunglasses, and from his reclined posture against the table, I wondered if he hadn't had another late night of . . . I didn't really want to think about what he did in his evenings.

"It wasn't a date, but it went well." *Thank you,* I mouthed.

He inclined his head and smiled.

"I'm Molly." My friend presented a weak hand, as if she were Lizzy Bennet waiting for Mr. Darcy to press his angsty lips upon it.

Ridley grinned, then lifted her hand, slapping it in a high five. "Ridley Estes."

"I know. *Oh, I know.*"

"You render females stupid," I said. "It's like your presence sucks all the brain cells from their heads."

"We all have our gifts," he said. "You're just jealous because you're immune to mine." He took a step closer, and I couldn't help but inhale his light cologne. "You're missing out on the experience. Most girls like me. Some of them even get to date me."

"And then they have to get their rabies shots. Did you want something, Ridley?"

The first bell rang, signaling we had seven minutes 'til we were tardy. I'd never had a tardy slip in my life. Ridley could probably use tardy slips to wallpaper his bedrooms walls.

"My comp professor emailed us the next assignment. It's a research paper." His voice lost some of that arrogance. "It's a big project, and I have to read a book."

I smiled. "Would you like me to show you what one of those looks like?" Beside me Molly gasped.

"I don't have time to read this thing," he said. "It's stupid."

"Need some help with the big words?" It hadn't taken me long to figure out that despite Ridley's sorry grades, he had a sharp brain in there. But it was still fun to tease him.

"I'm not sure you're hearing me," Ridley said. "I have to read 250 pages of this book and write a ten-page research paper to somehow go with it." He rifled through his bag until he produced a sheet of paper and handed it to me.

As I read the project requirements, I had to agree—it was intense. I guess this was college life.

Lines of tension bracketed Ridley's mouth, and I almost felt sorry for him. "So we make a plan for how to tackle it in chunks."

"I could help you with those chunks," Molly interjected. "I'm so good with chunks."

I ignored my friend. "It might require some extra time. Extra work."

"Which means extra study sessions," Ridley said. "Can you handle that?"

"I'm not sure." My left thumbnail had a chip in the pale pink polish, and I decided to slowly inspect the rest of my fingers, one at a time.

"Harper—" Ridley rested his hand on my sleeve. "This is major. I need help."

I looked up from my manicure. "Do you know how to dance?"

A bird called as it soared overhead. "What?"

"Do you know what Andrew likes to do? Dance. Do you know what he's going to expect from me at the dance?"

"If it involves some fantasy involving your band uniforms, keep it to yourself." Ridley plucked his project handout from my grip.

"Andrew's going to expect me to not trip over myself. To know what to shake on the fast songs and where to put my hands on the slow ones."

Molly popped a piece of gum in her mouth and leaned closer to watch the show.

"What's the problem here?" Ridley asked.

"You can teach me how to dance."

He had at least a day's worth of stubble on his face, and it nearly hid the dimples. "Fine."

"You will?"

"Yes. I'll teach you what to shake and . . . what was it, where to put your hands? And in return, you'll amp up the assistance on my comp class."

"Deal."

Ridley took two steps, then turned around. "Harper? Is this

guy worth all this?"

"Yes." Life had dangled this opportunity to be with Andrew, and I was not going to let it go. He was smart, kind, musical, and obviously not afraid to get down with his bad self.

"Okay," Ridley said. "I'll call you."

Molly and I both watched him walk away.

"What . . . was that?" She gradually pulled her rounded eyes from Ridley's butt to my face. "Seriously, you have major explaining to do. He has your number?"

"I'm tutoring him."

"And?"

"And in return, he's giving me insight into what guys want, how to be a girl who catches their attention. It's been a fascinating look into the male mind."

"Is that *all* you've looked at?"

"Yes, of course." Molly's crestfallen face made me laugh. "I'm not the least bit attracted to him. And obviously, I'm not his type."

"That boy—" She fanned herself with her ring-laden hand. "That boy is the epitome of beautiful. Do you get that? If you went to a museum of sexy, he'd be the main exhibit."

"We're just business partners." Though it felt pretty good to have a connection to a cool kid.

Molly picked up her backpack and fumbled with the strap, as if she were high on Eau de Ridley. "If you don't want him, then give him to me."

"Right."

"No, I'm serious."

"He goes through girls like you go through mascara. You want to be just another chick in his harem?"

"Yes," Molly said. "Yes, I do."

"Forget it."

Molly leaped from the table and swiveled on her glittery shoe. She tilted her head and inspected me closely. "Is there another reason you wouldn't want me to date your new friend?"

"No, I just wouldn't want you hurt."

"Because one might think you were developing a feeling or two for the fine Mr. Estes."

"I care about his grades."

"Grades." One dark brow arched. "Is that what we're calling it?"

"You know he's not my type."

"Right. Because you like the boring ones, and Ridley certainly does not meet that requirement."

Her words slid over me like sandpaper. "You don't even know him."

"No." Molly's lips curled in a winsome grin. "But I'd sure like to."

Chapter Seventeen

"I DON'T CARE if Molly dates Ridley. She can have him. Like that would bother me for one second." En route to an after-school home inspection at snooty Angela Smith's, I flipped on my left blinker and glanced at my passenger. I was pretty sure Roscoe the poodle was riveted by my conversation. Of course, he also found it enjoyable to lick his own butt, so his standards for entertainment were quite low.

"I'm just concerned for my friend, you know?" Roscoe panted in what I knew was agreement. "I don't want to see her hurt, and Ridley is . . . he's . . ." How did one describe him? Brooding, fiendishly handsome, unexpectedly endearing, deceptively intelligent, with a smile that could heat a Wisconsin winter. "But I do not like him, Roscoe. I adore Andrew." I braked as a red sports car squalled its fancy rimmed tires to pull out in front of me. "Andrew's my type. He's quiet. He's intellectual." He hadn't exactly warmed up to the animals yesterday. He'd made a valiant effort, helping me walk the dogs. But when we'd returned to the shelter, Andrew had pulled out his phone and taken a seat as I'd worked. A seat away from my furry friends. "Okay, so failing the animal test kind of worries me, but that doesn't mean he couldn't learn to love them." Roscoe planted his front paws on his door, nose flattened to the window, clearly done with our conversation.

We pulled into the drive of a two-story brick Colonial. Tall white pillars stood like sentry guards on either side of the front door. The landscaping was immaculate, with mums in full bloom, and shrubbery so symmetrical and tidy, a stray frond could not be found.

"Don't pee on anything expensive," I said to the dog as I clutched his leash in my hand and pushed the doorbell. "But if you don't like Mrs. Smith, we leave."

The door opened, and the middle-aged woman greeted me with the practiced smile of a former beauty queen. She wore a fitted blazer, a blouse the shade of butter, and linen pants creased in flawless lines that pointed straight down to the leather heels on her feet.

"Hi, I'm Harper from the Walnut Street Animal Rescue and—"

"Yes! Of course I remember you. You're right on time." Her eyes dropped to the dog. "I was kind of hoping you'd bring Trudy."

"Trudy? She's still not ready to be adopted."

"I see."

"Roscoe here is Mavis's dog. He comes with us on many home inspections." He had great people instincts, and he allowed us to see the potential adopters interacting with a dog.

"Oh. Of course." She rallied a smile. "Do come in then." Her heels *click-clicked* on her dark hardwood floor as we walked through her foyer into the living room. "Please sit down. Can I get you anything? Water? Cookies?"

"None for me. And Roscoe's watching his weight."

Mrs. Smith chortled with way too much gusto, as if I'd just told the most amazing joke. We attempted to do a home visit for every applicant seriously considered, and sometimes you got a person who simply tried too hard. Yes, homing the animals was serious business, but it wasn't like I was there representing the IRS.

"Such a sweet little boy." Mrs. Smith cooed to Roscoe, and the dog wagged his tail.

"He seems taken with you." Even Roscoe could have an off day. "Your application says it's you, your husband, and a son." There was a standard form we had to fill out for home visits, and I needed info on how the family would interact with the dog.

"My husband's at work. My son's a freshman at Stanford." She picked up Roscoe and placed him beside her on the couch, her hand absently stroking his fur.

I recalled from her file that she didn't work. Yet her clothes were definitely professional attire. "Tell me about you and Mr. Smith."

"Well, I'm a stay-at-home mom. I mean, I was. My husband and I have very full lives." She focused her gaze on Roscoe. "I just started volunteering. I spend most of my mornings with the Maple Grove Ladies League. A few afternoons a week I go to some yoga classes, and I help facilitate a book club. My husband Rob is the president of the bank there on First Street. Been there for fifteen years, I guess. He's a golfer."

"Your application said you've never had a family pet before."

"We had a beta fish." She gave a reflective pause, as if remembering a time standing over a swirling toilet. "That didn't end well."

"It never does."

"Other than that, no pets. My son was involved in everything, and we were so busy. Traveling baseball team, basketball, soccer, art lessons, school events. We didn't have time to give to a dog."

"But now you do?" It sure didn't sound like it.

She flashed me the beauty queen smile again. "Exactly."

"Did you have pets growing up?"

"No."

There was no way I was giving Trudy up for this inexperienced dog-convert. "I understand you've stopped by the shelter a few more times to see Trudy." And called a half-dozen times. "I appreciate your concern for her health, but we're trying to find you a smaller, more pedigreed-looking dog, like Roscoe here."

"I know it's crazy, but I can't get Trudy off my mind."

I couldn't either. Because she was going to be mine. "We think we have a home for Trudy lined up."

"Oh." Her disappointment suddenly made the fine wrinkles playing at the corners of her eyes appear more pronounced, her posture no longer holding at ninety degrees.

"As Mavis probably explained on the phone, I need to take a quick tour of the house and the yard."

Mrs. Smith recovered, her face lighting up again, as if she were not ready to concede defeat on custody of Trudy. "Right this way!" She was back to being chipper as a morning talk show host, and for some reason, it grated. It seemed I was perpetually in a bad mood these days, and apparently I was beginning to resent those who were not.

We first toured her backyard, which was outlined in a beautiful privacy fence. Roscoe would have plenty of room to run and play. With assurances of our return, we left him there to explore while Mrs. Smith walked me through the house.

Her home was decorated as neatly as her landscaping. Nothing out of place. Not a speck of dust to be found. A chef would've approved of her kitchen, and HGTV could easily have been her decorator. Family photos stood in a symmetrical line on the mantel, and the floors were so polished I could see myself frowning in the reflection.

"I took the liberty of buying a few things for our future dog," Mrs. Smith said as we came to a smaller, less formal family room. "I had a friend make an adorable dog bed. See the monogram? I've got some bowls, a few toys. My husband made me promise I won't embarrass the poor thing with silly outfits. Oh, and I've found *the* best teacher for obedience classes." She beamed with the expectant pride of a mother waiting for her adopted child to come home. "All we need is the dog. So you say you already have a home for Trudy? Are you certain? I really think she'd be happy here."

"Why do you feel like Trudy is the one for you?" I asked. "Out of all the dogs there, why her?"

"Despite her rough start, she's got good teeth, not too old, doesn't seem to be a shedder. Of course, I think with some grooming and some bows, she'd be an adorable dog. Even though she's a little bigger than we'd wanted, I believe Trudy will fit in here very nicely."

"Okay, then. I think I have all I need."

"Wonderful!" Her glossed lips grinned wide. "I have an excellent home and lots of space. I do hope you'll keep us in mind for Trudy. We could make her very comfortable."

"Mavis will be in touch."

Minutes later, I buckled Roscoe into his booster seat in my car.

And knew we were never coming back.

Chapter Eighteen

AFTER DRIVING AWAY from the most perfect house, which was run by the most perfect woman, I dropped Roscoe off at the shelter and had a quick visit with Trudy. She was improving a lot, and when she looked at me with those big, Hershey chocolate eyes, I knew her heart was for me only. Those eyes were saying, *Thank you for rescuing me. Take me home. Feed me your homemade puppy treats.* I just had to convince my mom.

I barely had time to swap insults with Mavis before I was back in the car, late for my next session with Ridley. Even though my relationship with him was all business, a small thrill fizzed within me. I, Harper O'Malley, low on the social food chain, was minutes away from being in Ridley's house. If this wasn't worth a selfie with some accompanying obnoxious bragging to post all over the internet, I didn't know what was. This one was for nerd girls all over the world. Who'd have thought I'd be invited into a popular boy's inner domain? It was like stepping from Kansas into the Emerald City. And I was ready to ease on down this road.

Ridley had left me a text after school that he needed to be home for his sisters, so tutoring would have to be at his house.

I recalled his directions and turned into the neighborhood. It was a part of town dotted with houses from the seventies, most of them in disrepair. It wasn't uncommon to see yards in desperate need of a mow, shingles hanging on for dear life, or sheets hung in windows in the place of blinds. Simply speaking, it was one of the poorest parts of town, and I was a little surprised this was where he called home.

I pulled into the driveway of 1200 Field Springs Drive and shut off the engine. The yard was trim, the paint a tad faded, but the porch of the one-story house sagged, as if it had given up the fight and couldn't properly rise to welcome me.

My hand rapped on the torn screen door, and inside I could hear the sonic blare of a TV, shouting, and possibly someone having a toddler-style meltdown.

The door swung open, and there stood a girl much younger than Ridley in a lilac dress. "Yeah?"

"You must be Faith." Ridley had told me there was an eight-year-old sister who liked the color purple about as much as she liked bossing him around.

"Ridleeeeeeey!" Her hefty bellow seemed at odds with her slight, delicate frame, her doe-eyed gaze, and the feminine face that showed no signs of Ridley's Hispanic heritage, but did hint at future modeling contracts or homecoming crowns. Like the O'Malleys, I guess you had to be beautiful to be born into this family.

"Faith, for the fourth time, come eat!"

I stepped into the living room just as Ridley appeared, one hand pointed at his sister, one holding little Emmie to his hip.

"Hey, there," I said.

He froze for a moment, and had I not been taking in every detail, I wouldn't have noticed the way his eyes briefly went wary and his shoulders tensed, as if he wasn't sure he should let me into his home. Was he afraid it was like the law of vampires, and once he bid me welcome, I'd just appear whenever I got the urge?

"Practice ran late." Ridley put Emmie down, and she waddled toward me, her fingers in her smiley, drooly mouth. "I need to get the kids' dinner, then we can hit the books." He walked toward the kitchen. "Want something to drink? We have water or water."

Faith climbed into her seat at the table. "Ridley says we have a very fine vintage on tap."

"Then that's what I'll have."

He lunged toward a chair and picked up a stack of coloring books, putting them on the counter. "Sit down. You hungry?"

"No, thanks. Smells good though."

"It's nuggets and mac-n-cheese," Faith said. "It's his specialty."

"Nuggies!" Emmie echoed.

"It's all about the dipping sauce." He scooped Emmie up and plopped her in her high chair. "Secret recipe passed down for generations. A sauce our ancestors carried over on the Mayflower."

Faith smiled. "I thought one of our ancestors clutched it in her teeth as she jumped off the *Titanic* and swam for her life."

Ridley put a hand over his heart and nodded his solemn head. "A little ice wasn't going to stop her." He took a cookie sheet of chicken nuggets out of the oven, making quick work of dividing them out between the sisters. I wondered where his share was. He dished macaroni and cheese onto plates, followed by one more final item.

"Ew, it's broccoli night?" Faith wrinkled her nose.

"Yucky." The baby shook her head, but maintained that killer grin.

"Harper can have mine," Faith said.

"Eat what I give you or it's double tomorrow." With practiced hands, Ridley cut Emmie's chicken into tiny bits. "And I don't mean stick them in the flowerpots on the back porch."

"You caught that, did you?"

Ridley scrubbed his hand over his sister's head. "Zero creativity."

I wondered how many got to see this side of the star football player. He was more than a brother to these girls—and more like a father. Where was his mom? Ridley never spoke of her, but maybe she worked nights? Ridley was known for being a fearsome opponent on the field, but as I watched him airplane a spoonful of noodles into Emmie's mouth, I wondered what his adversaries would think of this tableau.

"Harper and I are going into the living room." The girls received Ridley's best warning glare. "I want to hear chewing and that's it. Got it, team?" He put his hand toward the center of the table, and I watched as Faith and Emmie followed suit. "One-two-three, break!"

I followed him into the living room and settled onto the gray couch, only to jump back up at a squeak.

"That's Emmie's ball. The maid must be slacking again."

I studied Ridley over the screen of my laptop as I waited for it to power on. "You're really good with them."

"My sisters?" He shrugged it off, but he smiled like he was recalling a fond memory, a sweet time. "They're good kids."

"Do you babysit them often?"

He flipped open his own laptop, which was sheathed in a USK protective case. "I read the first two chapters of *1984*. It's a little slow."

He wasn't going to answer my question. "You'll get used to not having pictures."

"I'd rather read *Sports Illustrated.*"

"Be sure to put that on your college applications."

"If they fire your dad, I might not be going to college."

"Of course you are. And I don't even want to talk about that now."

He scooted over, his knee bumping mine. Nimble fingers stroked his track pad until his document finally appeared. "Have you heard anything?" Ridley was now all business. "You talk to those football guys. They have to know something."

"Haven't heard a word. The only one who knows what's going on right now is the athletic director. He's deliberating, I guess."

"It's taking forever."

"I'm sorry you're so inconvenienced."

"This is a big deal to me too."

"Really? Because are your parents weighing the idea of divorce? Are you going to have to pack up and move? Are you enduring the stares of everyone in town? Have you had complete strangers come up to you and say vile, cruel things like it was all somehow your fault?"

Ridley opened his mouth, then apparently thought better of it. He nudged me with his pointy elbow. "I'm sorry. I know it's hard for you."

It was impossible not to like the boy when he acted like that. "Michael said scouts have been showing up again at your games. He said you could go anywhere you wanted if you'd get your legal matters settled and get back on the team."

"That will have to work itself out."

"Do you have an attorney?"

"My uncle's helping me."

"So let's say you get your charges dropped and your suspension ends. You could play for another college."

Ridley leaned his head back, his hands covering his face. "It has to be the University of Southern Kentucky. That's my only option."

"Why?"

"Because they're the best."

"Maybe not if my dad leaves. What if they get an interim coach next year? Or hire some loser?"

Ridley angled his head toward me, his eyes searching mine. "That's not going to happen."

I had the strangest urge to reach out and brush the worry lines away from his forehead. "You don't know that."

"I don't have a choice." From the kitchen came the giggles of two little girls. "I've got to get that offer."

There was nothing else I could do for him. He could want the USK jersey with everything he had. We could work until he pulled an A in his class. And it still was probably too little, too late.

He tapped his pinkie to mine. "The second you hear anything, you call me." Then his finger wrapped around mine. "Promise me."

Somehow my face was within inches of his. Surely I hadn't been the one to lean in. "I promise."

Ridley's chest rose and fell with each breath, and I thought if I listened hard enough, I might be able to hear the steady tempo of his heart. His gaze remained steady on mine, and in those eyes I saw a Kentucky storm rolling, a hint of fear, desperation, and something I couldn't quite define.

"Ridley—" I didn't know what I was going to say. But it didn't matter. Because the front door flung open, and Ridley stiffened beside me.

A man and woman walked inside, arms around one another,

laughing at some delirious punch line we'd just missed.

"Mom."

The woman straightened and sobered, the man pulling her against his side.

Ridley stood to his feet, his hands balled into fists at his sides. "What's Dwayne doing here?"

The tension lit up like dynamite in the house, and I shrunk into the couch, afraid the walls would explode. This scene could've been ripped from the pages of my own past, and I desperately didn't want to be around to witness how this confrontation would end.

"I should go." I hated how meek my voice sounded.

Ridley drew himself up to his full six feet and walked up to the man leering right back at him. "The only one that's leaving . . . is him."

Chapter Nineteen

A TORNADO HAD been unleashed right in the living room, as Ridley and his mother's houseguest sized up one another like snarling dogs.

"You calm down right now!" His mom's angry words were slurred, as if her date with Dwayne had included a third party of liquor.

"Where've you been?" Ridley asked. "I had to leave practice early when the day care called. Said you hadn't picked up Emmie."

"You better watch your tone with your mama."

Ridley pretended like he hadn't heard the vine-thin man with the shiny bald head and torn snakeskin boots. The man had poison in his gaze, and I wanted Ridley to move out of his path.

"Dwayne and I are back together." His mom gave a half smile. "He came into the bar last night and—"

"You could've called. You could've picked up the phone and told me you weren't coming home. Do you have any idea how worried I was? What am I supposed to say to the girls when you just take off?"

"Shannon don't have to answer to you." Dwayne stepped in front of Ridley's mom and squared his shoulders. "You better back off before I wipe that look off your face, boy."

"Was last time not enough for you?" Ridley's voice boomed with a force that had Emmie crying in the kitchen. "I wiped the floor with you, and I'll do it again. You're a worthless drunk who gets his kicks out of beating women." I sucked in a breath as Ridley grabbed a wad of Dwayne's shirt and lifted him to his tiptoes. "Get out of my house before I call the cops."

"You go ahead," Dwayne hissed. "We'll just add those to your other charges."

"There won't be anything left of you when they get here."

"Stop! Stop it!" Shannon grabbed at Ridley's hands and tugged, tears streaming down her overly made-up face. "Let him go right now."

Ridley didn't budge. "You gonna let him hit you again? All that for nothing. I drag you out of that mess, and you just go back to it. I'm sick of it."

Dwayne swung his right fist, and it smashed into Ridley's face.

I leaped to my feet, the panic screaming in my head. The walls inched closer, and the air left my lungs as fear tried to smother me. No matter how similar, this wasn't my past. Wasn't another one of my nightmares. I had to pull it together and help.

Ridley dropped his hold on Dwayne and pulled back a fist. He delivered an uppercut to the man's gut that doubled him over. Dwayne collapsed to the ground, wheezing and spitting on the carpet.

I slid sideways off the couch and backed into the doorway of the kitchen. Faith was huddled in a corner, Emmie on her hip. I stretched out my arms, and Faith heaved herself into me. "It's okay." I held them both, moving my body in front to block them from seeing this. Or to block anything that came our way.

"Get out of this house." Ridley's voice was low and lethal. He didn't have to yell at Dwayne to intimidate. "Get out now."

"I love him." Shannon's mascara left watery tracks down her

red cheeks. "I forgave him!"

"Nice of you to pick him over us." Ridley glanced back at me and the girls, as if to assure himself we were safe.

His mom dropped to the floor and ran her hands over Dwayne's sweating head. "It's okay, baby. It's all right."

"Get off me." Dwayne threw off her fussy ministrations, then rolled to his feet, rising in pained increments. "Screw this. I don't need this."

"Don't go!" Shannon yelled, attaching herself to his back. "He didn't mean it."

"If he's not gone in thirty seconds, I'm calling the police." Ridley's words clipped out like bullets. "I'm pretty sure there's a thick file there with Dwayne's name on it already."

Dwayne was too stupid to know he was sticking his hand in the lion's cage. "I'll just press charges right back, sissy boy. Your big college gonna take you with a record? How's that suspension going, huh? You gonna send 'em your mug shot with your ACT?"

Ridley pressed his fingers to the gash over his brow, then pulled his phone from his back pocket. "Ten seconds."

"This ain't over," Dwayne threatened in a roar before slamming the door, shaking the house with the force of an earthquake.

"I gotta go after him," Shannon cried.

But Ridley beat her to the door. He stood there, arms out, ready to tackle his own mother to the ground. His eyes caught sight of me, then his sisters, shivering in my grip. "Don't do this, Mom." His voice softened, as if coaxing a feral dog. "Think of the girls. They need you here. Every day."

Shannon's shoulders shook as the sobs overtook her. "I hate you for doing that. For running him out. He was sorry. He said he was sorry."

"How many times you gonna believe that? You like getting beat up? You like your face all bruised?"

"He didn't mean to."

Ridley shook his head in disgust. "Listen to yourself."

"He's all I have!"

"You have us." Ridley wiped some blood from his cheek. "You know what, never mind. As long as you're back together, just get him to drop the charges."

"It'll just make him angry if I ask."

The way Ridley looked at his mom—I knew that look. You stared at this person who was supposed to love you, protect you. And didn't recognize them at all.

I felt moisture on my shirt, and I looked down to see Faith crying into her hands. "It's okay." I hugged her tighter. "It's gonna be okay."

But it wasn't. Ridley watched his sisters, and his face tore me apart. Hopeless. Dead end. A cycle of sick. I'd lived it. I knew it.

And so did he.

"Tell Mama good night, girls," Ridley said. "She's going to bed."

In silence sharp as a razor blade, Shannon looked around the room, taking in her daughters, her son, then finally me. "You want to date him?" Her laugh cackled like a Halloween witch. "His father was a worthless loser, and so is he." She snatched her purse that had fallen to the carpet and threw it over her shoulder. "Get out of my way."

Tired of the fight, Ridley eased to the left, held open the door, and watched his mother run into the night. Leaving him alone.

Ridley walked to us in the kitchen, first picking up Faith,

who wrapped her legs around his waist. Then he took Emmie from my hip. "It's over." He pressed a kiss to each girl's head. "You know I wouldn't let anything happen to you, right?"

His sisters cried all over their brother, and I stood there and watched him rub backs, right ponytails, and swipe away tears. His intense focus landed on me. "You need to go, Harper. You should've left as soon as my mom showed up."

I rested my hand on his shoulder, the action tugging my sleeve high enough to reveal a flash of mottled skin. "Leaving isn't what friends do."

An hour later, I sat at the end of Faith's bed as Ridley lounged back with both girls and read them the last pages of a story of a stuffed bunny trying to get back home.

"The end." He hugged Emmie first, then Faith, then climbed over them and stood to his feet. "Love you, girls."

They would be sleeping in one bed tonight, the night-light plugged in and standing ready.

"I'm sorry," he said as we walked back into the kitchen, plates with the remnants of unfinished dinners still where the girls had left them. "I'm really sorry."

"Don't apologize." I rummaged around in drawers until I found a clean rag, then ran it under warm water. "Sit down."

"You should've escaped out the back door." He eased into a seat.

"I couldn't leave your sisters." Couldn't have left him.

"Thank you." He looked up at me, his eyes capturing mine. "I owe you."

I was frozen in this moment, captivated by the raw intensity of his gaze, the soft caress of his voice. "I'm . . . I'm glad I could help."

"You probably don't see a lot of that in your golf course

community."

I pressed the rag to the wound over his cheek. The blood had mostly dried, but it still looked angry. "Actually I've seen a lot of it."

"Are you telling me Coach O'Malley—?"

"My mom. My biological mother." I stood between Ridley's long legs and dabbed at his skin, gently trying to clean it up. "I went into foster care when I was nine. The O'Malleys adopted me when I was eleven."

Ridley didn't look surprised. My dad's bio was pretty well-known, so it was no secret I wasn't their biological child.

"Was your mom a drunk?" Ridley asked.

"Alcohol, drugs. Kind of a powder keg of insanity. And those were the good days."

"What happened? I mean, what led you to getting removed from the home?"

I lightened my pressure on his wound when Ridley winced. "It was a long time ago."

"You just saw my family at its worst, and you're not gonna give me your story?"

I couldn't. Not yet. "I don't really talk about it."

"Where's your mom now?"

"A prison in Mississippi."

"Is she in there for hurting you?" Ridley waited two, three beats for me to answer before he moved on. "I guess the important thing is you have two parents who love you now. Two people who take care of you, who you can depend on. I mean, no matter what Coach O'Malley did, he's still your father. He's still a safe place, right?"

That was the ultimate question, wasn't it? Was my dad still the dad I knew? Did an affair make him less of a father?

"My mom was pretty wasted," Ridley said. "She's not always like that. She does so well, then she gets hooked up with guys like that."

"So that's why USK is your only choice." The picture was so much clearer now. "You don't want to leave Faith and Emmie."

"Nobody's ever seen that." Ridley pulled his dark gaze from the floor to my face, holding me in place. "All these years I was so careful to make sure nobody saw our crazy."

My hand slipped into his hair, and I brushed it back, as if I had a right to touch him. When had he made it to my safe list? "When you got arrested—that was Dwayne."

"I couldn't find my mom. When I finally did, she was at his place, and he was using her as a punching bag."

"And you came to her rescue."

"For all the good that did."

"So she saw it all?" I asked.

"And yet backed up Dwayne's story. Or at least wouldn't defend mine."

"Maybe she'll change her mind."

"I don't know what I'm going to do next year. How I'm going to take care of the girls."

I didn't know either. I wouldn't insult him with hollow attempts at encouragement.

I held the damp cloth away from his face and gave him a final assessment. "A butterfly bandage ought to do the trick. Maybe some of that antiseptic that stings enough to make grown men cry."

"Later I'm gonna lie awake regretting anyone had to see what went on tonight." Ridley pulled my sleeve over my wrist before bringing my hand to his heart. "But for some reason, O'Malley, I'm glad it was you."

Chapter Twenty

I SAT IN my car in my driveway Tuesday morning before school, my phone pressed to my ear, and listened to Mavis rattle on. While my boss yammered, I checked my pale face in the mirror. Molly and just about everyone else I knew liked to use their driver's seats to take selfies to post on social media. I personally found nothing about getting behind the wheel that made me think, *I should capture this moment with a photo.* Especially today. When I looked less like a high schooler and more like an extra from a zombie movie.

"Are you listening to me, girl?" Mavis said, interrupting my thoughts.

"Uh-huh."

When I walked into Washington High today, I would enter that building a different person—with a revised version of my friendship with Ridley. After witnessing the dysfunctional showdown at his house, then staying afterward to help with the fallout, I'd stepped into a new portal, taking me to a place where few had gone. Last night we had been unified by the ugly drama of life, and it was a strange bond. Not one I was totally comfortable with, but I was now tied to Ridley by this invisible, tattered cord all the same.

"You can't just throw away Angela Smith's application for a pet," said Mavis's Marlboro voice in my ear, pulling me back to the present. "She's a good home, O'Malley. I read the home visit notes."

"Did you?" I brushed gloss over my lips, hoping that would improve the corpse look I had going on. "Because it sounds like you skipped some of my comments. Like the ones that said 'neurotic and uptight with nervous tendencies'?"

"I thought that comment was a description of you."

"She's a no, Mavis. You've never doubted my instincts before, so why now?"

She coughed into the phone. "Because this is a conflict of interest. You want Trudy. She wants Trudy."

"Who saved Trudy? Me." And Ridley, of course. "Who does she belong to? Me."

"Have your parents heard that joyous news?"

"That's an irrelevant detail." I ignored her raspy laugh. "You don't think it's odd this Angela Smith suddenly dropped her need for a pedigreed dog and now wants a scruffy mess like my Trudy?"

"The heart wants what the heart wants."

I started my car. "Are you reading poetry again?"

"Frozen-dinner fortune cookies. Let us now move on to topic number two."

"Because the adoption status of Trudy is settled."

"Because you're boring me, and I've got two Great Danes playing *WWE SmackDown* in my lobby. Item number two, we have a Mrs. Henrietta Tucker, age eighty-five, who will not leave her home and move to Peach Tree Assisted Living because she can't take her beloved and likewise elderly schnauzer. Her son from Atlanta is coming in next week, and he'd like her to leave voluntarily rather than by force."

"He sounds like a jewel."

"He's actually a decent sort. Mrs. Tucker had her fifth fall in

JENNY B. JONES

a month yesterday, can't drive, can't see, and routinely points the TV remote at the oven to turn it off. He wants his mother taken care of, but he knows her heart is breaking over her dog."

And now mine was too. "And how do you have this intel?"

"My neighbor's son's cousin told Frankie, the owner of the Easy Street Bakery, who told Joe, who works at the lumberyard, who mentioned it to Joe's mama Ruth Anne, who owns the salon where I get my upper lip waxed."

Ugh. "And what do you want me to do?"

"This calls for some subterfuge, some shenanigans."

"Some lying?"

"Exactly."

"You know how I feel about that."

"I've got a great home lined up for her dog."

"Angela Smith?"

"No, you know she won't take a geriatric dog. The schnauzer's going to the Sacred Heart Convent off Highway 12."

"For last rites?"

"For a home with the sisters, sassy. Sister Mary Francis is a personal friend and has requested an older dog. It's a match made in heaven." She laughed, and I could hear her slap the counter. "Did you catch that pun?"

"Amazing. So why the deception? Why can't I just go retrieve the dog and tell Mrs. Tucker her dog is going to a good home?"

"Because she has a thing against nuns. Grew up in a Catholic school, taught by nuns. It didn't go well. Anyway, I'll send you more info. The point is, you're on the job, and I expect a flawless dog extraction. Today would be nice."

"I have an appointment after school." That stupid meeting with a counselor. "If I come up with an idea after that—"

"Over and out." Mavis hung up, through with all the talking.

Like I needed more stress. I pressed my foot to the brake, checked my rearview, waved to a man walking his dog who I knew was a reporter given the camera around his neck, and threw the car in reverse.

The Civic choked, sputtered, shook. And died.

"No." I gripped the steering wheel. "No, no, no. Not today. Not now." I twisted the key and tried to turn the engine again.

But nothing.

The car was dead.

I pressed my cheek to the cool glass window.

"Problems?" Michael appeared at my window.

I startled and glared. "Major."

"If this is a nerd meltdown, I'm zero help. I don't speak anime or Dr. Who."

"My car's dead."

"So ride with me."

"No."

"Afraid of raising your cool factor?"

I tried the key again, but the car only made clicking sounds, like it was drumming its nails in absolute boredom.

"It needs a jump," Michael said.

I opened my door. "You have cables."

"No time, señorita. I have basketball practice in five. I'm not running bleachers for being late. Either you're riding with me or you walk."

My life was one big sitcom. And every time I had it together, someone added a disaster to the scene.

"It's not that big of a deal, Harper."

But it was. I had plans for this car today. Places to go.

"Come on, Harper. It's either go with me or walk."

I slammed my car door. Kicked a tire. And caught a ride with my brother.

Practice normally lifted my spirits. If I had to do mornings, I liked when it could include music and my band friends. But today nothing was clearing my bad mood. Andrew marched along beside me for a solid hour—which brightened my spirits some, but not as much as it should've. I guess my heart was just too heavy after last night's soap opera. Ridley had texted me this morning, and his concern was undeniably sweet.

How are you doing? Worried about you after last night.

Minutes before first hour, I opened my locker and grabbed a textbook. I'd scoured the halls for Ridley, anxious to talk to him and see if his mom had ever shown up, but I couldn't find him anywhere. I went up on tiptoe to search for a binder.

An arm slipped around my shoulders, and I whirled around, my book falling to the floor.

"Whoa, hey!" Andrew took a step back, hands lifted in surrender. "Sorry. Didn't mean to scare you."

"Andrew." My breath came in bursts as I gave a shaky laugh. "It's fine." But if it was fine, why was I retreating even more, until my shoulders pressed against my locker?

"Mr. Sanchez caught me after practice, and when I looked up, you were gone."

A girl with a crush would've stuck around and waited on her boy, wouldn't she? I stunk at this stuff. I just had too much on my mind. "I have a test next hour and needed a few more minutes to study."

"You seemed quiet out there on the field."

I replaced my frown with a smile. This was the object of my

affection, and I needed to appreciate his attention. "I have a lot going on."

"Maybe I can cheer you up." From behind his back he produced a flower. An origami rose. "For you."

"Thank you." I took the offering, my heart perking a bit at the gesture. For me.

"Are you sure you're all right?"

"Yeah. I think I'm just a little overwhelmed with my dad, and there's this poor woman who needs to surrender her dog, and—"

"I totally have our newest song for Friday's game memorized. Isn't that awesome? I mean, the bridge on that thing is so fun to play, isn't it?"

I blinked. Okay, so Andrew wasn't into hearing about my sordid personal life. That was okay. I didn't really feel like talking about it anyway. "That's awesome." I ran my finger over the origami petals. "The rose is great. Very artistic."

"See you later, I hope."

The world moved in slow motion as Andrew leaned down and pressed a kiss onto my flushed cheek. My eyes went wide, and I suspended all attempts at breathing.

Straightening, he grinned. "Oh, and take another look at that flower."

I admired Andrew's retreating form as he walked down the hall, my pulse slowly returning to normal. He wore his usual uniform of dark jeans and an indie band shirt. His longish hair brushed the back of his collar, and in his back pocket was a protruding phone. He'd told me his phone housed photo collections of random things that inspired him to write some of his band's songs. Yesterday he'd put my picture in his collection.

It was all very sweet. I kept waiting for the crush feelings to intensify, but I think my system was too overloaded with everything else. A girl could only handle so many feels before she short-circuited. Or self-medicated with cookies.

Grabbing the rest of the necessities from my locker, I took off down the same hall. Dodging two couples and one janitor, I unfolded Andrew's intricate flower creation and found it was actually a note. How adorable. Who wrote notes anymore? I loved it already.

Harper,
For you I am over the moon.
Meet me outside at the giant oak.
Preferably at straight-up noon.

Your second trumpet,
Andrew

The day crawled on turtle's legs, and curiosity kept me on the edge 'til we had seconds left in English. When the bell finally rang, I was the first one out the door. I couldn't remember what we'd done in class, what homework Mrs. Patton had assigned. All I knew was that my presence had been mysteriously requested by Andrew.

The sky hanging over the commons was overcast, and the chill in the air had me wishing I hadn't left my jacket in my locker.

"Hello, Harper." Andrew pushed off from the giant oak at the north end of the campus. He reached out and took my hand, and I stared at our joined fingers. I was holding hands with a boy. *I was holding hands with a boy!* And I wasn't even sweating.

"Take a seat." Andrew gestured toward the blanket covering the sparse grass.

"What is this?"

"Lunch."

I laughed as giddy butterflies flitted in my chest. "For me?"

He released my hand and smiled. "For us."

For us. It had a nice sound to it. I had envisioned it. I'd wanted it for so long. He was exactly what I'd been looking for.

He unzipped his backpack. "I hope you like PB&J. It's the special today."

I rested my phone on the ground beside me. "It's exactly what I would've ordered."

"And a side dish, too, of course." He opened a bag of ranch-flavored chips. "I hope they're seasoned to your liking."

I reached in the bag and took a bite. "A hundred artificial ingredients crammed onto one tiny tortilla. You're totally speaking my love language here."

"And something to drink." He handed me a Dasani, uncapping the lid.

I smiled. "A bottle of your finest."

"Actually it's from the vending machine." Andrew's brow furrowed. "It's just water."

So sometimes the boy's humor failed him, but maybe it was just nerves.

"Let's eat." Andrew toasted my drink to his.

We ate in silence for a full minute, and my every bite was fraught with anxiety. Should I be talking? Did he want me to initiate a conversation? Was he not into talking? Should I have spent more time on my hair?

Rule one of conversation is to ask the person about themselves.

"So . . . what do you think of Washington High so far?"

He finished chewing hit bite, his lips curved in a beautiful grin. "So far I've made some good friends, joined a killer band, and now I'm hanging out with you." He scooted closer to me and rested his hand on my shoe. "Things are definitely looking up."

Every girl instinct in me said if I just inclined my head, if I simply leaned forward ever-so-slightly, Andrew would press his lips to mine.

So why wasn't I doing it?

Andrew's green eyes studied my face, and he slipped his fingers through a tendril of hair blowing in the breeze, tucking it behind my ear. "You could become the best part of this school," he whispered.

He leaned in.

I leaned in.

Close your eyes. Open your mouth. Lean into—

"O'Malley!"

I jerked away from Andrew, only to find Ridley walking toward our picnic.

"Impeccable timing," Andrew said, his hand resting on my knee like he was staking a claim.

"What is it?" I jumped up a little too quickly and brushed some crumbs from my shirt.

"Am I interrupting?" Ridley surveyed the scene before turning his attention back to me, a mocking grin telling me he knew perfectly well he was.

My voice was about as sweet as vinegar. "Did you want something?"

His expression sobered. "I need to talk to you."

"I'm busy," I said through gritted teeth.

"Gonna borrow your little lady here for just a minute. Very sorry." He grabbed me by my arm and pulled me out of earshot of my date.

"Let go of me." Bossy, impudent jerk. Where did he get the

idea he could just drag me off, that I was there to jump at his every bidding? I put the brakes on and crossed my arms. "I'm not going any further. Tell me what's going on, or I'm going back to Andrew. He doesn't shove me around."

Hurt slashed across Ridley's stricken face. "I've never shoved you."

"I . . . wrong choice of words. I . . . just tell me what the problem is. And where have you been?"

"With the USK athletic director. I had my meeting with him. Took the morning off, waited in his lobby over an hour, and he barely gave me five minutes."

Moncrief had promised me thirty. "What did he say?"

"He has no interest in having me on his team."

"You're working on your grades. You're going to graduate with all your credits. Surely that counts for something."

"He says the team has to continue working on cultivating its image, raising the bar for the Eagle reputation." His eyes flashed temper. "And I don't have what it takes to uphold that reputation."

"He doesn't understand. Did you tell him about your mom?"

"No." Clearly that was the dumbest idea ever. "I can't tell anyone about her. And neither can you."

"This could be so easy to straighten out."

"Harper, if the police find out the way that night really went down, it makes my mom look very bad. As in bad enough to attract the attention of child services. And it wouldn't be the first time. I can't let that happen."

"Well, did you mention you made a B on your last test in comp?"

"I didn't get that far. He spent the entire time telling me

what he was looking for, and how I wasn't it. Said he'd advised your dad to steer clear of me."

"But I saw your stats. You're nationally ranked. You're one of the best wide receivers in the state."

"Moncrief plans to sign his number one pick in the spring. Apparently I was his second choice, so with your dad out of the way, plus my rap sheet, I've been replaced."

"Maybe if you—"

"He's done, Harper. Chevy Moncrief looks at me and all he sees is a punk kid with a barely passing GPA and a white trash discipline record."

"But that's not you." I looked down and realized I was clutching his hand. "You're so much more than that. You're an incredible football player, you're surprisingly smart—"

"Gee, thanks."

"And you're all but raising your sisters by yourself."

Storm clouds loomed behind those eyes. Ridley was running out of options, running thin on hope. "I can't lose my sisters. Everything I do, it's for them."

"Ridley, you can't keep living like this. You can't go to college, play football, and be a full-time caregiver to Emmie and Faith."

"But that's what I have to do."

"They need a parent."

"I'm eighteen. I can be their parent."

"This isn't over yet," I said. "The season is still young, and there are months until spring signings."

He pushed a hand through his hair, his anguished eyes holding mine. "I feel it slipping out of my hands, Harper."

My heart ached to help him, but what could I do? The Eagles' athletic director was so wrong about this boy. Just like I had been.

"I've got to get out of here," Ridley said. "Clear my head."

"And go where?"

"I don't know. Anywhere but here."

I thought about the counseling appointment I was desperate to escape. "I think I've got just the place."

Chapter Twenty-One

"ANOTHER PUPPY ABDUCTION?" Ridley turned the Jeep a little too sharply onto the highway. "This is your big getaway? Your moment of busting loose?"

"Excuse me for combining my truancy with a noble deed." I consulted my text from Mavis one more time. "I was going to suggest holding up a liquor store and sexy wild sex, but that seemed entirely too unoriginal."

"Sexy wild sex?" Ridley held those full lips together but his laugh escaped anyway. "Please expand on that one."

"Just drive. There's a dog's life at stake here. Her neighbors say she forgets to feed him sometimes and is one accident away from burning down her house around them."

"Do you ever think your dognapping is crossing a line?"

"I don't cross lines. It's always on the up and up. I only take dogs who are severely abused."

"Will you need my muscles?" Ridley gave a sniff of feigned arrogance. "I could apply a little brute force."

"Henrietta Tucker is eighty-five, mostly blind, and partially deaf. Pretty sure I can handle her. Besides, she isn't intentionally hurting her dog, so it's not like I'm going to break in there, knock her down, and steal her precious schnauzer."

"That's a little disappointing. I was in the mood for more duck-and-cover like last time. But I should warn you—old ladies dig me."

"This one can't see, so she'll be immune to your hypnotic eyes."

"Hypnotic, huh?" He watched me a little too closely.

"I was teasing." My cheeks burned warm as a Kentucky sun in June. "It's not like I've studied your eyes." My laugh sounded a tad bit forced. "I don't even know what color they are." A deep brown like coffee with a teaspoon of cream, highlighted by flecks of olive green or mahogany, depending on the color of shirt Ridley was wearing.

"And what's my role in this dog extraction?"

"To sit pretty in your Jeep. I'll handle this one."

"And miss out on all the fun?"

"Despite our previous escapade, I work solo."

He turned down the radio then returned his arm to the console between us. "You normally conduct your dog espionage after hours. How about you tell me why you're really ditching school."

"I'm protesting the lack of meatless choices in the cafeteria."

"Try again."

My phone vibrated with a text from Andrew. I'd left him standing in the courtyard with a scowl, as he hadn't known what to say to my excuse of an urgent job for the shelter. But with an apology promise to call him later, I'd thanked him for the sweet picnic, then made a quick departure.

"I'm not skipping," I said to Ridley. "I'm merely exercising my right to experience new educational opportunities in the real world."

Ridley sighed. "I bet it's a long walk to this lady's house."

"Fine. My mom made me a counseling appointment, and I don't want to go."

He flicked on his turn signal and frowned. "That's it? You're skipping so you don't have to sit and talk to someone about your feelings for an hour?"

"Some things aren't worth talking about."

"Such as?"

"My bio-mom. The great Coach O'Malley."

"So you talk about it, make your parents happy, and you're done. What's the harm?"

Because when I thought about Becky Dallas, something black and dark unfurled in my stomach, and I wanted to keep the bad years where they belonged—in the past, under tight lock and key. "Make a left at this stoplight."

"Prison's pretty serious," Ridley continued. "What happened that was so bad your mom—"

"Andrew's going to kiss me." That shut him up.

Ridley reached for the radio. Switched it off. "You really need to work on your conversation transitions."

"I think he's going to kiss me, maybe at the dance."

"Congratulations."

I was sixteen. I was a firm believer in not giving up the goods, and going at your own pace. But still. The pressure to be like the other girls. To hear one of Molly's makeout stories and be able to do more than just listen. To put that flair on my girl-club sash that said, *I have been well and truly kissed*. I wanted that. I read five billboards and two exit signs before finally spitting out, "I don't have much kissing experience."

His voice sounded painfully careful. "How much *do* you have?"

"Danny Jacobson. Sixth grade on a class field trip to a carnival. I told him if he'd win me a teddy bear at the ring toss, I'd kiss him. I never thought the nearsighted idiot would make it." Ridley's lips quivered, and I continued. "The point is that kissing should be included in your tutorial."

He went the kind of still that usually required checking for a pulse.

I dared a closer look, and his face was completely void of expression. "Ridley?"

"I'm processing."

"You've made out with every girl on the Washington High campus." Yet he had to stop and consider whether he could make himself kiss me? Didn't *that* sting just a tiny bit. "What's one more?"

"First of all, I have not made out with every girl at school. We have at least five lesbians, and I've totally let them have their space."

I barely heard his words. I was too busy drowning in a river of my own humiliation. Had I not been so desperate to avoid making a total fool of myself with Andrew, I would have died before asking such a thing. But if I was choosing between being an idiot with Ridley or Andrew, it was a no-brainer.

"And second of all," Ridley continued, "I wasn't agonizing over the very idea of it. I just . . . You caught me off guard, that's all. Let's hear your plan. I know you have one."

"We meet at my house and you show me how a guy likes to be kissed."

"We guys really aren't that picky."

"There are a lot of variables."

"My part in this bargain is starting to feel a little bit sleazy."

"So you're in?"

He laughed and shook his head. "We'll see, Harper. We'll just have to see."

Ten minutes later Ridley pulled into Henrietta Tucker's driveway. Mrs. Tucker lived in a two-story Victorian the shade of watercolor sunshine. A white picket fence lined the edge of the property, and I imagined generations of families making memories in that home. Barren tree limbs waved hello from the stately oaks in her yard.

Ridley killed the engine. "What now?"

I quickly filled him in on what I knew of Henrietta Tucker. "I'm going to reason with her. Talk to her girl to girl. Dog person to dog person. And you're going to stay here and look pretty."

"You're really underestimating the power of my charm."

I doubted that.

Mentally rehearsing my spiel, I opened my door and marched up the sidewalk. Mrs. Tucker's doorbell buzzed as I pressed the button, and I patiently waited on her porch.

And waited.

And waited.

I mashed the doorbell again.

"I hear you! I hear you!" a voice called from the other side. I heard the sound of multiple locks being turned before the door finally inched open. "Yes?"

"Mrs. Tucker, I'm Harper O'Malley from—"

"I don't want any!" Henrietta opened the door wider, revealing white hair held captive by crooked curlers, knobby knees beneath a floral muumuu, and blue eyes behind thick glasses.

"Mrs. Tucker, I—"

"If you're a politician, I'm not voting for you. If you're selling something, I've already got two. And if you're that brat neighbor boy from down the lane who's supposed to cut my grass, don't think I don't know you didn't do the job. But you still took your envelope with money, didn't 'cha? Now go away."

"I'm not the neighbor boy. I'm—"

"Good afternoon, ma'am," came a voice behind me.

Mrs. Tucker stilled at Ridley's words, and I couldn't stifle the eye roll. I guess no female was immune, even at nearly ninety.

"Who are you people?" she asked. "I need to get back to my home-shopping program. The special buy this hour is two-for-one strapless bras."

"That sounds like quite a deal," Ridley said. He moved closer 'til he was right behind me, my shoulder blade touching some firm part of his chest that'd been thoroughly bench-pressed.

I turned around, speared Ridley with a glare, and jerked my chin toward his Jeep. "Go back," I whispered. "I can handle this."

He just looked down and smiled.

"Mrs. Tucker," I said, "I wondered if I could talk to you about your dog?"

"Mr. Wiggle Bottoms? Did my son send you? Because I am not interested in giving up my dog. No way, no how." She turned her head long enough to enjoy a coughing fit. "Not gonna happen."

"Ma'am, I'm Ridley Estes, and this is my girlfriend, Harper."

"Girlfriend?" I hissed. "I am not his girlfriend!"

"Fiancée," Ridley amended. "She gets upset when I forget that part, but it's still so new."

What in the world was he up to?

Ridley put a hand on my shoulder and squeezed. "We just moved into the neighborhood and have seen your dog Mr. . . . um, Mr.—"

"Wiggle Bottoms," the lady corrected. "He's Mr. Wiggle Bottoms."

"Right." Ridley nudged my ribs, and I knew that face of his

was smiling. "Harper and I have taken quite a few walks in the neighborhood, and we've seen your dog. We brought some treats for him to say hello."

"Well." Mrs. Tucker eased her war stance slightly. "He is a beauty, isn't he?"

At that moment, Mr. Wiggle Bottoms chose to limp toward his owner with matted black hair, reeking of something rotten and smacking his lips from what looked like barbecue sauce all over his face. I'd pulled prettier dogs from Dumpsters.

"Ma'am, there seems to be water coming from that door in the hall behind you," Ridley said.

Her eyes widened. "Again? That's my guest powder room. Toilet has a mind of its own." Her frail shoulders slumped in defeat. "I thought I called the plumber yesterday, but I couldn't see the numbers on the phone. When a birthday party clown showed up two hours later, I knew I'd called the wrong number." She pulled a tissue from her housedress and blotted her nose. "But Jangles sure did some impressive animal balloons if you're ever in the market. Well, nice to meet you, kids. I better take care of this."

"How about if I take a look at your toilet?" Ridley asked.

"I couldn't ask you to do that. It's too much trouble and I—"

"I'd be glad to." He gave me a reassuring grin as we stepped inside, and my pulse stuttered.

A few weeks ago I thought Ridley was such a different person. But now I knew him as a protector. A gentleman in disguise. I'd observed him with his sisters, witnessed his patience with me. Not once had he laughed at any of my stupid boy questions. He held open doors for girls, kissed his baby sister's boo-boos, and now he was fixing toilets for old, blind ladies. The cracks in his player persona were growing more cavernous by the day.

"Be right back, snookums." Ridley made a smacking kiss sound as he neared my face, but stopped just short of my cheek. "Miss me while I'm gone."

"If this doesn't get me a dog, I will make you suffer," I whispered.

"I'll make it up to you on our honeymoon."

I watched his handsome form walk away to the leaking bathroom, and I followed a cane-wielding Mrs. Tucker to the living room.

"Your feller sure is nice." Mrs. Tucker sat in a raised recliner and fumbled with a remote before the chair lowered her to a comfortable position. Her smelly dog flopped down at her feet, dust rising from the rug in a plume. "My son got me this chair. Only took me a year to figure out how to work it. I can't see the buttons. My eyes just do not work anymore. Another thing I can't see is your engagement ring. I bet it's a pretty one."

I looked at my bare finger. "It's completely unbelievable."

"You sound kinda young. Ladies these days wait 'til they're all out of college and careered up before tying the knot. In my day, we were married by eighteen."

"I've, um, I've done my time on a college campus." Oh, gosh. I was in over my head with the lies. *Thank you, Ridley, for throwing me into this deceptive charade.*

"My Stan went off to war at nineteen. Helping change the world before he was even twenty. Can you believe that?"

"He must've been a great man."

"He was. He's been gone for ten years," she said softly. "Don't ever get old, sweetie."

Behind us came the clanking of Ridley in her powder room. "I hope you had many happy years together."

"Oh, we did. We had two children. My daughter's in Spain with her military husband. And my son's in Atlanta. Wants me to move there to a home, but I can't leave Mr. Wiggle Bottoms. We're best friends." Her sigh was big enough to rattle her frail body. "I think I'm failing at taking care of him though. It's a hard decision."

I glanced around the room and saw evidence the house was also more than Mrs. Tucker could handle—dirty, molded dishes stacked on a coffee table, pee stains on her carpet, and smells that testified to how often the dog didn't make it outside in time. "I know you do your best," I said. "He's a great dog." *In serious need of a bath and an appointment with the groomers. And possibly a diet.*

"I can't get him outside as much as I should. The neighbors help me, but I know they're tired of it."

"Have you thought about letting someone else adopt him?" I pulled a dog treat out of my bag and waited for the dog to come to me. His black nose twitched twice before he lumbered toward me.

"I've had one offer from a convent, but my dog's not Catholic. We watch a lady preacher on Sunday nights, so we're whatever denomination she is." Mrs. Tucker bobbed her head in a nod, dislodging a few curlers.

"Toilet's all fixed." Ridley stepped into the room holding up two pairs of dripping panty hose. "Just a small clog of the hosiery variety."

"I hand washed my unmentionables last week," Mrs. Tucker said. "I might've misjudged the location of the sink."

Ridley disappeared long enough to find a trash can and wash his hands, then returned to the living room. He sat down beside me on the couch and scooted until his side was plastered to mine. I slid down to give us some space, but he wrapped his arm around my shoulders and hauled me to him. His grin only grew when he saw my scowl.

"How long have you two been engaged?" Mrs. Tucker asked.

I gave Ridley a look I called my Sour Mavis. "Seems like only minutes ago."

"We've known each other a long time. Not that this girl ever noticed me." There was mischief dancing in those eyes. "When I got the nerve to show up on her doorstep that first time, she didn't even remember my name."

"What a moron I was," I said dryly. "To go to school with you and not even know your name."

"I knew your name," he whispered. "But teasing you was more fun." He raised his voice for Mrs. Tucker's ears, his piercing gaze never leaving mine. "That first day I talked to her, I knew Harper was something else. I'd had a rough week, but when I saw her glaring at me, I smiled for the first time in days. And it's been an adventure ever since."

And right now my heart was on one wild ride. I wanted to cover my ears from the deep, entrancing pull of his voice, to look away from the voodoo spell Ridley was weaving with his eyes. Nobody spun magic like Ridley Estes.

Stop it. Stop it!

Charming girls was Ridley's superpower. *You're stronger than this, Harper. Resist! Resist!*

"Um . . ." I pulled my concentration away from Ridley and to the mangy dog sniffing the floor. "I, um, I sure do love dogs, Mrs. Tucker. Maybe I could come by and see Mr. Wiggle Bottoms some next week?" The bond between owner and dog was strong. She definitely wasn't going to let some fictional engaged couple walk out of there with her fuzzy beloved. But inroads had been made, and Mavis would have to be satisfied with that.

Mrs. Tucker pointed to a stack of magazines near Ridley's feet. "Mr. Wiggle Bottoms really seems to have taken to you." Across the room by the fireplace, the dog paused in the cleaning of his hind end. "My boy would love the company," she said. "I know he misses his walks. But you'd have to be very careful. He's old, like me."

"Harper's incredible with animals." Ridley gave my shoulders a squeeze. "She'd take a bullet for a dog."

"Well, no need to go to that extreme," Mrs. Tucker said. "But the neighbor on the corner's got a cat who's a real jerk."

"We should let you get back to your shows." I stood and wiped some dog hair from my jeans. "It was nice talking to you, Mrs. Tucker."

"Welcome to the neighborhood, dears. Mr. Wiggle Bottoms and I will look forward to seeing you. Young man, you keep an eye on that pretty lady of yours, now, you hear?"

"Yes, ma'am." Ridley shook the woman's delicate hand and grinned. "I'm trying."

"You can let go of me now," I said as Ridley and I walked to his Jeep.

He opened my car door and held it open. "We gotta sell this thing 'til the bitter end."

I slid inside. "She can't see six inches in front of her."

"We could do that kissing lesson now. For authenticity's sake."

I waved toward the porch at Mrs. Tucker. "Not on your life."

The crisp wind caught Ridley's hair as he laughed. "First day of our engagement, and we're already on the rocks."

Ridley jumped in the driver's seat, buckled his seat belt, and shoved the keys in the ignition. "I think you did the right thing—by taking this one slow."

"She's not ready," I said. "But she will be. She needs some time to adjust to the idea of a better place for her dog."

"Some things are hard to let go—how they used to be. How you want them to be."

Something we both knew.

"Mrs. Tucker's yard's a mess," Ridley said. "I'll get some of the guys on the team, and we'll take care of it this weekend."

"And I can clean her house when I go see her in a few days."

"We're a good team, O'Malley."

I tapped my knuckles to his outstretched fist. "I guess we are."

"But next time, keep your hands to yourself." He revved the engine to life. "Your handsy behavior in there was just embarrassing."

Chapter Twenty-Two

WHEN I WALKED into my house at six p.m., I knew I was in big trouble.

It was the silence that spoke volumes. The hardened expression on my mother's face as she sat beside my brothers at the dinner table. Or the way Cole stood up, pointed directly at me, and shouted, "You're in big trouble!"

My mother lowered her glass of merlot, pressed a napkin to her mouth, then stood, the dogs scattering into the other room. "Harper, in the kitchen. Now."

With no choice but to obey, I followed.

"Where have you been?" Mom planted her hands at her hips. "And don't tell me you went to the counseling appointment because they've already called to tell me you didn't show. And don't tell me you went to the animal rescue because I drove by there."

I was a horrible liar. That, combined with my mom's droid ability to track her children down, meant I never got away with anything. "I didn't want to go to counseling."

"I don't remember giving you a choice."

She had no idea what that forced oversharing did to me. "I don't need to talk to a counselor."

"But you did need to skip school? What has gotten into you?"

I shrugged a shoulder, which I knew she hated. "Counseling

is stupid. It's uncomfortable, and I don't see why I have to go when no one else does."

"The boys are starting soon. And I'm still waiting to hear where you were."

"I may not have been at the shelter, but I was doing shelter work. I went to check on an old lady who can't take care of her dog anymore."

My mom closed her eyes and held the bridge of her nose. When she spoke again, her voice was controlled, quieter. "Help me understand why you're so opposed to following through on a few sessions of therapy. I'm going to go. Your brothers are going to go. All the cool kids are doing it."

"Because . . ." Tears pressed at my stinging eyes. "She asked me about Becky Dallas."

"And it still hurts to talk about that." She brushed the hair from my face. "The fact is you've never talked about it."

"So why start now?"

"Because her probation's coming up. Because your dad's made national news. Because I see you falling apart and bravely trying to keep it together."

"Going back there, talking about that—it's not going to help."

Mom wrapped her warm arms around me and hugged me tight. "Years ago I held your hand and rocked you in my arms when you got out of the burn unit. All those nights you'd wake up screaming, crying. You carried the weight of the world in your eyes. That scared, haunted look you'd have—it tortured me."

"That was a long time ago."

She pressed a kiss to the top of my head. "When I look at you now, I see those same frightened eyes staring back at me."

Michael's voice preempted any response I might've had. "Mom!" he called, running into the kitchen. "Dad's here."

"This conversation isn't over." Mom used her index finger to swipe away the moisture from her cheeks. "Your father wants to talk to you and your brothers."

"I'd rather go to my room."

"Harper, you're on thin ice as it is. Don't push it."

My stomach flopped once, and suddenly the food sitting on the stove was far too pungent. I walked into the living room, breathing deep and hoping I wouldn't throw up that peanut butter and jelly sandwich I had eaten at lunch. That magical moment Andrew had created that now seemed so far away.

"Hello, Harper." Dad's face was dark, and his eyes lifeless, like that time I'd watched him bury his favorite old Labrador.

My body sank into the couch beside Cole and Michael, and Laz took the opportunity to jump into my lap. Mom occupied the chair beside us, her hands dangling from the armrests. Where was her wedding ring? Her left hand was completely bare. Had she just removed it to cook dinner?

Dad pulled the leather ottoman out and sat down. "Guys . . ." His pause was a painful movie cliff-hanger, an agonizing few seconds where panic clawed and scratched. "I, um, I wanted to talk to you about some stuff before it goes public."

It was not good news. A million possibilities sprinted through my frantic mind.

"The university has concluded their investigation. They've decided I violated my contract, and they've let me go."

Fired. Moving. Divorce. New home. Change.

Leaving friends—Molly, the team, Andrew, Ridley.

"What's going to happen to us?" Cole asked.

Dad stole a furtive glance at Mom. "I'm not sure. You're

going to be hearing a lot of things on the news, around town, at school. What I want you to know is that I made a mistake. And I'm sorry. I'm so sorry I hurt you. I love you guys." He turned his attention toward me. "Nothing will ever change that."

"Are you still seeing her?" Michael asked.

I held my breath and waited for Dad's answer. Could I even survive if this family fell apart? Was I some sort of curse on a home? I wanted to wake up from this, to realize it had all been nothing more than another one of my nightmares.

"I'm getting my act together," Dad finally said. "I want to be the man and father I should be. This family is everything to me." Dad had gone through years of media training. He knew how to answer a sticky question, how to spin it until it was manageable and threw him in a better light.

I was watching the expert in action right now. The master of talk.

The evidence was damning. And my heart desperately wanted to believe my father.

I had no idea where the truth really was.

The counselor had poked and prodded at my past, thinking my life with Becky Dallas was the source of all my angst. But she was wrong.

The one who had hurt me the most had never laid a hand on me. Never abused me a day in my life.

That honor fell to my dad.

BY TEN THIRTY I had eaten six cookies, flipped through two *People* magazines, and gone over my homework three times. I even called Mavis to see if there might be another dog in need of rescue, but no such luck. Where was a desperate animal in need of saving when I needed it?

The mattress bounced as I flopped on my bed and stared at the ceiling.

And remembered my promise to Ridley.

I had to tell him about Dad.

I pulled my hair into a ponytail and brushed my teeth. I leaned closer to my bathroom mirror to sweep some more eye shadow across my lids. It wasn't that seeing Ridley necessitated more makeup. It was just . . .

Okay, seeing Ridley made me want to get fixed up. That wasn't good. Not good at all.

I hastily removed my best pushup bra and traded it for the running bra that gave me the uniboob, throwing a plain gray sweatshirt over that. Nothing sexy to see here, boys.

"Where are you going?" Michael asked as I walked past the living room.

I held up my car keys. "Out."

"Where?" He sat alone on the couch, a bowl of popcorn beside him.

I looked over my shoulder for signs of Mom. I could've lied to my brother, but that skill hadn't exactly served me well lately. "I promised Ridley I would tell him when word came on Dad."

"You can't text him?"

Yes, I could've. That would've been the logical thing to do. "I think he needs to hear it in person. It's over. Dad was his last shot with the Eagles."

Michael took a bite of popcorn, chewing slow. My cat sat in his lap, something my brother never allowed. He couldn't stand Laz. "I'll cover for you. But if you're not back by midnight, you're on your own. And I jumped your battery this afternoon."

I smiled. We'd had our moments, but Michael had never

treated me like anything but a real sister. Even when I was the weird girl howling in the middle of the night, huddled in a corner on the floor of my bedroom. He never treated me like I wasn't part of the O'Malley team.

"I love you, you know," I said.

"Yeah." He nodded. "Back at you."

"I don't care what the girls at Washington High say about you." I reached over and gave him a quick hug. "You're not the worst thing ever."

"Girls love me!" my brother hollered as I sailed on by.

The drive to Ridley's took longer than it should have thanks to a family of deer crossing the road and getting behind a person driving so slow, he stepped on the brake more than the gas.

Finally I parked my Civic in Ridley's drive and ran up the steps of his porch. I knew it was late. The kids would be in bed. But the lights were on, and Ridley didn't strike me as the early to bed type.

When I knocked on the door, a white-haired woman pulled it open. "Yes?"

"Hi, is Ridley here?" Her frown was not the most welcoming. "I know it's late, but it's important."

"He's at work."

Work? "Where?"

"Blue Mountain Lodge."

"Are you sure? He's there now?"

"Every Tuesday night."

I looked past her into the dim living room, the TV casting colorful shadows on the wall. "But what about the girls?"

"What do you think I'm here for, to steal their cable? I'm telling you, Ridley's at work."

"What time does he get off?"

"He'll be there 'til two. Maybe later. Way too late for a kid to be up on a school night, but does he listen to me? No, he does not. Now I need to go. You interrupted my movie." She shut the door in my face without so much as a good-bye. I wondered if she was distantly related to Mavis.

The Blue Mountain Lodge was a good fifteen minutes out of town. It sat on a hill overlooking Avalon Lake, a beautiful lake Dad liked for fishing and boating with the family. The lodge had been many things throughout the years, but it was now a restaurant and inn that drew tourists and locals who wanted an evening or weekend retreat in the midst of nature while still enjoying the elegance of the posh lodge. I drove my Civic, and the closer I got, the windier the roads became.

I entered through heavy oak doors and walked on the native stone floor to the front desk. "I'm looking for Ridley Estes. Is he here?"

The woman behind the counter barely looked up from her computer screen. "In the restaurant. Probably in the kitchen."

Following the direction of her vague finger-pointing, I went down a hall, passing a banquet room that clearly was having a good time from the sounds of their eighties music and loud laughter. Rounding a corner, I finally came to the restaurant. A Closed sign hung in the window. The door unlocked, I went inside anyway.

A man turned off his vacuum as I approached. "I'm sorry, miss, we're closed."

"I'm looking for Ridley Estes."

"Ridley!" he yelled into the quiet room. "Your girlfriend's here to see you!"

"No, I'm not his girlfriend. I'm just—"

"What are you doing here?" Ridley strolled from the kitchen, that angular jaw tight, as if he were considering escorting me right back out.

"The university made their decision." I did a terrible job of keeping the quiver out of my voice. "My dad got fired tonight." Had I sucker punched Ridley, his face would've held the same mix of hurt and shock. "You told me to let you know. I'm sorry." I turned to leave, and with each step, I felt more alone, more hollow than ever.

"Harper, wait." Ridley met me in the hallway. "Stop."

I took in his blazer, his white button-down, his khaki dress pants. The name tag pinned to his chest. "How many days a week do you work?"

His frown was quick, confused. "A few."

"How many?"

"Depends how often my uncle calls me in. Sometimes three or four."

The music from the banquet room pulsed and pushed at the doors beside us. "This is why you roll into school looking like you've spent the entire night partying with the Kappa Sigma boys at the university."

He was through discussing his job. "Is your dad going to appeal?"

"No. He knows he screwed up."

Ridley dropped his head and stared at the brown and gray rocks beneath his feet.

"I'm sorry." My words were a tiny offering, so lame and useless.

"I was so close, Harper. I had it all planned out." He shoved his hands over that short, dark hair and finally lifted his face. This was a guy in need of some sleep. "I'd get college paid for, be close to my sisters. Still work when I needed to. And now . . .

nothing. It's all gone."

"Maybe you just need a different plan. There must be options."

"It's over."

"I don't believe that."

His voice was heartbreakingly hoarse. "You gonna save me, too, O'Malley?"

In that moment, I wanted nothing more. "You'll get other offers."

"None that I can take."

"Ridley, your sisters need more than a brother as a parent."

He didn't even acknowledge that. "What about you?" Ridley's sad smile had me blinking back tears. "How are you holding up?"

"I'd hoped for something else." I really didn't know how I felt. My heart was one big black hole at the moment.

Ridley stepped closer and rubbed his hand down my arm. "You've had quite a day."

I pulled a tissue from my purse and dabbed at my leaky eyes. "Let's cancel tomorrow's lesson."

"Dancing 101?" Ridley turned as a man in a suit stumbled out of the banquet room, a busty blonde under his arm and a drink in his hand. They laughed as they made their way down the hall, as if life were one big party.

"Yeah, forget it," I said. "I need a day off."

"I guess we both do." Ridley nodded his head to the beat of a tune that signaled the group within had now moved on to the nineties. "Or," he said, taking my hand, "we get to that dancing lesson right now."

Chapter Twenty-Three

"Y OU'RE TOO STIFF. Relax."

Ridley had patiently tried to show me some moves for thirty agonizingly long minutes as we crashed the revelry in the banquet room. None of the partygoers seemed to even notice us. Who would've thought Ridley could dance? He was a bulky football player. He attributed it to his Latin roots, but I was the one who knew music and rhythm. Yet he had this instinct for the beat, as if his body just knew when to move an arm, where to place a leg. He didn't attempt anything complicated. Ridley wasn't ready to star in his own music video, but his low-key efforts were the type that blended in perfectly in a crush of dancing people. My attempts made me look like I was mid-seizure and in need of medical attention.

I wanted to shout with relief when the rap song ended. "I need a break. Gonna get some water."

"Hold up." His dimpled smile curved as the first ballad of the night began to play. "My tutorial wouldn't be complete if I didn't cover the slow dance."

"I think I got that one. He puts his arms around me, I wrap my arms around him. He thinks about making out. I think about puppies. Is that about it?"

"Are you sure you actually like this Andrew guy?"

"Yes, I do." I sighed and righted my ponytail. I must've dislodged it when I was headbanging, something Ridley said I should never again do in public.

"I'm starting to doubt." Ridley reached for my hand. "Let's take this out to the terrace."

"Andrew's perfect," I said as he pulled me through the dwindling crowd and past the double doors that led outside. "Did you hear me?"

"Yeah, keep telling yourself that."

Andrew *was* perfect. Everything about him was right. Though my initial manic butterflies had faded to monarchs floating on a spring breeze, I knew it was just the pressure of all the romance material I was learning—plus the mess my life had become.

"Here." Before the evening chill swept over me, Ridley shrugged out of his jacket and eased my arms into it. I tried to imagine it was Andrew's, but for some reason I couldn't even bring up a memory of his face. All I could see was this boy in front of me.

"If the guy is the right one"—I sucked in a breath as Ridley pulled me to him—"and if he's holding you right, you won't be thinking about stray dogs."

Those eyes. So dark, a brown that held mysteries and promises I knew better than to think were for me. Yet when they were trained on me like they were now, my insides melted like gooey Nutella.

"This seems to be more your thing," Ridley said, his voice near my ears as we swayed to the slow-moving song. His body was warm, and I had the strongest urge to rest my head on his shoulder, to shut my eyes and let all my problems disappear in the fog that swirled around me. The terrace was empty, save for the two of us. Gaslit lamps stood on iron stands, giving the look of rustic candlelight. Crickets harmonized to the music that poured from inside. The chilled lake air slid across my skin, and I moved closer into Ridley's embrace.

I did not have feelings for this boy.

I couldn't.

We were barely friends.

So different.

He dated beauty queens and cheerleaders. Usually at the same time.

And I wanted Andrew.

"Did you hear me, Harper?"

"No." Holy trumpets, he smelled nice. "Did you say something?"

His laugh tickled my ear. "I think it's time we took the next step . . . in your tutorial."

Ridley leaned closer. His face hovered inches from my own. His eyes searched mine, and his challenge levitated in the sliver of space between us. "Kissing."

"Kissing," I repeated dumbly.

"That's right." His gaze dropped to my lips. "You're going to want to take notes."

"Is that so?" I wondered if he could hear my heart thudding in my chest.

"The lesson's already started, in case you're wondering."

"I don't know that this is really necessary."

"Oh, kissing is very necessary. And I recall it being your idea." Ridley had yet to retreat. If anything, he had somehow gotten closer. His left hand reached out, slid up my stiffened arm. It slowly journeyed back down. Rested on my hand. "I'm not going to hurt you." He gave my fingers a squeeze. "Do you believe that?"

My answer left my lips before I had time to think. "Yes."

"Have you noticed you don't totally recoil anymore when I touch you?"

I had noticed. He had somehow made the short list of people who could handle me without making me want to barf on their shoes.

"Do you want to proceed?"

I nodded. Then let out the air I didn't know I'd been holding.

"You stay stop, I stop. Got it?" His smile was kind, heartbreaking even. "It's just a kiss."

Just a kiss.

He was in my space in every sense of the word. But it was . . . different. I could hardly draw in oxygen, but it wasn't that same sensation. The fear still pulsed, but instead of shackling my limbs, it seemed to push me forward. It became something else entirely.

"Let us continue." That gentle smile turned a little wicked, lifting his cheeks, lighting his eyes. He picked up my hand, and his skin, roughened from football, was an electric abrasion on mine. He waited a long moment, as if letting me adjust to the feel. Lifting my fingers to his lips, his eyes now on mine, daring me to look away, he turned over my palm. And pressed his lips in the warm center.

"Lesson twelve." His breath was a caress on my hand. "An amateur goes straight for the lips, stays there."

Good heavens, I couldn't move if a tornado screamed into the room and spun us about.

"But someone who knows what he's doing," Ridley continued, his voice gravelly and deep, "he knows there's more ground to cover. To explore." Ridley's gaze dipped to my hand then back to me. "Just part of the fun." And with that, he pressed his open mouth to my palm again. As if the nerve endings were directly connected to my heart, my chest fluttered and jumped. My thoughts tripped over themselves, caught as a new heat wrapped around me and filled my every cell. I couldn't think. All I could do was . . . feel. This was *so* going in the diary.

"And then," he said, "you might use that hand to pull the person in." He did just that. So close my hand landed on his chest to keep my balance. A prayer couldn't have fit between us. "You getting this?"

Words eluded me, sentences beyond possibility. "Yes."

He looked at me as if I were a mystery he wanted to solve, a present he wanted to unwrap. "Then you focus on your target."

His attention on my mouth had me sucking in my bottom lip, worrying it with my teeth. With a faint laugh, Ridley framed my face with his hands. He rubbed his thumb over that same lip. "You might say something complimentary at this point." That thumb teased my lip again in a slow, excruciating slide. "Like how I love the scent of you. Or how I think about your lips. Too often." He began to close the distance again, his head tilting, leaning.

"Ridley—"

He lazily lifted his eyes to mine, his mouth hovering so close. He quirked a dark brow in question.

"I . . . I don't know where to put my hands."

His thumbs now aimlessly caressed my cheeks. "Lots of places for hands. It's like a multiple choice test you can't get wrong." He waited. Smiled. Watched. "Give it a try."

"Right," I breathed.

I thought of every romance novel I had ever read, every movie makeout scene I'd watched.

My hands seemed to be detached, almost robotic as I lifted

them.

Started at Ridley's chest.

Wondered about his back.

Considered his neck.

Stayed away from his butt.

"You're thinking too hard." Then, as if trusting me to figure it out, he pressed a featherlight kiss to my cheekbone. Then two more just like it, creating a trail of shivery sensations. "Go with what you feel." He continued to kiss. And when his lips closed on my neck, I sucked in a breath and slinked my arms around his waist and pulled him tight. Whatever he was doing, it was heaven.

His laugh vibrated against my chest. "Good girl."

Was it okay to move my hands? What were the rules? I hesitantly walked my fingers up his back, felt the muscle, traced it through his shirt.

"O'Malley?"

"Yes?"

His lips moved from my neck to the space near my ear. "I'm going to kiss you now."

"I thought that's what you've been doing."

"Just the warm-up."

Ridley's mouth descended, and I lost all sense of time and space. Gravity eluded me, and my heart floated about. I felt just the slightest touch, his lips on mine, his—

He stopped. "You're not breathing."

What was with all this talking? "Of course I am."

"Do you want me to stop?"

"No." The single word came out a little too loud.

"I don't want to push this."

"But it's just a tutorial," I said. The stars flickered overhead, the night breeze sang all around. "It means nothing. Right?"

A wayward strand of hair escaped, and Ridley reached out and slid it behind my ear. "It's okay to tell this dude to go slow. It's okay to say you have . . . boundaries."

Ridley was worried about me. Me and my odd assortment of mismatched baggage. "Maybe I'm tired of the boundaries."

"Not in this department. Do not make it open season for this guy."

I laid my hand on his chest, felt the rapid beat of his heart. "You're a good guy, Ridley Estes."

Then he crushed his smiling lips to mine.

Good heavens.

Ridley Estes kissed like a Beethoven symphony. It was power and beauty, a crescendo of fire and grace. His lips on mine, his hands now holding my face, angling it to draw me closer. His tongue traced my bottom lip before capturing it again. "Close your eyes, O'Malley."

And I did.

But not before seeing that hard face soften, his features relax as if completely unguarded.

Then Ridley seemed to pull back, slow it down. As if he'd decided to savor and take his time. I knew I was awkward. My nose hit his more than once. But he didn't laugh, didn't say a word. Just held me tight and kept his mouth fused to mine. My hands slid up his chest and around his neck. I marveled at the heat of his skin. The heat within me.

He drew his lips away from mine, and I heard him sigh heavily before pressing one final kiss to my forehead. "You think you've got it?"

While I willed my legs to keep me upright, my eyes drifted open to find Ridley watching me, an unreadable expression on his dark face. "Not bad," I said.

He grinned at that. "You've had better?"

"Danny Jacobson's kiss did come with nachos."

Chapter Twenty-Four

SO THAT'S WHAT I had been missing all this time. I'd never felt that before—as if I would vaporize into a million fragments of dust if Ridley had continued.

Oh, but he could have. My mouth tingled where his had been. My pulse raced. My skin—

"O'Malley?"

"Yes?"

"You're gonna have to let me go sometime."

The fog made one last swirl through my brain before my thoughts finally cleared.

I was still holding onto Ridley like he was my anchor in a tropical storm.

I dropped my hands and took a giant step back, the embarrassment like a blowtorch to my cheeks. "Okay, good lesson. I think we've got it. I should be going. Thank you very much. Nice kissing. Good work. See you tomorrow. Tomorrow is personal narrative, paragraph structure, descriptive language. I'll bring cookies." Suave as ever, I turned on my heel to go, but he caught me and reeled me back in.

"Hey," he said. There was laughter in his voice, and I could not do anything but study the ground. "Harper?"

"Yes?"

"Look at me."

He gently lifted my chin until we were eye to eye. I wanted a portal to open up in the ground and suck me right in. It had been so awkward, then . . . so nice. And I'd gotten swept away. Like an actress morphing into her character.

"You did good," he said. "It takes practice."

What did that mean? Were we going to *practice* more?

"Thank you." It was a lame response on my part. Thanks for making out with me? Who said that? "I'm . . . I'm not good at this sort of thing."

We still stood a mere breath apart. He was in my bubble, and my tension was returning by the second. I automatically backed up a step. But he only followed. Reached for my hand and followed.

"You want to tell me what happened?"

"During the kissing?" Seriously, was he so practiced at it he'd just gone on autopilot and not been aware of his every move?

His gaze briefly dropped to my wrist. "Before you came to live with the O'Malleys."

This boy was worse than any counselor.

Ridley let the silence linger like an invisible third member of our party before finally speaking. "Come with me."

"Where?"

"To my second-favorite spot."

I knew his very favorite was the football field. "I don't know that this is a good idea."

But Ridley wasn't hearing the rest of my protest as he laced his fingers with mine and tugged me to the edge of the terrace and down two flights of stairs. Small garden lights illuminated the path he took as he guided me through a winding trail that finally ended at the lake's edge.

His hand let go of mine, and I was immediately colder. And more confused. Our intertwined hands meant something, didn't it? Probably not.

Definitely not.

"The pier's right over here."

Clutching his coat tighter and trying not to audibly inhale the delicious scent of it, I walked behind him to a wooden pier that jutted into the lake. The wind seemed to still for us, as if it knew I needed a reprieve. Our shoes thudded on the boards as we stepped onto the pier, the water lapping at the underside, and the moon peeking out from a nest of clouds. It was beautiful out here.

"Front row seats." Ridley sat down next to the edge and held out his hand for me to join him.

"Do you come here often?" I settled in beside him, staring out at the dark expanse of the lake. The waves ebbed and flowed in a dance that soothed and calmed.

"I take my breaks out here. Even in the winter." He angled his head, an eyebrow lifted. "You were telling me about your life before the O'Malleys."

"I already answered that. I said there wasn't much to tell."

"You know I don't believe that, right?"

The clouds clustered to cover the full moon above us, and I thought of all those nights I would sit in my room in the dark, staring out my window at the night sky, wondering where my mother was and who she'd be when she came home.

"Things before the O'Malleys were bad," I finally sad. "My mom didn't want me around, but wasn't smart enough to give me up. She didn't like me very much." The words, the very thought was still a wound. No longer a gaping hole, but more like a paper cut that never goes away. A thin razor slice that irritates, even stings. One you forget about until something occasionally snags it.

"And she hit you?"

"Yeah."

"And your dad?"

"Not a nice man. She eventually kicked him out when I was four. But other guys would move in. They weren't much better."

"I've never met my dad. I just got stuck with his last name." He said it with the confidence of knowing he was talking to a kindred soul. "So . . . did anyone ever . . . I mean, did those guys try to—"

"Mostly I was just a punching bag."

"Mostly?"

"Things could've been much worse." He frowned, and I didn't like the sympathy that was starting to come over his expression.

"I think it must've been plenty bad. You wear those long sleeves like a shield. You jump when someone you don't know lays a hand on you."

"Some men were meaner than others." I absently rubbed my forearm. "It was a toxic house. I was alone a lot. My mom would leave for work or for some date, and she'd lock me in my room." I could feel invisible walls closing in. My lungs worked to drag in air. "Tell me to be quiet or . . . I'd be in trouble. The week I first got put in foster care, my mom had been gone for almost twenty-four hours. The neighbor had heard me screaming for help." But that hadn't been the worst of it. The worst came six months later when the state returned me to her. If I closed my eyes I could smell the smoke, hear my own screams.

The O'Malleys had immediately gotten me therapy. And it had helped. But the real bandage on the wound had been their love. They'd held me when I'd cried for no reason. Hadn't suggested it odd that I'd slept with a night-light 'til just last year.

Hadn't given up on me even though it had taken me two solid years before I'd let any of the O'Malleys near me with a kiss or a hug.

"But you survived it," Ridley said. "And you're stronger now because of it."

Was I? Stronger than I'd been at age five or six, yes. But if that had never happened, I'd be normal. I probably wouldn't have hired a high school senior to teach me how to be a girl a boy would notice, would want to date. Would kiss.

"I'd be nothing without the O'Malleys," I said. "I probably wouldn't be alive." The courts had tried to return me to Becky Dallas. But Cristy and John had moved mountains to make sure that hadn't happened. "We lived for six months not knowing if I would have to go back to my bio-mom. I wouldn't let John touch me, but he loved me like his own anyway." I swiped away a stupid tear. "He taught me how to throw a punch. How to defend myself. At the time he'd made it a game, but I knew. Even at that age, I knew he was just protecting me in case the worse happened."

"But it didn't. You're an O'Malley."

Was I? Would I always be? I wasn't sure what that meant these days. "Ridley, what you do for your siblings, it's every-thing. I didn't have someone to take up for me. To make sure I'd eaten or gotten on the bus for school. But you can't keep it up. You have a life to lead. You can't work, go to college, play football *and* be a parent."

"I guess football isn't an option right now," he said. "And neither is giving up my family."

"There are foster parents out there who could—"

"Split them up? Parcel them out? Can you promise me they'd be together? Can you promise me they'd both go to a home as good as yours? No, you can't. No matter what it takes, my family stays together."

"My mom, those men—they left bruises. Your mother might not be hitting you and your sisters, but it's abuse just the same."

"It's *not* the same. Their lives are completely different."

"And how do you figure that?"

"They've got me."

Chapter Twenty-Five

I HAD KISSED RIDLEY Estes.

That was the single thought in my head as I tried to march backward on the football field at Wednesday morning band practice. I relived those dreamlike moments over and over, stumbling three times, playing five wrong notes, and earning a blast from Mr. Sanchez's bullhorn before he finally let us go.

"Hey, everything okay?" Andrew walked beside me as our group migrated back to the high school.

"Yes! Just fine!" Too much? My forced pep would rival a cheerleader's.

"You seemed distracted back there. You never mess up."

"I'm full of mistakes." Kissing Ridley last night—had that been one of them? Had I unleashed a Pandora's box of lust and depravity whose only antidote was a football player I could never have, should never want?

No, this was ridiculous. It had merely been two mouths smashed together. Meaningless, merely a tutorial in the art of romance. When someone kissed that good, I'd have felt electric jolts no matter who he was. If Andrew kissed me right now, I'm sure it would be just as all-consuming, just as toe-curling, just as—

Stop thinking about it!

"Harper, I was wondering about yesterday." Andrew's words all but shoved me back to the present. "Maybe we could talk about—"

"Levin!" Mr. Sanchez yelled. "I need to see you now!"

Andrew opened his mouth, his eyes serious on mine. "Never mind." He gave my free hand a squeeze. "I guess I'll talk to you later."

I floated from the field to inside the school, somehow ending up standing before my open locker. My fingers traced the spines of my books as I tried to figure out what I was supposed to be grabbing. First hour . . . Wednesday . . .

"The big blue one that says *Econ*." Molly appeared next to me, her neon pink mouth curved in a mischievous smile.

I pulled the text and slid it into my backpack. "I knew that. I was just—"

"Thinking of a certain boy?"

"It's not like that at all. He and I—"

"Are a completely adorable couple. I gotta give you credit, Harper." Molly bit into an apple she pulled from her purse. "That Andrew's quite the romantic."

Andrew. Right. The boy who had captivated my heart, made me a swoon-worthy picnic, and sweetly kissed me on the cheek.

Not Ridley. The one who had made me laugh as he showed me how to dance—and forget my own name as he'd kissed me senseless. How was it I could still smell his cologne, feel his skin beneath my fingertips, taste his lips?

"Hello?" Molly waved her gloved hand in front of my face. "Are you listening to a word I'm saying?"

Today Molly wore black-and-white striped leggings, gold glittery flats, a pink miniskirt, and ruffled white blouse, topped off by an acid-washed denim jacket.

"I'm sorry," I said.

"What's up with you? It was like an alien invaded your body

at practice out there."

"I just got distracted by your outfit."

"You like?"

"Very early Madonna."

"I wanted to wear my black hat, but Principal Sparacino just took it away."

"He has no clue who he's dealing with."

"And no appreciation for artistic expression."

Molly and I joined the masses in the hall, moving in wads like schools of fish. You just had to find a gap in the lines and jump in, swimming with the flow.

"You look tired."

She had no idea. "The university let my dad go. Press conference this afternoon, I guess."

"Oh, Harper. I'm sorry. Do you need a hug?"

That pulled a laugh out of me. Molly knew those things were usually about as comforting to me as sticking my hand in a blender.

"Seriously, what can I do?"

I dodged a senior who had no respect for the implied rules of the hall. "There's nothing you can do."

"I can't believe it's come to this."

Neither could I.

"Oh my gosh. There he is." Molly gave a little squeal beside me, and I fought not to hightail it the other direction as I saw the source of her girly fit. Coming toward us was Ridley. My heart lurched at the sight of him. He'd yet to see us, and I made a quick study of every inch of him. He had his arm around some cute brunette from the dance team, and as he said something to her, she tossed her glossy hair and laughed. The tiny darts of jealousy came swiftly and unexpectedly. I didn't care if he flirted with that girl! Heck, he could have a girlfriend for all I knew. Five of them.

Yet he had kissed *me* last night.

Kissed me like he'd meant it.

Except that moment had meant nothing to him.

And nothing to me.

"Hey, girls." Ridley smiled as he approached. His bemused gaze dared me to look away.

Did the nameless brunette see the shadows beneath his eyes? Did she notice how his posture bent the slightest bit, as if he carried the weight of the world on those shoulders?

"Hello!" Molly chirped. "I want you to know I think it's an outrage you're not playing right now."

Ridley smiled, then kept moving with the flow of traffic, his attention pulled back to his skinny dancer.

"You don't even know who we play," I said to Molly.

She sighed. "Who cares? All I know is I'll be at that game, and Ridley could be as well. The band geek and the football god. It would make a great romance novel."

"Or fantasy."

"Talk to him for me. You see him all the time. Do you have any idea what kind of gift that is? It's like being handed a key to Macy's. A check with lots of zeroes. A chocolate fountain that never runs dry."

It was right there on the tip of my tongue to tell her about yesterday. Ridley's ridiculous farce that we were engaged, my going to his work, his kissing me senseless. But instead I kept walking, keeping my secrets to myself.

"Talk to him, Harper. That girl doesn't love him like I do."

"You don't love him."

"I know. It's much too soon," she said. "But after our first date, he would realize I was all he'd been looking for and be blinded to all those other girls."

"And by your outfit."

"Can you even imagine what it would be like to kiss that boy?"

"Yeah." I looked back, but Ridley had disappeared in the crowd. "I think I can."

Econ class flew by in a blur. Unfortunately, a blur that included a quiz and some group work that had me thinking villainous thoughts about my teacher.

When the third-hour bell rang, I went to the band room's instrument closet and once again retrieved my beloved trumpet. Finding my seat, I ran a cloth over the silver metal, polishing it until it shined like the day I'd first got it. My trumpet had been one of the first things the O'Malleys had given me when I'd come to them as a foster kid. My bio-mom hadn't been able to afford an instrument, so I hadn't gotten to sign up for elementary school band. My dad had found out on a Monday, and by Tuesday, I'd come home from school to my very own trumpet. All mine. In the world of scraps and secondhand, so very little had been completely mine.

"Hey, Harper." Andrew sat down in his number two seat, a hint of caution on his face. That didn't bode well. "So . . . you took off pretty quickly yesterday."

"I'm sorry. Something came up." Andrew was such a stark contrast to Ridley. Andrew was slender to the point of needing a cheeseburger, while Ridley could probably deadlift a refrigerator. Andrew had longer hair, where Ridley's was short. Andrew was vintage T-shirts, while Ridley dressed like a Latin Abercrombie model. Andrew told me he thought he might be allergic to dogs, and Ridley braved bullets and fake engagements to help me save them.

Yet Andrew was the boy I liked. The one who was right for me.

"Lunch was great though," I said. "I think it's one of the best dates I've ever had." And the only one.

A hesitant smile lit up his face. "I had a great time, Harper."

"It was incredibly sweet."

"So, uh, you and that Ridley guy . . ."

"We're just friends. I—"

"Tutor him, yeah, I know. But—" Andrew scratched his neck, pausing on a thought. "You two seem to be pretty close."

I opened my mouth to deny it, but Andrew was right. Ridley and I had become friends, confidants. I'd shared things with him even Molly didn't know. And I knew few, if any other girls, had been to his house. Yet he had let me in. We'd invited each other into the dark and secret places of our lives.

Just enough to create a strange brew of a friendship.

And a maelstrom of confusion in my mind.

"Are you sure you wouldn't rather invite him to the dance?"

"What? No!" Did Andrew not want to go anymore? "You're the one I want to go with. Unless you'd rather take someone else?"

"I was just checking." Andrew gave a small laugh. "I'm not good at this dating stuff. I've only dated a few girls, so I'm still learning."

Oh, wasn't that absolutely charming? Lack of experience—I would later add this to my document titled: "Things Totally Adorbs About Andrew Levin."

"I thought I could pick you up early before the dance," Andrew said. "We could get something to eat."

"That would be awesome," I said. "I'm a big fan of food."

My repartee was still a perfect example of a natural disaster, along with spewing volcanoes and cataclysmic floods.

Andrew placed his music folder on his stand. "You wanna hang out today after school? Maybe listen to my band practice?"

"I'd love to. I would. But I have tutoring."

"With Ridley."

Was Andrew jealous? "Yes."

"No big deal." But Andrew's jaunty shrug said otherwise.

"Andrew." The thought of this boy walking away from what we were starting . . . I was not going to let that happen. We were too close to becoming a real couple. "Tutoring is a job. That's all it is."

"Are you sure?"

"Yes." That was all it ever could be. Nothing more.

WHEN I GOT home, there was a For Sale sign stuck in my yard.

After a quick trip to the Walnut Street Animal Rescue and Mrs. Henrietta Tucker's after school, I pulled into our driveway just as a Maple Grove Realty car drove away.

"Mom?" I slammed the front door behind me, jumped over one of my two foster dogs, and sailed through the foyer, coming to a jaunty halt.

"Hello, Harper." Dad stood in the doorway between the foyer and living room. He wore jeans and an Eagles sweatshirt, looking painfully normal. Even though not one single thing was.

"What are you doing here?"

"I'm moving back in."

Somewhere in the house a door shut. The roof creaked. A dog snored.

And I tried to think of something to say.

"Are you okay with that?" Dad watched me closely, like there was only one correct answer.

"I don't know."

And that wasn't it.

"Harper, I'm your father. You can't just write me off after one mistake."

"It was more than a mistake. It was an atom bomb to our family." And to my illusion that I was finally safe and secure.

"I know I broke your trust," Dad said. "But that means you're done with me?"

"No," I whispered. Why was this so confusing? Mom and Dad didn't understand anything I did right now, and my thoughts hadn't unraveled enough to explain it.

"Give me a second chance."

"I'm afraid to."

"John, I—" Mom walked out of the living room, stopping when she saw us. "Harper."

Yeah, Harper. Your daughter. The one you've forgotten to mention a few updates to. "Just saw the For Sale sign."

"We decided last night. Your dad and I were going to talk to you about it, but Michael said you'd gone to bed."

I owed my brother. "So we're moving? As a family?"

Mom glanced at Dad. "Your father is here to help us get the house ready to sell. We can't stay in Maple Grove. You know that."

"He's moved back in to help us box up some clothes?"

Mom hesitated, as if she wasn't too sure herself. "We want to do what's best for everyone. Right now it makes financial sense for your father and me to not live in two separate homes. And we thought it would be nice to be together as a family for the holidays. So your dad's moving into the room over the garage."

This seemed sudden. And weird.

"Cole's grades are slipping. He's been getting in some trouble. You're struggling," Dad said.

Now I was confused *and* offended. "I'm not struggling."

"You skipped school. Skipped your counseling appointment. You cleaned the baseboards and baked a hundred cookies this morning," Mom said.

"So I deal with things through carbs, cleaning, and avoiding intrusive conversation. Pretty sure that doesn't mean I'm falling apart."

"I love your mom, Harper. And I miss you kids." Dad had that injured look on his face, like that time in sixth grade I failed to invite him to my first daddy-daughter dance. "And this family belongs together. I would think you of all people would agree."

If Dad was moving into the suite over the garage, was this a reconciliation? And what if it didn't work? What if I let myself believe we were this untouchable family once again, only to have it ripped away? "Where are we moving?"

"I've already got a few job offers." Dad reached down to pet the dog that had plopped down at his feet. "It's for next season, but one' a very definite possibility."

"Where?"

"I can't say yet."

"Make an exception."

Confidentiality was the way of the athletic world when it came to contracts and deal terms. We all knew that. If I stitched our family motto onto a pillow, it would read Keep Your Mouth Shut. So I was surprised when my dad inhaled deep then had the nerve to smile. "Mississippi Tech. It's going to take a few weeks to finalize."

I didn't *want* to move. My life was in Maple Grove. "My

friends are here. I'm finally first chair."

"I know you've worked hard for that, but moving is part of my job and—"

"Not this time," I said. "This isn't some career advancement. We're moving because you—"

"Harper." My mom stood in front of my dad, like a warrior queen ready to take a dagger for her king. "Let's sit down and discuss this . . . calmly."

"I don't want to." The house for sale made this all too real. Change always tipped my canoe, but this was more. This was speedboating toward Niagara Falls.

"We have a family counseling session tomorrow night," Mom said.

I walked toward the stairs. "I won't be there."

Chapter Twenty-Six

"**H**ARPER, YOUR DATE is here."

Dad stepped inside my room just as I snapped a selfie to send to Molly.

"Wow, babe." He smiled as he took in the curls Mom had created with a flatiron and the ivory lace dress that stopped well above my knees, revealing legs that could possibly go down as my best feature. A thin black belt circled my waist.

"You look beautiful." Dad braved a kiss to my cheek, and for a moment, I breathed in his familiar scent and remembered how normal things were only a month ago. How solid my world had been. I wanted to go back, to rewind it all and be that family again.

"Thank you." I reached for the little clutch that matched my shoes.

"It's such a pretty dress. Are you sure you want to wear that cardigan over it?"

"Yes." The dress had vintage-inspired three-quarter-length sleeves, but there was no way I was putting even a hint of my arms on display. "It's chilly out."

"Have a great time."

"I will."

Dad had been back in the house three nights and three days, and it was . . . weird. I wanted to hope that my parents would stay together, but they were bunking in separate spaces and were so painfully polite to one another, they were more like new roommates than husband and wife. I feared the worst, that divorce was inevitable, and they were merely buying time.

I walked downstairs, where Michael intercepted me. "Have fun at your nerd party. You look nice and stuff."

I smiled. "Thanks. And stuff."

Andrew stood in the living room, talking to Mom and Cole. He turned as I came into the room, his face brightening like the lights on the Wildcat football field as he smiled. Now that was how a girl dreamed of a boy looking at her.

"Whoa." Andrew walked to me and pressed a quick peck to my cheek. "The other guys are gonna be so jealous of me."

My face warmed. "Probably not after they see me dance."

"Any guy would kill to have you as his date tonight."

"You're very good at the flattery."

"I only speak the truth."

I didn't believe him for a second, but I repeated the words in my head three times, committing them to memory so I could record them later.

"Are you ready? Our chariot awaits." Andrew gave me his arm. "And by chariot, I mean my dad's Toyota."

I glanced up at his face, hopeful he had just made a joke. But no. The expression staring back at me was that of Literal Andrew.

"You guys have fun," Mom said.

"Don't do anything I wouldn't do," Michael added.

I pulled Andrew toward the door. "That's a very short list."

I couldn't help but notice that Andrew didn't open my car door like Ridley. He didn't drive with one hand on the wheel and the other a mere centimeter from mine. Nor did he occasionally look away from the road to stare at me broodily.

Stop thinking about Ridley!

You're with Andrew. He's kind, he's smart, he's cute. He's perfect for you.

Andrew took me to an Italian restaurant on one of the side streets off the square. We sat in a corner booth as Dean Martin tunes played softly. A candle lit our table, making Andrew's eyes movie-star beautiful and easy to look into. We both got lasagna—Andrew's was traditional, while I ordered one made with eggplant. I worried the accompanying salad would guarantee green things in my teeth, or that the bread would make me bloat like a Macy's Thanksgiving Day Parade balloon, but the talking went down much easier with a little calorie consumption. Plus the bread came with this melted butter that made me want to stand up and give glory to God Almighty. I mentally referred to Ridley's rules throughout the meal. *Compliment Andrew. Ask him about himself.* By the time dessert came, I had graduated from awkward conversationalist to at least mediocre. I learned he'd been a Boy Scout, helped on his grandma's farm every summer, and gone on three mission trips to dig wells for orphans. He was pretty much the boyfriend jackpot.

But someone needed to give Andrew some conversational lessons.

"And then I grabbed my rifle and took out that deer right from the window of our hunting cabin. Can you believe that?"

My throat closed around a bite of cheesecake. "I can hardly stand it."

"I know, right? So cool. It was at least a twelve point."

Taking a few sips of water, I tried again to steer him back to a topic that didn't make me want to cry into my napkin. "You know what I love?"

He smiled as he sliced his fork into his warm brownie à la mode. "Tell me."

"I love movies. Every Sunday night my family has a B-movie night." Not that we'd done it lately. "We watch really terrible, cheesy ones with horrible special effects, low budgets, bad dialogue."

"Interesting." Andrew chewed his brownie for a lengthy period of time, and I realized that was all he was going to say about that.

"So . . ." Ridley had told me this was a good topic, and so far he was wrong. "Have you seen any movies lately?"

"No." Andrew scraped some hot fudge sauce from his bowl. "I mostly watch Japanese TV shows online."

"Oh, like anime?" I could totally talk about this.

"No, more like reality shows. Really funny stuff."

Funny stuff? What about *my* funny stuff? I'd thrown out my best jokes tonight. I'd told Andrew the story of Molly accidentally losing her bra onstage in her last play, the tale of my youngest brother barfing on Santa Claus, even mentioning the time Mavis and I had each stuffed three puppies down our shirts to sneak them by a confirmed dogfighter.

What did that get me? A few courtesy laughs. But Japanese reality shows flicked his funny bone?

By the time the waiter brought the check, I was all out of questions. I'd gone through my entire repertoire. I needed to ask Ridley what to do when Andrew answered my questions, but didn't ask me any back. How was I supposed to keep the flow of conversation going? Maybe we were both having an off night. Maybe I was just so upset over the idea of moving that I was being hypercritical. That had to be it. Probably nothing would please me tonight. Or this decade. Though it wouldn't have hurt for Andrew to offer a bite of that brownie thing. Just for comparison purposes.

Andrew reached for my hand as we walked back to his Camry. His skin felt cold on mine, his palm a little clammy. Andrew had me listen to his favorite tracks from his band on the way to the school cafeteria. I couldn't make out most of the words, but his band seemed to have a lot of enthusiasm.

He parked the car, cut the engine, and turned to me. "I like hanging out with you."

Was something going to happen here? "I feel the same."

But he just opened the door and hopped out, meeting me on the sidewalk and walking me to the door.

I wished I could ask Andrew what his expectations were. For me, for us. For this night. Was this a kissing night? I assumed it probably was. Would I be able to recall all I'd learned? What if I screwed that up? What if I had only been decent at it because Ridley had been such the aficionado?

The unknowns ran like a dripping faucet in my head, and I couldn't turn it off.

"Harper!" Molly flung her arms around me as soon as we entered the disco ball–lit cafeteria. "Come dance with me!"

The room vibrated with a rock song, and already a large group of bandies gathered on the floor, thrashing and moving to the words, the beat, or whatever else propelled their limbs.

"They're all terrible dancers," I said. "I've been worried for weeks about this, and look at them." I laughed as I watched my friends and classmates do their thing. "Most of them are absolutely awful."

"It's our curse." Molly tossed back a cup of red punch. "Most of the WHS band members are completely incapable of looking even remotely cool on the floor." She flung an arm around Andrew and me. "But that's the fun of it! Come on!"

So I did.

I set my clutch and inhibitions on a table, then joined a mob surrounding my best friend and just flung and flailed like the rest of the crowd. It was exhilarating. It was liberating. Andrew and I laughed at the others. We laughed at ourselves. He did have a sense of humor! There were a few students who looked like they knew what they were doing, but they were the minority. Bad dancers ruled the night.

Andrew was in a class of his own. He moved like Justin Timberlake. It was something of beauty, something to be envied. He tried to show me a few moves, but it was hopeless. Yet instead of hyperventilating over my lack, I just laughed. And threw my hands over my head and continued my rhythmic fit.

"This one's for all you couples out there," said the DJ, changing the music to a slow song and nearly clearing the floor. "Guys, grab your ladies."

Andrew extended his hand. "Can I have this dance?"

As the music floated around us, he pulled me in tight, his arms holding me close. My hands played at his neck, and I thought of how different he felt than the boy I'd danced with last.

"Harper?"

I lifted my head.

And saw hazy purpose in those eyes.

I might not know jack about the mechanics of kissing, but I knew that look.

"Yes?" I smiled up at my date, my heart tripping wildly.

"I really like you."

"I'm glad," I said. "Because I like you."

His head lowered even more. "I think we should date. Be a

couple. Exclusive."

I had waited a lifetime for those words—or at least since the moment I saw Andrew Levin step his foot onto campus. I had just known he would be right for me. And now here we were, wrapped in each other's arms, bodies swaying to one really bad love song, his lips inches from mine.

"Are you asking me to be your girlfriend?"

"That depends on what your answer is."

I recreated one of Molly's flirty smiles. "And if the answer is no?"

"Then I'm going to go drink myself into a stupor on watery punch, grab one of those cheese trays, and cry all the way home."

I laughed. "And if my answer's yes?"

"Then I'd probably still steal a cheese tray." His face sobered. "I'm kidding. You get that, right? I wouldn't really steal a cheese tray. I'm not a thief and—"

"Andrew." I patted his shoulder. "I know."

His grin widened as his nose brushed against mine. "And then I'd kiss you."

Oh, gosh. Here it was. *Be brave, Harper. You can do this.* "Andrew?"

He tilted his head, raised a brow.

"My answer is yes."

"The punch bowl is safe." His smiling lips lowered to mine, and all dancing stopped. Andrew's mouth took possession and I sighed and slid my hands into his hair. His kiss was sweet and slow. It didn't have the fire and skill of Ridley's, but somehow that was a relief. I didn't lose all thought as Andrew kissed me, didn't forget where I was. Nope, I could pretty much do long division in my head with this lip-lock.

"Harper!" Behind me I heard Molly's voice.

"Ignore her," Andrew said against my cheek.

"Harper!"

I stepped from Andrew as Molly broke through the slow dancers, bearing toward us, waving my cell phone.

"You have a text," Molly said.

Andrew had the good grace to laugh. "Seriously?"

"I'm kind of busy," I said. "I'll check it later."

She shook her head. "It's Ridley."

Andrew tensed beside me. "I'll talk to him later."

"Your phone was on the table and it kept ringing. Then when it beeped with a text, I picked it up to check it. Here."

Emmie's burning up with fever. Tried everything to get it down. No idea what to do. Call me.

"I need to call Ridley," I said. "I'll be back."

Andrew's face as I walked away reminded me of an angry grizzly, but all I could think about was Emmie. Ridley must be worried out of his mind.

Ignoring the warnings of two parent chaperones, I walked outside where I pulled up Ridley's number and called.

He answered on the third ring.

"Ridley? What's going on?"

"Are you home?"

"No. I'm at the dance."

I heard his muffled curse. "I forgot. I'm sorry. Have a good time."

"No, wait! Is Emmie okay?"

"I'll take care of it."

"Tell me what's going on."

"I wouldn't have called if I'd remembered the stupid band dance. I just . . . I just didn't know what else to do. I've been with her all day, doing everything I was supposed to. And the fever's not budging. My mom hasn't been around. I'd thought you could ask your mother what to do. I think I need to take her to the emergency room."

"What's Emmie's fever—"

"A hundred and four."

"I'll grab my dad and be there in fifteen minutes." Grab my dad? Where had that come from?

"Don't be crazy. Stay at the dance. I'll handle this myself."

Like he did everything else. "See you soon."

"Do not leave that dance or—"

I ended the call and made another to my mom. But it was my dad who picked up, as if he'd known I'd thought of him first.

"What's wrong?"

I filled him in, my stress decreasing. He would take care of it. I knew it.

"Your mom's out with some friends. I'll be right there, Harper."

When I turned to go back inside, Andrew stood at the door, his face bathed in the overhead light, his hands shoved in the pockets of his dark slacks. The autumn night air stirred, blowing Andrew's hair across his frowning forehead.

"I'm sorry," I said. "I have to go."

"Ridley."

"His baby sister is very sick. He can't find his mom."

"So he needs you to take care of it?"

"He's a friend, and he's scared." Andrew had no idea what it was like to be on your own, to need a parent, but not have one who clocked in for the job.

"We still have the bonfire."

"My dad's on the way."

"I could've taken you home."

"No, I want you to stay."

"You're the only reason I'm here."

A pinprick right to my heart. "I'm sorry."

Andrew reached for my hand, warmed it in both of his, and gave a mirthless laugh. "From dogs to people, saving is just what you do, isn't it?"

I didn't know if that was a quality he liked or one he wished I'd overcome. "I had a great time."

He leaned in and kissed my cold cheek. "Call me later."

I had just ditched my new boyfriend.

To be with Ridley Estes.

Chapter Twenty-Seven

"TELL ME AGAIN why you're leaving your date to go help Ridley Estes?" Dad turned onto Cherry Street and into Ridley's neighborhood.

"Because his sister—"

"I get that his sister needs help. But why you?" Dad pulled into the drive of the little gray house. "Where's Ridley's mother?"

"She's out of pocket."

Dad turned off the car and just looked at me. If he had any more questions about Ridley's mom, he kept them to himself.

I had no more opened my car door than Ridley met us on the porch. He wore a black T-shirt, half-untucked, jeans with a stain of something on the thigh, and dark circles beneath his haunted eyes. In his arms he held his baby sister, who rested against him like a limp doll.

"Hello, Ridley," Dad said.

"Coach O'Malley."

"Look at this sweet girl." Dad pressed his hand to Emmie's red cheek. "You're going to be just fine. We'll get you better in no time." His voice remained gentle, the same tone I heard whispered over me in the hospital years ago—calm, reassuring, safe. Dad turned his attention to Ridley. "What's her temp now?"

"Still a hundred and four. Has been for most of the day."

"Is she drinking anything?"

"No."

With a frown, Dad tilted his head and inspected Emmie. "Tell me what you've tried."

"Everything. Cold baths, meds, rubbed alcohol at the bottom of her feet."

"Alcohol?" I asked.

"Old remedy," Dad said. "You've done a good job, Ridley."

"She's just lifeless." The self-assured football hero was gone. In his place stood a brother whose voice held a tremor of fear, his face etched with lines of frustration, alarm. "This isn't like her. Normally she can't sit still. Her eyes are so vacant."

"It's going to be okay," I said. An overwhelming urge to wrap Ridley in my arms pulsed through me, foreign and strong. Me, who barely tolerated hugs. And now I just wanted to draw Ridley and Emmie near and take some of that pain.

"I think we need to get her to the ER," Dad said.

"Where's Faith?" I asked.

"At a friend's." Ridley pressed a kiss to his sister's hair. "If my mom has insurance on the girls, I can't find it. What if they won't see us?"

"A doctor will see your sister," Dad said. "I'll make sure of it. Don't worry about the cost."

"I'll pay you back," Ridley said.

"No need."

"I *will* pay you back."

Dad hesitated for only a moment. "If that's how you want it. We should probably go."

We moved the car seat to my Dad's truck then flew to the hospital. Ridley sat in the back with Emmie, his hand caressing her hair, her little hands. He spoke to her in hushed croons, the passing streetlights revealing the shadows of fear on his face.

The wheels of the truck seemed to barely spin as the minutes yawned along the ten long miles to St. Vincent's Hospital. I took a deep yoga breath as we finally arrived, and Dad pulled up to the sliding front doors.

Ridley already had Emmie out of the car seat, and he covered her head with her pink blanket to block the wind and rush her inside.

"I'll see you in there, Dad." I followed Ridley.

A woman at the front desk quizzed Ridley about the whereabouts of Emmie's legal guardian. The lady had to be as tall as Ridley's six feet, though her shoulders could've been twice as wide. She had a hint of a mustache above her top lip, and I had a feeling she had missed her true calling of wrestling or operating heavy machinery.

"My mom's out of town. I can't get hold of her."

"I have paperwork I need her to sign."

"I'm Emmie's brother."

"And I'm the receptionist. Neither one of us is this baby's mama."

"Just give me the paperwork," Ridley said. "She needs a doctor now."

She harrumphed but slid over a clipboard. "Fill this out."

"When can a doctor see Emmie?" Ridley asked.

"There's a long line of folks ahead of you. It's probably gonna be a while. So take my clipboard, your baby sister, and go sit down. We have a lovely selection of magazines for you to peruse while you wait."

I sat in a navy chair and watched Ridley scribble the info onto the form. "Do you want me to take her?" He could barely write for holding Emmie.

"No." He filled in three more lines, then put down his pen, his gaze finding mine. "Thank you."

I slowly smiled. "You're welcome."

"I didn't mean for you to do this."

"I care about her too." *And you.*

"I didn't know who to call."

"I'm glad you called me."

He twisted the cap on his pen. "I'm sorry I ruined your date."

"I wanted to be here." He watched me closely, and I wondered what was going through that head of his. I reached over the chair arm and placed my hand on his. "She's going to be okay."

He watched our joined hands. "She has to be. If anything happens to her—"

"It won't."

"Why are you still in the waiting room?" Dad asked, appearing beside me like an angel ready to do battle.

"Secretary Smiley said there's a wait," I said.

"I'll take care of this." Dad disappeared as fast as he arrived, beelining toward the front desk. The woman's eyes widened, and I knew the second she recognized the infamous Coach O'Malley. This was either going to go very badly, or Ridley was going to get the St. Vincent's version of first class.

Whatever Dad and the lady discussed, it involved lots of hand motions on her part. Finally, the woman waddled over to us. "Exam room four. Follow me."

Ridley scooped up a whining Emmie and let the receptionist lead the way.

Dad plopped down beside me in the seat Ridley had just vacated.

"Thank you," I said.

He slid lower in the seat and leaned his head back. "Want to tell me the real story on his mom?"

I could've lied, but I didn't. "No."

"I assume that kid takes care of his sisters?"

Dad probably couldn't know the depth of that statement. "Ridley chose USK because it was the number one football program," I said. "But also because it's important he's near his family."

Dad pulled a pack of gum from the pocket of his track pants and held it toward me. "How long's he been the man of the house?"

"I think forever."

"What happens to his sisters if he moves to a different college?"

I looked toward the metal doors that Ridley had carried a pale Emmie through. "He's going to make sure they never find out."

An hour later, Emmie was admitted to the hospital. The children's wing was decorated with brightly colored zoo animals, but it did nothing to cheer up Ridley.

"Emmie has a virus," the doctor explained after they settled her in a room the color of butter. "Probably the strand of crud that's been going around." He pointed to the IV that was connected to her tiny arm. "She just got dehydrated. It's more common than you'd think. You did the right thing bringing her in."

"How long until she feels better?" Ridley asked, staring down at his sister sleeping in the bed.

"We'll watch her tonight, see how she feels in the morning. Fever ought to break anytime now."

The doctor gave Ridley some final instructions, shook my dad's hand, then left.

Dad, Ridley, and I stood around Emmie's bed. Her cheeks were no longer as pink, and her little forehead no longer pulled into a frown.

Ridley checked his phone, only to stuff it right back in his pocket. His mother still had not checked in. This was too much for someone Ridley's age to deal with, and it angered me that his mom was so absent.

"Do you need anything?" Dad asked.

"No," Ridley said. "I'll stay here with Emmie. We have all we need. But I'm grateful for your help."

"I'm just glad the doctor was an Eagle fan," Dad said. "If he was an Aggie, we'd still be in the waiting room this time tomorrow." Dad glanced at his sports watch. "Sis, it's after one. You ready to go?"

I looked at Ridley. Then back at my Dad. "I . . . I think I'll stay here too." Dad started to protest. "I'll be fine," I said. "Trust me."

"You can stay for a few hours." He reached for a strand of my hair and gave it a small tug. "Call me when you're ready to come home. I'll be right here."

I'll be right here.

I didn't know whether it was from the fatigue or my dad's words, but my eyes misted, and I had to look away.

"Anything else you need?" Dad asked Ridley.

"I hate to ask, but I left the house open. Any chance you could swing by and lock up? I don't exactly live in the safest neighborhood."

"Consider it done." Dad gave Emmie one more assessing peek, an *atta girl* wink to me, then shut the door behind him.

A faint light radiated through the room, as if bathing it in moonlight. The sounds of beeps and hisses from far away filled the silence as Ridley and I had nothing to say for the next half hour. He just sat in his chair, elbows resting on his knees, and watched his sister sleep.

And I watched him. His body became so still, I thought he had fallen asleep. Until I heard his voice.

"Sometimes I have this dream." His words sounded hoarse, raw. "I dream that something's coming for Faith and Emmie. It's dark and big, and I don't know what it is. But I can't get to them in time." He tunneled his hands through his hair. "I wake up in a sweat. Sometimes I go check on them, just to reassure myself they're still there, they're okay."

My throat thickened. "You'd never let anything happen to them."

"You're right, though—I can't always be there. You have no idea how that thought chills me. I'd die without those two."

I slid my hand up his back, felt the warmth there, the strength beneath my fingers. "They're lucky to have you."

"I think about what you said a lot. That I can't keep pretending to be the parent. But Harper, it's all I've known. And the thought of them split up, or living with some other family—without me." He lifted anguished eyes to mine. "That's worse than any nightmare I've ever had."

My hand fell back to the armrest, and he reached for it. Pressed my palm to his cheek and leaned into it. My heart swelled and gravitated within my chest. My feelings for Ridley . . . I feared they were shifting and morphing into something I couldn't tame. And that couldn't happen. He was a friend. That's all we could be. I had sworn my romantic allegiance to Andrew. And I couldn't let someone so undeniably wrong for me get in the way of that.

I let my hand drop back to my lap, studied my fingernails, wondered why I felt saddened by the loss of my skin on his.

"Did Levin kiss you tonight?" His question could barely be heard above the drip of the IV, the faraway blare of an alarm.

"Yes."

Ridley slowly nodded, his eyes never leaving mine. "Was it everything you hoped for?"

No.

It was night to Ridley's day, moon to Ridley's sun. A small fuse to the liquid lightning that had been Ridley's mouth on mine. But this boy was out of my league.

And maybe I was out of his.

"I think," I said, "it was all that I needed."

Chapter Twenty-Eight

A BOLT OF *lightning crashed into the tree outside my window. I coughed as the smoke filled my lungs and my eyes watered with the sting. In vain, I banged on the door, but no one was coming. The door was warm to the touch, and I quickly moved away.*

"Help me!" I yelled. "Someone help me!" But there was no use. The rain fell in torrents, but somehow the fire raged on. I was trapped in my house.

Alone.

I would die alone.

"No!"

I sat straight up in bed, my panting breaths barely audible above the storm blowing outside. A tree scratched against my window, and I clutched my pillow to my chest, tears streaming down my face, desperately trying to bring the room, my mind in focus.

I was safe. In the O'Malleys' house.

And I wasn't ten.

Sweat dotted my forehead, and I crashed back into my pillows as thunder shook my walls.

I was so tired of this. Tired of never knowing when my past would reach out and tap me on the shoulder, whispering memories in my ear like a phantom enemy.

My bedside clock read six a.m., and I knew it was no use

trying to go back to sleep, though my head ached and swelled with fatigue.

I had lain down mere hours ago. Taking up my dad's offer, I had called him at three in the morning to pick me up from the hospital. Ridley's mother had never shown, but Emmie had stabilized, improved even, and Ridley had finally convinced me to go home.

The weird thing was, as draining and frightening as last night had been, I'd had fun. With Emmie sleeping soundly, Ridley and I had watched old movies on TV before breaking out a pack of cards someone had left in a bedside drawer. I'd taught Ridley gin rummy, despite his initial request to play strip poker. He'd made me laugh, and we'd talked for long stretches of time before falling into a comfortable silence. The kind that didn't poke at you to fill it.

I'd sent Andrew a text last night, but he'd yet to respond. I would deal with him later.

I brushed my teeth and threw on a sweatshirt and pajama bottoms before trudging downstairs. My stomach hadn't awakened yet, so I skipped breakfast and mopped the kitchen floor instead. Grabbing a feather duster, I walked down the long hall, trying to find something peaceful about the sound of the falling rain.

I swept the duster over the black frames that held our family pictures. Dad with his arms around a smiling Mom. The five of us all in white linen shirts on the beach in Gulf Shores. Cole and Michael's baby picture. A black-and-white of my adoption day.

"Cristy?"

I jumped as Dad's voice came from his office at the end of the hall.

"It's me." I stepped inside his man cave, a room that both

fascinated me and made me long for the Pottery Barn fairy to have her wicked, girly way with every wall.

Wood paneling stopped halfway up walls that were painted fire-engine red, one of the USK colors. Sports memorabilia piled everywhere. On his desk sat a glass case that held a football from some game I didn't remember and signed by some NFL guy I didn't know. Collages of team photos hung proudly on the walls, a chronology of the schools my dad had coached, and the guys who had become part of our lives. Many of those players, now long graduated, still called my dad. Last year a few even stopped by for Christmas.

"Storm wake you up?" Dad sat in my favorite part of the office, a seating area that included an old, beige, mushy couch and matching chair with a flat screen large enough to serve a drive-in.

"The thunder was pretty loud." I eased into the room. "What are you doing?"

He waved the remote toward the TV. "Watching some scouting footage I had."

The uniforms on the screen looked familiar, and I realized it was from my high school. Dad rewound a play and zoomed in. "Your friend Ridley Estes plays a mean game of football. I've had my eye on him since he was in the tenth grade. I came to a game to see you march, and when I saw that kid run with the ball, I knew I was looking at college potential."

"I wish things could be different." I sat on the arm of the couch.

Dad fast-forwarded a few seconds, and the team went into motion again. "Ridley's rap sheet . . . want to tell me the real story behind that arrest?"

"I can't."

Dad reached for a mug of coffee beside him. "When I went back to his house to lock up last night, his mom was there."

"Are you sure it was her?"

"Skinny blonde with a purple shiner?"

"Yep."

"She seemed pretty out of it. I told her about her daughter. She said she knew. I offered to take her to the hospital and see Emmie, but—"

"She was too gone?" It felt disloyal to talk about the woman, though I didn't know why. "She's not always like that."

"Did Ridley put those bruises on her face?"

"You saw him with his sister. What do you think?"

Dad took a sip of coffee. "I think he'd as soon sever his own hamstring."

"He'd never hit his mom."

"What about beating up grown men?"

I put my feather duster on the coffee table, but said nothing.

"I'm going to assume this particular grown man deserved it," Dad said. "Does that sound about right?" He gave me a moment to answer, and when I didn't, he continued to piece together the world's easiest puzzle. "But I have to wonder why Ridley wouldn't defend himself. He seems smarter than that."

I picked up a red throw pillow and hugged it to me. "There are some mean people in this world."

Dad swallowed a drink of coffee as the game footage played on mute. "I'm gonna take another wild guess and assume the man Ridley punched is good friends with Ridley's mother."

"I believe they know one another."

"What kind of mother lets her son take up for her, then says nothing when he's arrested?"

I'd read the police report online. "She backed up Dwayne's

story."

"What Ridley needs is a way to clear his name. Get back on the field so coaches can see him play. He's got to tell his side."

"He's not going to do that."

Dad lifted the remote and paused the game. "Does the name Terrence Simpson mean anything to you?"

My laugh was small and tired. "You know I always fail your sports trivia."

"He's the wide receiver for the New Falls Mustangs. New Falls, Oklahoma."

"Is that the guy Chevy Moncrief took instead of Ridley?"

"Indeed it is. He's probably the best high school wide receiver in the country. I watched him play, spent some time with him, but it felt off. So I didn't offer for him." Dad watched the TV, Ridley frozen on-screen as he intercepted a pass. "Got busted for possession with intent to sell last night."

A door in my heart cracked open an inch, and hope walked in. "Are you saying he's no longer eligible to be a USK Eagle?"

"What I'm saying is, I know the coaching staff is on the hunt once again. And your boy needs to decide what he's going to do about it."

My boy. I stood up, my slippers *shush*ing across the wood floor. "Thanks, Dad."

"Anything for you."

"You were great last night." It had been my old dad, the guy who fixed everything. Who was a rock I could depend on.

"You know"—his hand linked to mine—"I keep thinking about the way Estes couldn't take his eyes off his sister. He looked at her . . . like a father."

"That's pretty much what he is."

"A father would do anything to see his kids safe, happy. To

keep them near."

"You didn't think that when you were with Josie last week."

He pulled his attention from the TV. "I was at her house." Dad stood up, walked to the window where the November rain had decreased to a mere sprinkle. "That day she'd been released from the hospital, and not one person in her life would pick her up. She was completely alone, had lost her job, and I'd been the cause of that."

I had zero sympathy for the story so far.

"Her fiancé kicked her out," he said. "Her parents wouldn't return her calls. So I picked her up, got her settled. Then I told her it was over." Dad turned and looked right at me, bold and unflinching. "The second time I was with her, it was to say that her legal team coming after me wasn't going to persuade me to keep seeing her. What those photos didn't show was my own attorney, conveniently cropped out. As your mom knows, Josie had made several threats to blackmail us, something I couldn't talk about. I told her I was ready for anything she wanted to disclose, and I haven't had communication with her since. Cheating on this family was the worst mistake I've ever made. I'm not going to get into the why of it all, but being unfaithful is not who I am. I stepped away from church, I practically lived at work, and I lost sight of what truly mattered. But Josie Blevins and I are over."

"How can I believe you?"

He gave a tired shrug. "I guess you can't know for sure."

"You're a risk, Dad."

"I was from the day you came into our lives. This family never promised to be perfect, but we swore before a judge to always be there with you. Harper, I can't promise you our family's going to ever be like it was. Your mom may decide next week she can't continue to live in the same house as me. Next year Michael goes to college. I'll have a new job, a new state. Soon you'll graduate. But no matter what, we're still your family. I'm your dad. And Cristy O'Malley will always be your mom."

The tears were immediate and swift, as my heart recognized something my head had denied. "Just tell me this isn't the end of the O'Malleys. Tell me I'll always be one of you."

"Dear God." Dad crushed me to him. "Is that what you think? That we'd ever let you go?"

"I don't know." My voice shuddered. "No." The word packed little conviction. "Sometimes I'm so aware of how fragile my connection is to you guys. When Cole or Michael wonder why they have brown hair or why they're so good at sports, all they have to do is look at you and Mom. I'm nothing like you guys. I'll never be your blood relative."

Dad stepped back, his hands bracketing my arms. "Our family wasn't complete until the day we met you. I knew the first time I saw you that you were our missing piece. We'd been waiting for you and hadn't even known it. You have your mom's intelligence, my sense of humor. You have your mom's fierce protective nature, and my questionable taste in music. You make us laugh, you challenge us. Harper, just think about Ridley's face last night and imagine that heartache a hundred times worse. That's what your mom and I felt the day we had to give you back. We were broken. You mother and I just sat in a huddle and cried and prayed and cried some more. We knew our family would be broken until you were back in our home where you belonged."

"Becky Dallas couldn't love me." My nose dripped as the tears flowed unchecked. "She threw me away."

"That's not what I did."

"You did. You did, Dad."

"I'm asking you to stop expecting the people who are supposed to love you to discard you. No matter how much I screw up, I will always be the father who wished he could've walked through that burning apartment to get to you. You'll always be mine. Do you hear me, Harper? You can stop talking to me, you can avoid me. But I'll never give up on you."

I nodded my head, letting the words settle over me. I simply couldn't speak.

He ran his hand over my hair. "Why'd you call me last night?"

Seconds passed before I found enough air to voice my hesitant truth. "Because I knew you'd take care of it. I knew you'd come through."

I DIDN'T KNOW what made me wearier: my inhumane lack of sleep or the tug-of-war in my head.

After attending a church service in which I only nodded off twice, I spent the rest of the afternoon at the dog rescue. Trudy was a tail-wagging bundle of energy now, and soon, she would be ready to go to her own home. And that home would be mine.

I had a seven o'clock tutoring appointment with Ridley. It was probably safe to assume my own lessons were complete, but Ridley still had another month of English comp.

When I pulled into his driveway, his car wasn't there. But a brown Ford sedan was.

I knocked on the door, and a new face answered it. "Yes?" The man wore a button-down white shirt and khaki pants, similar to Ridley's restaurant uniform. "Can I help you?"

"Is Ridley here?"

"Just left. Are you Harper?"

"Yes."

"I'm Tim, his uncle."

"The manager of Blue Mountain Lodge?"

His large cheeks bunched as he smiled. "That's my place. Ridley said to tell you he's at the football field."

I tried to catch a peek over his shoulder. "How's Emmie?"

"Sleeping, but she's doing great. I'm babysitting the girls. Giving our tough guy a break."

"I'm glad she's okay."

"I heard how you came through for Ridley and Emmie last night." He dug into the pocket of his khaki pants. "For you." He pressed a card into my hand.

"Free onion rings." I read the coupon and grinned. "Nice."

"Nothing says thank-you like batter-fried vegetables, eh?"

Uncle Tim went back inside, and I stepped off the porch. Three steps away from my car, Ridley's mother pulled in beside me. She eased out, wobbly in a pair of heels, but she didn't have the crazy eyes of someone high on drugs.

"Wait!" she called.

I clutched my keys in my grip, the jagged metal edges biting my skin. I flung open my car door, desperate to get away before I said something I'd regret.

"Harper!"

There was no avoiding her. "Yes?"

"I wanted to . . . thank you for what you and your dad did. For helping my kids."

I knew my face did not radiate grace and mercy. "Ma'am, you didn't do the right thing last night by not being there for your daughter. And you can't go back and fix it. But you do still have the chance to help your son." I swung into my seat and revved the motor to life. "Clear Ridley's name."

Chapter Twenty-Nine

THE WASHINGTON HIGH football stadium had witnessed generations of heartache and victories. It was the best place in town to get a burger on Friday nights, and two bucks more got you caramel apples, served up fresh by the band booster club. On game nights, most of the town would pour into the stands, cheering on the players who fought to keep their traditions alive. The place was empty now, save for one solitary boy.

Ridley stood on the twenty-yard line, a football in one arm, staring into the near-dark sky. The lights perched on tall poles, shining down on this tortured guy who just wanted to play, yet had so much more at stake.

"If you'd like, I could stand on the sidelines and be your cheerleader."

He turned at my voice, with eyes that held too much. "You in a short skirt." His smile didn't quite lift his lips. "That I'd like to see."

"I do quite the toe touch." My damp shoes carried me to him, and I zipped my jacket against the evening chill. "How are you?"

He palmed that football, studying the lines and ridges. "I've kept it together a long time, you know?"

The lackluster grades, the hungover appearance. Not years of partying, but millions of moments of being a dad to two girls. "You've done a great job."

He looked past me and toward the goal line. "I come here sometimes when I get off work, late at night. It's like . . . church. Just me and the field. I know all the rules here. I have control of my part in the game. I know who I am, who my opponent is."

"My dad says you're one of the best."

"I practiced my butt off from the time I was just a little kid. Faith's dad stuck around for a while, and he got me started. He'd make me run drills, throw the ball. Playing football's all I ever wanted to do. And I knew it was my meal ticket, you know? I knew it was my ride to college."

"It still can be."

He wore the face of a guy digging a shovel into the cold earth, burying his dream. "I think it's time to admit it's truly over."

But I had a little something up my long sleeve. "Terrance Simpson won't be signing with the USK Eagles."

Ridley stilled. "What do you mean?"

"He got picked up for drugs last night. My dad told me."

"The dad you're not talking to?"

"Dad also said that he was never wrong about selecting you for the team. He said you have to get back on the field and finish this season."

"Don't you think I would if I could?"

"You know what it takes. Tell the police the truth about that night you hit Dwayne."

"I'm not throwing my mom under the bus."

"Why not? She's tied you under a semi."

"Harper, if I do that, it's another red flag to child services about my home, my mom. I can't risk that. I know it's not fair, but you haven't lived with the O'Malleys so long that you've forgotten that sometimes you're just dealt a hand. My sisters are my priority."

"You have choices here. At least consider them."

He slowly walked to the thirty. "I'm going to miss this field. My team. I wanted to be more than some forty-year-old man whose greatest accomplishment was a state champ ring in high school."

"And you will."

"I've held onto that hope for so long, knowing guys like me, from homes like mine—the odds were never in my favor." He tossed the ball into the air, and it spiraled as it came back down, slapping into his waiting hands. "It's not just a sport. It's . . . its' a high." Ridley gave me a crooked grin. "It's my Beethoven, my being part of that symphony."

Rule one of conversation is to ask the person about themselves. "Tell me what you like about it."

"All of it." His voice was filled with passion, wonder. "When you've hustled until your lungs are on fire, and you walk back to the huddle. There's just something about standing shoulder to shoulder with your teammates huffing and wincing right with you, seeing that matching determination in everyone's face. It resets the exhaustion, pushes you on. And you dig down deep and pull out the reserves you didn't know you had for that next play. Or when that next play is the breakout, the play that scores and turns everything around. And it wasn't just you, it was the team, together."

"They've been your family."

"Yes," he whispered. "They took me just as I was. And I was *someone* out here."

"Ridley Estes, you're someone everywhere you go."

"I feel alive out here. I forget all the crap going on at home. Where the money for the electric bill's gonna come from, who's picking Emmie up from day care. It's just me and the game. It's running with the ball like demons are right behind me. Or when I'm on defense and lower my head at full speed and launch my body into another guy as hard as I can. Then you just stand over him, waiting for that next play so you can do it all again."

"Sounds exactly like marching band."

His wry smile gave way to the dimples, and I grinned in return. The trees shook as the wind swooped around us, and I shivered when the breeze passed through my thin jacket.

Ridley took off his scarf and looped it around my neck, his hands resting on my shoulders, bringing me closer. "Nobody's believed in me for a very long time," he said. "But you did."

His eyes almost looked black in the dimming light, and they held me pinned to the spot, unable to look away.

My lips tingled as his gaze dropped to my mouth. "I didn't intend to."

"Sometimes," Ridley said, his husky rasp straight out of a teenage girl's fantasy, "just every once in a while . . . I let myself think about having it all. College, football, a life."

"It can still be yours."

He reached out, slid his finger over the arc of my ear. "And sometimes I think about you."

Had I closed that distance or had he? My chest now pressed against his sweater, so close I could feel his valiant heart beating. "And what do you think about?"

"Doing something like this." Ridley's head descended, and his lips, soft and warm, covered mine. My heart humming with wonder, I knew my movements were artless, unpracticed. But Ridley just held my face in his hands, his mouth a caress, an endearment.

Cherished

Wanted

That's how I felt as I slipped my hands up his sweater and around his neck. I'd never been this close to a boy before, never dreamed I'd want to. When I was in Ridley's arms, the old fears slipped away, the past forgotten. All I knew was here and now. His gentleness, his heart beating against mine. His kisses comforted and consumed. Teased and soothed. Voices of caution called out from the recesses of my mind, but I muted all that out. I didn't want to think about logic and reason now.

Ridley pressed a kiss to my temple. "You are not what I expected."

"Is that good or bad?"

His eyes darkened. "I don't know."

His lips claimed mine again, and I felt his smile as the kiss deepened. It both thrilled and frightened, these feelings that whirled in my center like a wind tunnel within me. And just like that tornado of my childhood, a relationship with Ridley could destroy the safe haven I craved. He was not the boy I'd thought he'd be, but he was still not the one who would be the wisest choice.

"Ridley," I whispered, as he held his lips to my forehead. "We're supposed to be studying."

He lifted his head, and arrogant eyes stared down at me. "Your nerd ways can be really inconvenient."

My pulse still hammered, and the thoughts bounced like fireflies in my head. What was I doing? This was Ridley Estes. And who was I? "We can't do this."

Ridley lifted one solitary brow. "Why not?"

"Because . . ." So many reasons. And any second I was going to remember what they were.

"Of Andrew Levin?"

"Yes." Right. That name did sound familiar. "And because we have your research paper to do." And because socially speaking, I was the nerd peasant to his prince. And clearly a temporary lapse in judgment for him. For both of us.

Ridley reached for the end of his scarf around my neck and slowly looped it once. "Harper?"

"Yes?"

For a second I thought he would kiss me again, thought he was on the verge of some bold, glitter-dipped declaration that would light my world on fire.

But Ridley only shook his head. "Nothing."

Disappointment was insistent and loud, but I refused to let it in. "Let's go study at the coffee shop," I said. "I'll buy."

"You're not buying."

"Rule number thirty-one." I walked on ahead of him. "Never turn down free lattes."

As we got in Ridley's Jeep, I knew two things with absolute certainty.

I could not fall in love with Ridley Estes.

And I knew just how to get him back on the team.

IT WAS NINE o'clock and dark as road tar when I got home. The stars hid behind distant clouds, and I could smell winter coming.

Entering through the garage, I stepped into the kitchen, where my mom and dad stood on opposite sides of the bar. Tension hovered like smog, and my mom's suddenly pleasant face turned my way. It did nothing to persuade me I hadn't just interrupted a fight.

"Hey, babe." Mom's arm slipped around me as she pulled me in for a side hug.

"What's up?" I looked from one parent to the other.

"First item of business is that Mavis dropped off a terrier. Said it's well enough to be socialized." Mom crossed her arms and leaned against the counter. "You didn't mention we were fostering a third dog."

"It totally escaped my mind."

Mom rolled her eyes. "Harper—"

"You know, some parents have to hear their daughters tell them they're pregnant. You? The worst you have to hear is I brought home a dog." It made perfect sense to me. "So really, you should be thanking me."

"Every dog in this house is temporary," Mom said. "It's hard to show this place when it looks like a petting zoo."

The dogs were deterring our house sale? Sometimes even *I* didn't know the depth of my intelligence.

"Trudy's kenneled in your room," Mom said. "Make sure she stays there."

"The dog you're going to let me keep forever?"

"No deal."

"Second," Dad added, "Andrew Levin's sitting in our living room."

"By himself?"

"Don't be crazy," Mom said. "We wouldn't leave him alone." She took a slow drink from a coffee mug. "We sent Cole to entertain him."

Even worse! I raced down the hall and nearly twisted my ankle as I skidded into the living room.

"You're right, Andrew, that is a fun app. But my favorite thing on Harper's laptop is her diary. If you open this icon right here—"

"That'll be enough of that." I grabbed the laptop from Cole's thieving hands and pointed my finger right to his black, corrupt heart. "You have five seconds to leave this room."

"Or else?"

"Or else I tell Andrew how you still like to play with sailboats in the bathtub."

"Stop! Shut up!"

"And then I'll tell him about your baby blanket you still—" Cole ran out, carried by Nikes and utter humiliation.

"So." Andrew stood up from the couch. "You keep a diary."

"Yep." Could he tell I'd just been kissed by Ridley? Was it written all over my face? Could you get hickeys from mentally replaying your own makeout scenes?

"Anything in there written about me?"

"At least a line or two." Neither one of us closed the distance. I stood by the TV, unable to make myself walk those ten steps that would take me to him. I had a boyfriend, yet I had kissed someone else. Was I no better than my dad? "I'm really sorry about last night."

"How is Ridley's sister?"

"I texted you." I had told him about the hospital, then later sending another text to let him know Emmie was okay. "I even called. Left a voice mail."

Andrew sat back down, hands planted on his knees. "I was mad. And I'm sorry."

"You don't have to apologize, I—"

"No, I do. You have this friendship with Ridley, and I'm jealous."

I couldn't quite look him in the eye. "Don't be."

"I thought about it all day. Couldn't sleep last night. It was stupid of me to get mad. We've barely started seeing each other, and I'm getting territorial. I'm not that guy."

Having an intimate conversation with someone from across the room probably broke some rule, so I crossed the floor and settled myself at the end of the couch, a mere two cushions away.

"I like you a lot, Harper. And I've never really felt that way about anyone."

"I . . ." Make out with boys on football fields. "I like you a lot too." I still liked him. I was sure of it. Andrew gave a pointed look at the laptop in my hands. "I want you to write good things in there about me." He scooted toward me 'til his hip bumped mine. "I want to be the best boyfriend you've ever had."

I had to laugh at that. "You're the only boyfriend I've ever had."

Andrew took my hand, his thumb grazing over my skin. "I need to know you're in this."

"I am." I was. Pretty sure. Mostly sure. Definitely thinking I was probably sure.

"When I kiss you, can you tell me I'm the only guy you're thinking of?"

The feel of Ridley's skin against my fingers, the slide of his lips over mine, the warmth of his arms holding me tight. All of that rushed back from memory.

"Yes," I told Andrew. "Yes, I think I can."

Andrew's smile was a little crooked, a little uncertain.

Because both of us knew I was lying.

Chapter Thirty

ON MONDAY MORNING, I woke up to a text from Andrew. Because boyfriends send texts.

At three a.m., I had put the terrier in bed with me, and she was now curled in a ball, resting peacefully against my legs. Her ear was wiry to the touch, and she opened sleepy eyes when I petted her. "Good morning, Trudy."

The dog wagged her tail, and I smiled. She had been given a new life. I loved my work at the rescue, and when we moved, I would have to let it go. I could volunteer at another shelter in another town, but it wouldn't be the same. At least this dog would be coming with me.

I ran my hand across Trudy's face, and the dog sniffed my fingers.

"Trudy, have you ever had a boyfriend? I'm not sure I'm ready for it." The dog rolled over on her back, more concerned with getting her tummy scratched than being my therapist. Laz batted at a stuffed mouse from the end of the bed, unfazed by yet another new addition.

What were the rules to a relationship? Did we always hold hands? Did we call each other every night? I was light-years from being the one to initiate a kiss. Would that bother Andrew? Did I have to rehash my life story so he'd understand me?

Surely every girl agonized over these things with her first boyfriend. Ridley would probably tell me I was overthinking.

Tired of stewing in my thoughts, I pried myself out of bed at five thirty, tended to all three foster dogs and one uppity cat, then padded to the kitchen to get breakfast started. Cooking was a stress reliever, but it was also where I'd first bonded with my mom. In the early days, conversations flowed better when she was showing me how to roll the pizza dough or press a fork to the top of peanut butter cookies. I always worked by her side as she prepared the Thanksgiving dinner, and I wondered if I'd even want to this time. The holiday was in a matter of days, and I dreaded the farce it would be. Eating our sweet potatoes and pretending everything was okay.

Thirty minutes later when my mom came down, I had coffee perking, biscuits in the oven, and a broccoli quiche sitting on the stove.

"Coffee or juice?" I asked as Mom pulled out a bar stool at the counter.

"What are you doing?"

I blinked. "Making breakfast."

"Why?"

"Because I was hungry."

"Are you sleeping at all?" Mom asked.

"Yes." Mom looked like she hadn't gotten much rest herself. "I slept a bit last night."

"Really? Because I thought I heard another nightmare. I know you're worried about everything, and Becky Dallas is probably heavy on your mind, but—"

"It must've been the new dog." I drew my knife through the quiche and slid a piece onto my plate. "I'm sure that was it."

Mom studied me for long, painful moments, but finally let it go. "You've had a busy weekend."

"Yeah." I poured my own glass of juice and sat at the bar

beside her. "I guess Dad told you we talked."

"He told me a lot of things. Harper, you know I love you, right?"

"Yes."

"And that you're an O'Malley on the good days and the bad days? I mean, sis, you're stuck with us no matter what." Mom nudged me with her shoulder and smiled. "Your dad said you mentioned not having O'Malley blood."

I sneaked a bite of quiche to the two dogs at my feet. "I can't help how I feel. I know I'm your daughter, but—"

"When you were in the burn unit, you had a blood transfusion three different times. Did you know that?"

I shook my head and pushed a crumb on my plate with my fork.

"You happen to be an O positive. Know who else is?" She didn't wait for my response. "Your dad and I." Mom tapped the top of my hand. "So yeah, Becky Dallas's blood runs through your veins, but so does mine. And so does your father's. You're a mix of all of us. And that makes you perfect." She hugged me to her and kissed my cheek. "And it makes you ours. Forever. Got it?"

I blinked my leaky eyes. Lately, I had more waterworks going on than the fountain downtown. "Got it."

"Next month your dad is going to Becky's hearing to remind that judge what happened, how she treated you. He'll never stop fighting for you. But it's time you fought for you, as well. One day Becky's going to walk the streets a free woman." Mom tapped the soft indention at my temple. "Don't let yourself be the only one who's locked up. It's okay to talk to the counselor. To tell her how you feel. To tell her what happened. Harper," Mom said, "it's okay to let go."

But what if I shared my whole story . . . and all that ugly was still there? What if I never got closure? What if I always recoiled whenever someone stood too close?

What if someone saw all my scars?

"You seem pretty close to this Ridley," Mom said. "Is there anything I need to know?"

"We're just friends. That's all I want to be."

"Because you like Andrew." It was a statement, but it came out more like a question.

"He's not quite what I thought he'd be, but there's still a lot to like."

She smiled behind her "Coffee Before Talky" mug. "That sounds completely boring."

"It's not boring. It's logical." Why couldn't anyone see how smart I was being here? Too many people rushed into relationships based on nothing more than feelings. I wasn't going to make those mistakes. "When I list the reasons he's right for me, it's irrefutable."

"You made a list?" Mom asked.

"Yeah. Pros, cons. Didn't you do that with Dad?"

She inspected a nail in need of a polish touch-up. "Maybe I should have. Tell me about this list. Give me the reasons you like Andrew."

"He's smart. He's reliable. He's predictable."

"You could be talking about one of your dogs."

"Which is basically the ultimate compliment."

Mom laughed. "No, it's not. What about fun? Does he make you laugh?"

"He tries to. That counts, right?"

She didn't look convinced. "Is he someone you can talk to for hours?"

"We haven't known each other long."

"Does he seem to get you?"

Not like someone else I knew. "Andrew likes me. No boy's ever liked me before."

"I bet lots of boys have." Mom pointed a piece of bacon right at me. "You just didn't give them a chance."

"YOU SEEM PREOCCUPIED."

Andrew's voice pulled me away from my thorough scanning of the lunchtime cafeteria. "I guess I just have a lot on my mind," I said. Like wondering where Ridley was. I hadn't seen him all day.

"My band just got another gig lined up for next week," Andrew said. "Are you ready to be a rocker's girlfriend?"

Molly snorted beside me.

"What's the other gig?" I asked, kicking my best friend beneath the table.

"A party at Jamal Horton's."

Molly put down her fork and gaped at Andrew like he'd just offered her Madonna tickets. "Jamal Horton's? I've *never* gotten an invite to one of his parties. Harper, they're such a big deal. He always has live music. College kids show up. And tacos. He throws killer parties with tacos."

Which was totally lost on the vegetarian at the table. "I'm not really the party type of girl."

"But you're still going to my show tonight, right?" Andrew asked. "I thought you could go hang out with the other band girlfriends, get to know them." He sounded like he was doubting my groupie abilities already. "You could help us set up, and, I dunno, be there for moral support."

Molly picked up her tray and stood. "He means kissing between sets. And speaking of that, I'm late for play rehearsal."

"If you don't want to go, I understand," Andrew said as we watched Molly flounce away. "The band's a pretty big part of my life, so I thought you'd want to go and—"

"Of course I do." Yep, I could do this. "I'll be there."

"I think I'm about to get a job," Andrew added. "So we should hang out while we can."

I waited for the sinking bomb of disappointment to hit at the news I'd be seeing Andrew less. It sailed right past me. "Where are you going to be working?" I asked.

He popped a chicken nugget in his mouth. "You're looking at a future fry cook at Smitty's Burgers. If you play your cards right, you can have me *and* discounts on value meals."

"I've struck boyfriend gold." My eyes flicked to the doors, as if Ridley might come in any moment. Where was he?

"If you're interested, I think I could get you on at the burger place."

I forced myself to tune back into the conversation. "I work at the shelter. And I tutor."

"Yeah, um . . ." Andrew's expression dimmed as he reached for my hand. "How long are you gonna tutor Ridley Estes?"

My hand in Andrew's went cold. "Is my tutoring him a problem?"

"I'm not sure," Andrew said. "You tell me."

"Ridley and I are friends."

"There are three of us in this relationship, Harper. And one of us needs to go."

"Oh." Life without talking to Ridley every day. Laughing without Ridley every day. "I wasn't expecting this."

"It doesn't have to happen now. But maybe soon?"

"It's really important he passes his college class. He has a lot riding on it."

Andrew's brow furrowed and he released my hand. "Just give it some thought."

No more Ridley.

No more who I was with Ridley.

It was all too much at once.

"I need to go make a phone call." I got up from the table and grabbed my backpack.

"Harper, are you okay?" Andrew asked.

But I didn't answer. I just kept walking. Past the table of cheerleaders. Past the table of kids most likely to blow up the school. And past the three tables of football players that normally included Ridley Estes.

I pulled out my phone in the shelter of the third bathroom stall and pulled out the business card my mom had given me weeks ago.

Someone picked up on the third ring.

"Vital Roots," a female voice answered. "How can I help you?"

Chapter Thirty-One

"HARPER!" DEVON MCTAVISH clapped her hands together and waved me into her office. "I'm so glad to see you!"

Her enthusiasm was bolstering. If not a little weird. And now that I was here, I was already regretting it. "Thanks for seeing me at the last minute."

"I had a cancellation," Devon said. "What serendipitous timing."

"Uh-huh." I settled myself onto her love seat while she did her contortion pose to get comfy in her own chair.

"So you skipped our last appointment. I knew you'd miss me."

Oh, to have some of this lady's confidence.

"What brings you by today?" she asked.

"I don't want to be here." I was just a ray of sunshine these days. "But I think . . . I know I need to deal with some stuff before things change."

"What do you want to change?"

"The uncertainty. The voices of doubt. The nightmares."

Devon nodded, seeming to be satisfied. "Are you ready to roll up your sleeves and get to work?"

My sleeves would be staying where they were. "I think so. I guess I'm also ready to talk to you about Becky Dallas."

"Oh, you're not going to talk to me." Devon pulled her hair back and secured it with the elastic from her wrist. "You're going to talk to Becky."

Fear shoved me hard. "What?"

"Today we're going to role-play."

Role-play? "Aren't there some inkblots I could look at? Some puppets I could talk to?"

"You should know I've talked to your parents about your bio-mom," Devon said. "Done a little research. This could get very authentic."

I doubted that. I wasn't exactly the type to go for emotional theatrics.

Devon slipped off her glasses and looked at me with calculating eyes. Her voice lowered. "Hello, daughter. I haven't seen you in a long time."

"Is that supposed to be my mother?" I rolled my eyes. "Seriously?"

She crossed her arms and leaned back in her chair. "Why don't we talk about the night of the fire? I think we have two very different ideas of what happened."

"This is stupid." I was getting better at this honesty stuff. "Maybe this was a bad idea. I don't think I'm ready for this yet."

"You always were whiny," Devon said.

Her words hit their target. It was exactly what Becky Dallas would've said. "I think that's enough for today. This is so not what I came for."

Devon's lips pulled in a mocking smile. "You're so weak. So very weak."

Good gosh, it was my mother. Those words were straight from Becky Dallas, as if she were taking over Devon's body. "I'm not weak."

"You're a weak little girl who couldn't keep her mouth shut. Who couldn't take care of herself. And who could never earn my love."

It was impossible to not defend myself. I'd waited too long. "Nothing I did made you happy. I did everything I could to be the best daughter to you."

"It wasn't enough. You were never enough."

You were never enough. Words that had been tattooed on my heart my whole life. "The O'Malleys would tell you otherwise."

"And what else do these O'Malleys tell you?"

"That I'm loved. That I'm worth it. That I don't have to earn their love."

"You think your dad's going to be there for you? He cheated on your mother. He cheated on your family."

"That's still nothing compared to what you did. And you know why? Because he's sorry. Because he's contrite. Because he cares how it's affected me."

"How convenient."

I sniffed back tears. "Forgiving him isn't easy. I'm not even sure I'm there yet."

"You're such a self-righteous brat. You never could keep your mouth shut."

"I never told anyone what my life was like. I never knew it could be better until I went to live with the O'Malleys. I have a real mother and a real father."

"Is that what they are?"

"Yes!" My voice echoed in the small room. "You were supposed to take care of me. But you didn't. You treated me like some annoyance you had to put up with. You never really loved me, did you?"

"What do you think?"

"I guess it doesn't matter. Because I have what I need now. And you can't matter to me anymore. I don't have to stay locked in that room."

"Maybe you don't deserve to be loved."

I could see Becky Dallas sitting there, and I wanted to tear her apart. "Every moment I'm an O'Malley smothers out the dark you were in my life. They'd never hit me, never starve me, and they would set themselves on fire before they'd ever lock me in a room and leave me to fend for myself."

Her twangy voice filled with venom. "It was an accident."

"I didn't deserve that. I didn't deserve any of that. And I'm through paying for it and letting it control my life."

"You'll never be anything more than my daughter. You're going to be just like me, aren't you?"

"You don't know me." I stood up and threw the couch cushion to the floor. "You're never going to know me, so let me tell you about myself. It turns out I'm a fabulous person. I'm smart, kind, I have friends and a future. I have no idea where I'll be this time next year, but I know the O'Malleys will be right beside me. They taught me about faith and love. They gave me hope and safety. They showed me what real love looks like. It's unconditional and constant." The words burned like a brand in my head, and I finally knew they would be permanent. "I hope you know it one day. I pray you wake up and regret what you gave up, all the years you've wasted. I don't know what anyone ever did to you, but I hope you never treat another human being like you've treated me. I used to beg God every night that you'd love me. I thought I wasn't good enough for my prayers to be answered. Then the O'Malleys came for me. And they never let me go."

"You can have them. Go back to your rich life."

"I'm not rich, but I am better than this. I deserve to be loved and protected. I deserve happiness and a chance. With you, I didn't have any of that. And you still can't offer it to me now. I'm through trying to be someone you could love. I'm not the problem. All this time, it's been you."

"And what are you going to do about it?"

"I . . . I want you to know I intend on forgiving you. One day. One day soon."

Becky Dallas scoffed. "I don't believe I asked you to."

"Consider it a free gift. When I quit hating your guts, I'm going to absolve you of every slap, every time you turned your head while some new boyfriend did whatever he wanted, every ugly, evil word out of your mouth. It's over, Becky. I refuse to let those things have a hold over me anymore." I breathed in the victory and exhaled a little bit more of the past. "My name is Harper O'Malley, and I'm the best thing that ever happened to you."

My voice reverberated in my head, and I suddenly became aware of where I was. Of who I was.

And who the woman in front of me was *not*. "Oh my gosh."

I stood in front of Devon McTavish with my legs braced, as if I was about to deflect a blow—my finger pointed in accusation, and fire flaming in my belly. The sleeve on my extended arm had drawn up, flashing my scars.

And I didn't even care.

My skin tingled with invisible electricity, and my head spun as if the pressure in the room had leaked away.

I collapsed into the love seat, threw my head in my hands.

And cried.

"Harper?" Devon asked after some moments. "Harper, are you okay?" Her voice was softer now. I no longer heard Becky Dallas.

"I don't know what came over me."

Devon handed me a box of tissues. "Healing," she said. "Healing just came over you."

"Just like that?" I blew my nose into the pink Kleenex.

"You've still got a long road. You've kept all that stuffed inside a long time. It can't be fixed with one conversation. But you just took some giant leaps."

"And yet what does it change?" I grabbed another tissue and blotted my eyes. "My dad's still the guy who cheated on my family. I'm still the girl who can't get it together and be a girlfriend."

"I think once you get Becky Dallas totally out of your head, you're going to get the clarity you're looking for. Today you just threw out a bunch of her baggage."

"There's still a very heavy carry-on somewhere in my head," I said.

Devon smiled. "Then that will give us something to talk about next week."

Oh, geez. She expected me to come back.

"You said you were up for this," Devon reminded me. "It's time to fight for your happiness. Do you believe you can do this?"

I did.

It was time to stop being the child of Becky Dallas.

And time to be an O'Malley.

Chapter Thirty-Two

AN HOUR LATER, I sat in my car in Ridley's driveway, wondering what I was doing there. I'd gone home after seeing the counselor, intending to do homework until time to leave for Andrew's show, but it had been impossible to focus. I felt like I'd sprinted a marathon carrying a refrigerator. My body was exhausted, my soul was spent. I had to talk to someone.

And I was watching the house of the only person who'd understand.

I dropped my head to the steering wheel, letting the cool of the leather press against my hot cheeks. I closed my eyes and whispered a prayer.

Then jumped when someone knocked on my window.

"You going to camp out in my driveway?"

Ridley leaned against my door, and I couldn't help but notice the way his henley tugged over his chest. While my attention to boy parts was a welcome sign of improving mental health, I didn't want to be aware of his. I made a mental note to fantasize about Andrew at first opportunity. And not this boy wearing a rakish grin, whose superhuman arrogance seeped through the steel of the car.

"Couldn't stay away from me?" Ridley asked from the other side of the window.

"I thought it was a tutoring night."

"It's not." He walked around the car and got in the passenger side. My little Civic was not made to carry big boys of football. He shut the door, his body filling up the space, his nearness filling my senses. "Want to tell me what's going on?"

"I was in the neighborhood."

"Selling Girl Scout cookies?"

"No." I would not cry.

"Hey." He palmed my cheek, running his thumb across my skin. "Talk to me, O'Malley."

The words tumbled out in a frenzied mess. "I saw my mom today. I mean, I went back to that counselor lady, and she pretended to be my mom, and it was really, really dumb, but then it got seriously real, and I have no idea why, but I yelled at her, and it felt so good just to say all that because I meant every one of those things."

"I have no idea what you just said."

"I went to see the counselor today."

"The nosy one who keeps asking about Becky Dallas?"

"That's the one. She acted like she was my mom, and I told her how I felt."

"And how do you feel?" Ridley asked.

"I'm not sure."

"Maybe you're charging some of Becky's hurts on your dad's account?"

"She really screwed me over. I'll never know why she did the things she did. Why she couldn't love me like I needed her to." I knew he understood this part.

"Substance abusers are selfish people."

"Is that all it was? If it wasn't just the drugs, then I never truly mattered. And I wasn't enough."

"Maybe not. But I've seen you with your parents. You're enough for them." Ridley gathered me to him, pressing his lips to my hair. "You have no idea what the rest of us see, do you?"

"A supermodel in denial?"

"You don't need Becky Dallas to love you to be amazing. You're smart, you're funny. You like cutesy music and you have the biggest heart I've ever seen."

"It's just padding."

He framed my face now, and I met his stare in the dark of the car. "I think you're beautiful."

My heart folded like an origami swan. This was the boy I couldn't have. Saying all the right things. "You don't mean that."

"I think I know pretty girls. But you're more than that. You're the best person I know. You try to see the best in people, and if you can't, you try to fix them. And you agonize over everyone in your life, even some dog you pass on the street. There's no one more caring than you."

"I bet your sisters would say the same about you."

"It kills me to see you judge yourself by mistakes other people have made."

"I can't help it." Though I was a tiny bit closer to leaving it behind.

"It's a choice," Ridley said.

"Kind of like your football future?"

He sighed. "You had to ruin the moment."

I smiled. "We should probably make a rule for that. By the way, where were you today?"

"Home with Emmie. She can't go back to day care until tomorrow. Did you miss me?"

"I think . . ." I thought of the kiss that we'd yet to discuss. Andrew's request to end tutoring. "We should probably talk about—"

His passenger door opened and Faith leaned in. "Are you guys kissing out here?"

"No." Ridley kept his eyes trained on me. "Harper got handsy, but I pushed her away."

Faith rolled her eyes with tween precision. "There's a guy on the phone. Says he's from Ohio State and wants to talk to you."

Ridley didn't even hesitate. "I'm not home."

"Yes, he is." My phone lit up in the console, and Andrew's name flashed on the screen. "The concert!" I snapped my seat belt back in place. "I'm late for Andrew's show."

Ridley took his time getting out of the car, only to duck his head back in. "I'm glad I was the one you came to," he said.

I turned the key. "Thanks for listening."

"Oh, and Harper?"

"Yes?"

"We will have that conversation."

I DROVE FASTER than a respectable citizen of Maple Grove should've, speeding through two yellow lights and rolling through a final Stop sign, finally arriving at the Ulysses Theater on 21st Street. Once an old opera house, it now served as an art venue, home of concerts and really bad community theater.

"Five dollars, miss," the man at the door said.

I frantically searched my wallet in vain. "Do you take debit card?"

"No, I'm sorry, we—"

"You're too late."

I turned at the familiar voice, dread sinking in like a feral cat's claws. "Andrew."

He stood there in his Mushroom Cloud Raincoats shirt and

his disappointed frown. "We played a half hour ago."

"I'm so sorry. Something really important came up, then I kind of got delayed."

"With Ridley."

"No." The lie slid right off my tongue, and I tried to call it back. "I mean, that's not why I'm late."

"But you saw him."

"I did, but that's not—"

He turned, pushing through the doors and walking into the dark.

Leaving me.

I rushed after him, finding him standing in the parking lot, his face shadowed in the glow of the theater marquee. "Don't be mad," I said. "You have no idea what that does to me."

"How about what it does to *me* to know you're seeing Ridley Estes?"

"I'm not dating him. We're friends. That's it."

"Is it?"

"Yes."

"You left school today, then didn't answer any of my texts. I've been worried. And then you tell me you've been with Estes?"

"That doesn't mean we're huddled up and making out."

Andrew ran a hand over the light scruff on his face. "I can't do this, Harper."

I had wanted him for so long. I had a list of required attributes for boyfriends, and Andrew checked every box. Only a fool would let this go. "You're the one I want to be with."

"It doesn't look that way."

"I can't share everything with you. Not yet."

"But you can with him."

There was quicksand beneath me, and I was sinking fast.

"I'm . . ." I couldn't quite make sense of it myself. "It takes me a long time to open up. I haven't known you long enough to tell you about the wreck that's my life. The mess that's me."

"Have I done anything to make you not trust me?"

"It's not that simple."

"Have I?"

"No, of course not."

"You tell me what you want, Harper. Are you in this relationship or not?"

A line had been drawn. On one side stood Ridley, that enigmatic, heat-inducing boy who had become my confidant, my friend. But he was just as scarred as I was, irrational, unpredictable—and God only knew where he was headed.

On the other side was Andrew. Sweet, gentle, Andrew. With his musician's heart and that innocent face. He was stable, solid. A boy you brought home to meet Dad. One who Becky Dallas would've never gone for. One would make me picnics under shade trees. The other was out of my league and serial-dated girls pretty enough to be in perfume ads. Ridley would break my heart, and I didn't know if I could survive any more hurt. All my life I had longed for safety. Nice, calm, predictable safety. Andrew was just that.

"It's you," I said. "I choose you."

A lonesome tune sounded from inside as another band took the stage. The base thudded hard enough to rattle the doors, and I wondered how many choruses they'd sung before Andrew finally spoke.

"I want you to be sure."

There was too much space between us, and I closed it. "You're the right guy for me."

Andrew reached into the pocket of his jeans and pulled out

what appeared to be a necklace. "I made something for you. It's probably stupid. I was gonna give it to you before the show." He opened his hand. Sitting in his palm was a guitar pick on a silver chain. "It's my first pick. I carry it with me everywhere I go. It means a lot to me, and I thought . . . I thought you might wear it."

Something heavy pressed at my chest, pushed on my heart. But I smiled into my boyfriend's eyes. "I'd love to."

I turned and lifted my hair, and Andrew placed the necklace around my neck. When he was finished, a piece of him rested against my collarbone.

It was time to be Andrew Levin's girlfriend.

And that meant letting Ridley Estes go.

Chapter Thirty-Three

"I'M ABOUT TO disobey you."

Dad looked up from his computer in his office, then spun in his leather rolling chair to face me. "What?"

"I'm going to the university. Mom banned me from campus, so instead of sneaking out, I thought I would just . . . tell you."

He wore his black-rimmed glasses, the ones that were rarely caught on camera but made him look more like a professor than a dethroned coach. "It must be important."

"I'm not going to steal a dog or do anything illegal. You have my word."

"If I let you go, your mom will kill me. You just made me an accomplice."

"A normal teenager would've just bolted. I don't know why I can't get this adolescence stuff right."

"What's this about?"

"I need to see the team."

"Emergency tutoring session?"

No, this time I needed their help. "I'll explain later. Can you just trust me on this?"

"Do you think one day you'll be able to extend the same courtesy to me?"

"Give you permission to ignore your grounding instead of sneaking out your window?"

Dad didn't smile. He stood, his face grave and tired. "Do

you think you can put your trust in me again? Believe me when I say no matter what happens, I'm not going anywhere? Maybe take me at my word when I tell you this family is all I want?"

"I'm trying."

He slowly nodded. "It's a good start." Dad hugged me with his good side, and for the first time in weeks, I didn't pull away. "I'm sorry, sis." These were the arms that had held me after nightmares, made pancakes on lazy Saturdays, grabbed the steering wheel when he'd taught me to drive. I would break in two if that was all truly over.

"I know."

Dad consulted his watch. "It's already eight. Can you be back in a few hours?"

"I hope so."

I blinked past the dampness in my eyes. "Dad, last week you asked me if there was anything you could do."

"Yes?"

"If you have any friends left on the Eagles coaching staff, I want you to get one to next Friday's game at Washington."

"Is Ridley no longer suspended?"

"He won't be after tonight."

IF THE ANIMAL rescue was my second home, the University of Southern Kentucky was next in line. The glass doors of the athletic dorm posted fliers for concerts and university events, and one lonely ad requesting a study group for trig.

"I'm not done talking!" Marcus Ross called as I stepped inside. Five of his teammates simultaneously grabbed slices of pizza and lifted their hulking bodies from cushy seats.

"Dude, we said we'd watch CNN with you tonight, and we

did," Dominic Vago said. "We don't want to have a discussion on foreign policy."

Marcus tried again. "Nuclear disarmament?"

DeShawn took a bite of pepperoni. "Turn it to *SportsCenter.*"

"Is it so wrong to want to connect with global events?" Marcus threw Dominic the remote. "To want to share our thoughts on the wars gripping our planet?"

Dominic changed the channel. "Pretty much."

I cleared my throat, and fifteen intimidating heads turned my way. "Hey, guys."

The boys leaped over couches, knocking carryout boxes to the floor as they welcomed me back.

"Harper!"

"I'm flunking accounting. Marry me now."

"Girl, we need you like protein shakes."

"You dating that stupid boy?"

"You pretty as a bowl ring."

"You got cookies in that bag?"

I was high-fived and fist-bumped 'til my hand shined red. These boys were my family. Their stories were so intertwined with mine, from those of us who shared hard beginnings, to now—when our futures were filled with cloudy uncertainty because of the actions of Coach John O'Malley.

"I need a favor," I said.

"You want to do my Spanish homework?" Tyler Nicholson asked. "I'll let you do that."

"What is it?" Marcus stood in front, ready to pick up his sword for the old friends we had become.

"Name it," said DeShawn.

"You're our girl." Dominic pounded his fist to his heart.

"You tell us what you want."

"I wondered if a few of you would follow me to Sedalia Springs." I had the attention of every player in the room. "I'd like to have a chat with a man named Dwayne."

Chapter Thirty-Four

T HE DELMAR APARTMENTS were known for three things: roaches, drug busts, and a cast of characters that kept the nightly news hopping and the county jail full.

Dwayne lived in Sedalia Springs, an old railroad town about thirty minutes outside of Maple Grove. It was an armpit of a city, and aside from a few restaurants, there was nothing to redeem it.

Including Dwayne Woods.

His door was not illuminated by a porch light, and when I stood on his step, it reeked of must, decay, and whatever depravity held inside.

My hand pounded on the paint-scarred wooden door.

No answer, but the TV shone through the window, and I heard motion inside.

I knocked again. Harder.

A shirtless Dwayne flung open the door, a beer dangling from his fist. "What?"

"My name is Harper O'Malley and—"

"I don't care who you are. Go away."

Charming specimen of mankind. "I've come to ask you to drop the charges against Ridley Estes."

His hoarse chortle revealed a stunning lack of dental hygiene. "That kid's finally gonna get what's coming to him. He think he can push me around, tell me what to do? I hope they lock him up forever."

It was hard to ignore the way Dwayne's leer traveled over my form. "Mr. Woods, I really think it would be in your best interest to reconsider."

He took a long, noisy draw from his beer, then wiped a hairy arm across his mouth. This man was a ghost from my past— different name, different face. But I knew him well. It was everything I could do to stand there under his chilling scrutiny, the creepiness he wore like a cheap aftershave.

"I don't know who you think you are, little girl. But unless you want to come in and talk about this further, you best get off my porch."

He took a drunken lurch toward me, but Marcus appeared, placing himself between me and Dwayne. "The lady said you need to drop the charges."

A sober man would take one glance at Marcus and know he needed to back down. My intellectual friend could turn on the mean like a switch. But Dwayne possessed neither smarts nor a respectable blood alcohol level.

"I ain't afraid of you." Dwayne gave Marcus a little shove.

"I didn't expect you would be." Marcus pushed up the sleeves of his Eagles sweatshirt. "That's why I brought some friends."

Three wide receivers and two quarterbacks flanked us in battle formation.

"You think you can intimidate me?" Dwayne yelled. "I got rights!"

"I'm pre-law," Dominic said, taking Dwayne's beer and tossing it to the ground. "I'd be glad to review those *rights* with you."

Six more Eagles stepped into the yard, game faces firmly in

place.

"We'd like to escort you to the sheriff's office where you can drop the charges," Marcus said.

"No." Dwayne shook his head like a fool choosing to walk the plank.

"My friends and I do not like that answer," Tyler said. "And when I say friends, I mean the entire defensive line."

Soon I was surrounded by men.

And I'd never felt safer.

"Mr. Woods, you have two choices." I punched some bravado into my voice. Because I, too, was an Eagle. "You can either let these guys give you a ride so you can do the right thing, and leave Ridley Estes and his family alone forever. Or you can finish up your party with my friends."

Marcus threw an arm around my shoulders. "Your family."

Tyler cracked the knuckles on both hands and gave me a wink. "Your brothers."

Dwayne tried to slam the door shut, but it was no use for the brute squad.

Tyler grinned as he reached in and grabbed Dwayne by the shoulders, lifting him 'til his socked feet dangled. "What do you want me to do with him, Harper?"

"Remember what you did to that Aggie right tackle last fall?"

"That was pretty bloody."

"The quarterback for the Razorbacks?"

He grimaced and tightened his hold. "Dislocation involves a lot of screaming."

"Perfect," I said. "Let's combine the two."

"No!" Dwayne kicked his feet and flailed as best he could in Tyler's iron grip. "Let me go."

"Desmond and Marcus are still upset over last week's loss," I said. "Got lots of energy to burn."

"Okay!" Dwayne spat. "I'll do it. I'll let your sissy boyfriend off. But—"

"No butts," Marcus said. "You drop the charges, and we walk away. But if we ever hear of you messing with Ridley or Harper, we come and find you." Tyler released his hold, and Dwayne fell into a pathetic heap. "And when we do, that's a game we *won't* lose. Are we clear?"

"Yes." Dwayne didn't bother picking himself up. "I'll drop the charges."

"Consider this taken care of," Tyler said to me. And I knew they would see it through.

While the boys went over some of the finer points of how the rest of the evening would go down, Marcus and I slipped away from the crowd, and he walked me back to my car.

"Thank you," I said.

"Don't thank us yet. The real challenge is gonna be getting out of here without letting Dominic throw at least one punch."

I smiled at my friend. "Just don't leave evidence."

He opened my car door. "We meant what we said. We're your family. And real family sticks together no matter what."

"I know the athletic director is on you guys to avoid trouble at all costs, so I appreciate that you'd do this for me."

"Harper," Marcus said in his big brother voice, "when it comes to the people we love, the right thing is always worth the risk."

DEALING WITH DWAYNE Woods was a cakewalk compared to where I headed next.

After driving by Ridley's house and seeing his car gone, I

drove up to Blue Mountain Lodge. It was after ten, and once again, the restaurant was shutting down. Luckily I found Ridley's Uncle Tim bussing a table.

"Is Ridley here?" I asked.

"He's on break. Out on the terrace."

I thanked the man, then found the nearest exit that would let me outside.

Ridley sat at a table, alone in the dark. Hunched over a keyboard and a novel, he worked by the light of the laptop, taking warmth from the gas heater that hummed next to him. He was the most handsome boy I'd ever laid eyes on. Who'd have ever thought that beneath that tough, devil-may-care exterior, beat the heart of a brother who'd sacrifice it all to take care of his family? He'd changed this scarred girl's life forever. But even if I dated bad boys, I was way beneath him on the social food chain. And we both knew it. I would be nothing more than a brief diversion for him. And he'd be devastation for me.

"Hello, Ridley."

He jerked at the intrusion, his cautious eyes widening in surprise. "Harper. Is something wrong?"

"No." I figured everything was close to being as right as I could make it. "Doing some homework?"

He lifted the book *1984.* "Have you read the ending?"

I nodded.

He thumped it with his fingers. "That's not right."

Endings rarely were. "I came to talk to you."

He stood, and I took a step back when he moved to touch me. "I'm ending our arrangement, Ridley." It was out. I'd said it. "I've found a friend from the university who's agreed to help you with the last few weeks of your class. She'll—"

"No. We had a deal."

"I can't keep doing whatever it is this is becoming. I'm with Andrew now, and it's not fair to him."

"You make it sound like we're just messing around."

"Aren't we?"

"It could be more."

"It's not what I want." He was so close, and it almost hurt not to have his hands on me.

"You're lying."

"I don't think so. I appreciate everything you've done for me, and—"

"Don't do that." His words punched holes in my forced bravado. "Do *not* thank me for—"

"For what? What do you want to call what we have?"

"I didn't expect to fall for you," he said. "It was the last thing I saw coming. But it's there, and you can't tell me you don't feel it too."

I told my heart we couldn't have this, couldn't give into the emotional land mine that dating Ridley would be. "I've made up my mind."

"Right, for the sake of your plan. God forbid you veer from your carefully constructed plan, this safe house you've built for yourself. I'm sorry I don't fit your idea of what a boyfriend should be."

"Don't talk to me about deviating from a plan. Like you're not running away from your entire future right now? Maybe you're using your sisters as an excuse. Maybe you're afraid, deep down, that you're not good enough. We both know what it's like to hear that from people who are supposed to love us. It worms into your head, and you think you can't dig it out, but you can. Ridley, you have to go to college. You were born to play football."

"You want to go home to my sisters, tuck them in, kiss their cheeks, then tell them you're going away forever?" The breeze was no match for the steel resolve in his voice. "Whisper you love them, then tell them they have to move in with total strangers? Or live apart?"

"You're sacrificing your life to be a hero. It's still not enough. When are you going to see that you can't give your sisters all they need? They need parents, Ridley. And you're not it."

"They're fine with me. They have everything they could want."

"And ten years from now when you're working some hourly gig at the hotel because you threw it all away, will *that* be all they could want? How are they going to feel when they're old enough to realize you sacrificed your entire life for them?"

"I can go to college later."

"Or you could get help now."

"You have no idea what you're asking. I will *never* walk away from them."

"No one's asking you to! There are colleges out there begging for you to come play for them. You will never have this chance again. How can you just throw that away?"

"Without me, Emmie and Faith go into the system."

"You're in total denial. It doesn't have to be like this—"

"Does it sound simple, Harper? Brave talk coming from you. Why don't we discuss your life? Let's count all the ways you're so brave. You're running away from dealing with your dad because you don't know where he fits in your black-and-white little world anymore."

"I'm working on that."

"And when are you going to make your decision?"

"When I can trust him again."

"So two years, five years, ten? Until then you'll ignore him and pretend like the last seven years he poured into you didn't matter? He's just this conditional dad you can toss away when he screws up?"

"Screws up? He wrecked my family." He wrecked me.

"Do you have any idea what I'd give to have a dad? Someone to love me and my sisters? To help me and take care of my mom? Your dad is crazy about you. He messed up, Harper. But he's desperate for a relationship with you. Unlike your biological mom, unlike *my* mom, Coach O'Malley wants the job of parent."

"It's not that simple."

"And let's not forget about the issue of Andrew."

"Leave him out of this."

"You feel nothing for him."

"That's not true. I wouldn't have humiliated myself by coming to *you* for advice if I hadn't wanted to be with him."

Ridley shook his dark head, his eyes alight with fire. "He's just a prop. Someone you wish you liked. Because he's perfect, after all. He's safe, isn't he, Harper? He's a nice, middle-class white boy who marches in the band, makes good grades, and says all the right things."

"Oh, when you put it that way, he sounds positively awful. What *was* I thinking?"

"I'll tell you what you're thinking. That he's too nice to ever hurt you. That his record's too clean to ever let you down. He's the idea of what you thought you wanted. But now that you've got him, he bores you."

"Kind of like this conversation?"

"He doesn't make you feel a thing, does he?"

"Andrew is kind and gentle, and he—"

"When he kisses you, does it make you feel like you can't get enough? Do you forget your own name and where you are? Do you count the hours 'til you see him again, until you can be with him? Does he consume your thoughts until nothing's left in your head?"

No, Andrew did not. "Are you suggesting that you're the answer?"

"You tell me."

"You don't want a serious relationship with me."

"I can't stand to see you with him."

"If you think that's jealousy you're feeling, you're mistaken. You're just upset because I'm the only girl who hasn't thrown myself at you. All you've ever done is win—football, girls. And then I came along and became some game to you."

His jaw tightened and those brown eyes narrowed to slits. "You have no idea what you are to me."

"Then why don't you tell me?"

"What difference does it make? I'm nothing like Andrew." He jabbed one accusing finger in my direction. "Because you feel something when you're with me. And that's what scares you."

"Of course it scares me. You go through girls like disposable razors. Why would I want to sign up for that?"

"No girl has ever seen my house. Hung out with my sisters. Met my mother. Not one girl at Washington knows I work my butt off at this hotel. If it looks like I had lots of girlfriends, it's because I tossed them out before they could see what I really was, where I come from. I never gave myself the luxury of a real relationship. It was never worth it—until you. I've never let anyone into my life like I have you."

"I'm just a means to an end. You pass your class, you graduate."

"Stop being the girl who tells herself crap like that!"

I shivered against the cold and moved to the edge of the terrace. I couldn't see the lake, but I heard the distant melody of waves crashing against the rock. "Ridley, I can't do this anymore."

"Andrew is not what you want."

"He's exactly what I'm looking for."

"You have this plan for your life, right down to this mythical perfect guy. No one is perfect. Not your dad, certainly not me, and not even Andrew Levin. God only knows what hell you saw in your mother's house, but the life you're creating for yourself now, it's making you miserable."

"Actually I've never been happier."

"Liar."

"You and I can't happen."

"And why is that?" He walked closer, stood behind me. "I want to hear it. From your lips."

There were too many reasons, so I just narrowed it down to one. "Can you promise me you'd never hurt me?"

"No."

"Then I have nothing else—"

"But neither can Andrew. Or any man walking this planet." His hands on my shoulders, Ridley slowly turned me 'til I faced him. "I think in that battered heart of yours, you know I'm right. Just like you know I'd never intentionally hurt you. Want to know how many girls I've cheated on? Zero. How many I've raised my voice to? Just you." His gentle hands cupped my face. "Because you make me insane, Harper O'Malley. I think about you a lot—too much. Somehow you became my friend, and we both know . . . something more. It's complicated, and it's messy." His head lowered, and his lips hovered a breath away. "If it wasn't, it wouldn't be worth the fight."

My heart pounded, my breath shuddered. Somehow my hands had slinked around to rest on his back.

"Do you want me to kiss you?" he asked.

My chin lifted in the tiniest of nods.

"You should ask yourself why." Ridley's eyes pierced mine, held my gaze for seconds that stretched into minutes, hours, an eternity. Then finally, *finally* his mouth lowered . . .

Bypassed my lips.

And whispered in my ear.

"I don't kiss other people's girlfriends."

Chapter Thirty-Five

NIGHTMARES DID NOT take holidays.

I pushed the sweat-drenched hair from my face and sat up in bed on Thanksgiving morning. I thought when I'd talked to my counselor, my big breakthrough would start mending things. The nightmares would cease. The nagging voices of doubt and derision would go away. I'd be excited for Andrew's text. Look forward to his phone call.

Ridley told me I needed to stop running. I needed to be done with the meekness.

He was right.

That was exactly what I had to do. It was time to live life on a little more faith and a whole lot less fear.

Trudy stirred beside me, and I rubbed my hand across her happy face. In the right home, dogs had it so easy. No worries, no concerns. They didn't even seem to be too choosy in their mates. Just whoever walked by and smelled right.

For the third night in a row, I had cried myself to sleep, and awakened with my pulse beating triple-time and eyes as puffy as marshmallows. I hadn't heard from Ridley. Not that I'd expected to. Still, it seemed like there was a vacancy in my heart, and it was a lot of pressure on Andrew to fill it.

Before the dog and I made our way downstairs, I brushed my teeth, threw my hair in a ponytail, and spackled on enough makeup to resemble a funeral home specimen. The concealer hid the dark circles, but my skill with eyeliner was too limited to draw over the swell of my lids. Finally, I spritzed on some perfume because if I was going to look like something the dog puked up, at least I would smell pretty. Thanksgiving was my annual tradition of running goodie bags to the USK athletic dorm, delivering them to the players who stayed on campus instead of going home for the short holiday.

I took all three dogs out, then fed our menagerie. Lazarus the cat hissed at Trudy, but my new dog just wagged her tail, blissfully ignorant of the rejection.

If only I could do the same.

In the kitchen, Mom stood at the oven and pulled out yet another pie.

"Smells good," I said.

She kissed my cheek. "You're looking a little rough, sis. Did you sleep last night?"

"Some. I've just got a lot on my mind." But didn't we all? "Permission to have an exception to visit campus this morning?" I hugged my mom to my side and rested my head on her shoulder. "I promise I'll be back before lunch."

She rolled her eyes, but not before I saw that smile. "I went ahead and sacked up your care packages."

"You did that? For me?"

"Twenty-three bags of your cookies, some candy, and a note reminding the boys to call their mamas."

Just like I would've done. "Thank you. You're the best."

"The best, huh? Then I'm about to graduate to legendary status because your dad and I have decided you can keep Trudy."

"Seriously?"

"Yes." She held up her hand in warning. "But you've got to find homes for the other two. We're not running a petting zoo around here. I'm sick of vacuuming up—"

I stopped her sweet rant with a smacking kiss. "Thank you."

She held my face, the way she had hundreds of times before. "You have a good heart. You know that?"

"Thanks," I said. "I hear I get it from you."

IF I WERE painting the USK campus today, my palette would require only variations on the color gray. The temperature had slid to a biting forty-five degrees, as if winter was hinting it would soon take its rightful place. I made quick work of the deliveries, as most of the players were anxious to be the first in line for the cafeteria's special Thanksgiving lunch. I stayed long enough to thank them again for their help with Dwayne, and to tell them hello from their beloved coach. These guys were part of my family, and I would miss them. I could only hope the next place we landed would give us a team just as special.

I saved the best for last, stopping by room 302 on my way out.

When my friend Marcus answered his door, I surprised the both of us by bursting into tears.

"Harper?" He tugged on my hand and pulled me inside. "What's wrong? Did that creep guy come after you? Did that boyfriend of yours break your heart? You tell me who to punch, and I'll do it."

I swished my hands over my eyes like windshield wipers and shook my head. "I'm going to miss you, Marcus." He was my favorite. Nerdy, sensitive Marcus. A beast on the field and a Renaissance man on campus.

"Did your dad get news?" He pulled out his desk chair and gestured for me to sit.

"No. But it's coming." I handed him his care package, which was filled with more cookies than anyone else's. And a few books. "We won't be staying."

"There's a petition on campus to get him reinstated."

"It won't work. Chevy Moncrief has made up his mind."

Marcus pushed up his ever-sagging glasses. "It's already gone viral and gotten five thousand signatures."

"And that's what you want? My dad back as coach?"

"It's what we all want."

"Why? Why would you take him back after what he did?"

"Because he's still our Coach O'Malley." Marcus settled onto his neatly made twin bed. "Do you know he still stops by and checks on our grades? Still rides us about our homework? Last week he gave Vago fifty bucks so he could go home and see his mama this week. Vago hasn't seen his mom all semester. Two weeks ago he drove groceries all the way to Newton County so Hashish Batra's grandma would have some food. He still watches our game films and sends us secret messages about what we need to work on."

"He loves you guys."

"You're still mad at him."

"It's all very confusing," I said. "It's not as simple as your situation, I guess. I don't need him to restore my team."

"Don't you?" Marcus leaned forward, his elbows planted on his legs. "You need him even more than we do, Harper. And it wasn't an easy decision. The team has met so many times together. We've gathered in that commons room downstairs with our bags of chips and Gatorade and hashed it out so many times. We talked about all the things Coach has done for us, all the ways he's been a father to us. The way he still is. And we also talked about the crap he's put us through. But in the end, Coach is a good man. I believe that. And we're standing behind him."

"Maybe I need a team to talk to," I said. "All I've got are all the fighting voices in my head."

Marcus reached into his care package and pulled out a cookie. "I'm taking this psychology class, right?"

"The one with all the ridiculous reading?"

"Yeah, but I've learned a thing or two. I've learned when I get overwhelmed and confused, I focus on what I *do* know. So tell me—what do you know for sure about your dad?"

"He cheated on my mom."

"Naw, what else?" He bit into his cookie and gave me a brief smile of approval. "Why was Coach O'Malley the one you went to when your friend Ridley called you about his sick sister?"

I'd shared that story with Marcus on our way to finding Dwayne. "Because I knew my dad would take care of it."

"Why?"

"Because he's responsible."

"Is that all?"

He was seriously channeling a counselor. "Because he's kind. He's good with kids. And . . . he's never turned down a chance to help me."

"So he's been there for you?"

"Yes." A flood of memories washed through my mind. I had few memories without him, where he wasn't right there. "I guess he's been there for all of us."

"When else has your dad been there for you?"

"You know about as well as I do."

"Humor me and tell me anyway, or I'll let the team know they should've held out for a bigger goodie bag."

Oh, for heaven's sake. "He goes to court every two years and defends me. He reminds them what happened." I looked at

Marcus's peeling ceiling as my throat tightened. "He tells my story." Even when I couldn't. "When I was little, he got the best legal team in Mississippi for my custody hearing. When I was finally removed from Becky Dallas's care, he sat in my hospital room for three weeks straight, even though he was needed at his job at Mississippi State. He taught me to ride a bicycle. He taught me to drive. He taught me how to throw a punch if someone ever tried to hurt me again." And along with my mom and brothers, he taught me to be part of a family. To love someone and receive love in return. "But things might never be the same again."

"They might not," Marcus said. "Your dad could mess up again. Maybe your mom does the same. Maybe they divorce. Maybe they don't. You have to decide if you're going to cower every time that happens, Harper, or if you're going to carry on as part of your family. If you're going to love them, flaws and all, or only on their perfect days. Your brothers don't get to just cut ties with your dad, so why should you? You're an O'Malley, right?"

Yes, I was. My mom and dad had made sure of that. "So I'm supposed to be brave and just love people anyway?"

"I think that's what happy people do," Marcus said. "People are going to disappoint us all over the place, even the ones we love. Last week Dominic set me up with a girl."

"What's wrong with that?"

"She was forty-five." Marcus did a slow shake of his head. "Disappointing. Though she had some excellent tips on retirement planning."

Any other time, that would've made me laugh. But I was too hung up on everything else he'd said. "So I just press on even when I'm scared?"

"Was going to see that Dwayne guy scary?"

"Yes."

"But you did it. And look how well that turned out."

"Because I had you guys behind me. I wasn't alone."

"You have your own team behind you—your family. And lots of folks wouldn't have gone after that dude like you did. You were brave, Harper."

I was?

Maybe . . . maybe I was.

"But Marcus, what if something's permanently broken in me? I finally got Andrew Levin as my boyfriend, and I don't feel for him like I should. I'm taking a risk and pushing through that. So why am I so hesitant to be in a relationship with a boy?"

"Easy." He reached for another cookie and pointed it at me like Harry Potter's wand. "He's not the right boy. Any more questions?"

Andrew wasn't the one for me. Just like that.

Just like that I knew he was right, this football-playing sage. I was so busy trying not to get hurt and trying to date a safe boy, the kind of boy my mother never would've gone for. At first I *had* liked Andrew. On paper, he had made so much sense.

But then life happened.

Ridley happened.

"Ridley's still a huge risk," I said. "He could stomp all over my heart."

"Yeah." Marcus grinned. "But what if he doesn't?"

Chapter Thirty-Six

E VEN THOUGH I hadn't been to Andrew's house before, I knew his neighborhood. I'd cruised through it multiple times, doing drive-bys of Josie Blevins's house. While I didn't want to be insane like Becky Dallas, I could own up to an occasional moment of crazy. It was my prerogative as a female. Andrew's house was a two-story home with beige siding and maroon shutters. It was as tidy and efficient as he was. And like him, no doubt very functional, but also a little plain and boring.

My hands shook as I knocked on his door. I had nothing prepared to say and no idea how to go about breaking up with a boy. If I'd had time, I would've Googled it. Written out a plan.

The door opened on a gust of wind, and Andrew appeared wearing his band T-shirt and sweats. His hair was adorably disheveled. "Harper. Hey." His smile quickly faded when he saw my face. "Come on in."

I hesitantly stepped inside the small foyer and followed him into the living room.

"My parents are picking up my grandma." He gestured to a leather couch and sat down on one end. "I think I know what you're about to tell me."

My gosh, this maturity crap was so hard. The big baby in me wanted to go back home and text this conversation from the comfort of my bedroom where I didn't have to see his face.

I eased onto the sofa, sitting on the edge, as if I couldn't even fully commit to a piece of furniture. "I'm sorry, Andrew. I never meant to be unkind or hurt you."

He scrubbed a hand over his face and looked away. "But that's kind of what happened."

"And I apologize—for how I've treated you. Suddenly life just overwhelmed me, and my careful plan got overrun by—"

"Ridley."

"By my heart," I said. "I didn't intend to fall for him."

Andrew turned his head at those words. "So you are with him?"

"No. He actually wants nothing to do with me. We had a little . . . disagreement."

"And I'm tired of being your second choice."

"I'm through asking you to." I took in a deep breath, letting my lungs fill with a little bit of the grace I was extending to myself, even if Andrew wouldn't. "I still think you're handsome, talented, smart, and incredibly nice. You're first chair material when it comes to boyfriends, and you deserve to be with someone who puts you first."

"And that girl's not going to be you?"

"I liked you so much, still like you, and saw us together. You were exactly what I thought was the ideal guy for me. And then my dad's scandal was like this meteor that hit my carefully ordered planet and totally knocked everything out of alignment."

"Are you going to wait on Ridley?"

"I don't know what's going to happen there."

"He has a terrible reputation, Harper."

"He does." Nobody could argue with that. "Maybe he's earned some of it, but I know the rest of the story." And whether or not Ridley ever spoke to me again, I wanted to be with someone who set my spirit on fire and captured my frightened heart in his hands. "I feel terrible for how I've handled this, but I want you to know I appreciated how sweet, how patient you were. Some of us girls need that."

He said nothing, but stared at the patterned rug on the floor.

"I feel so guilty," I said. "If there's anything I can say, anything I can do—"

With a faint smile, Andrew lifted his head. "You could give me your chair in band."

"I don't feel quite *that* guilty."

Andrew gave a small laugh as he walked me to the door. "Be careful out there, Harper."

"I will." I handed him his guitar pick necklace, letting the chain pool in his hand. "Whoever wears that is going to be one lucky girl."

He clasped his necklace and pulled the door toward him. "See you on the field, O'Malley."

I HAD NEARLY missed Thanksgiving lunch. Try as I might, my trip had not allowed me enough time to get back home by noon. I'd stayed and talked to Marcus, stopped by Mrs. Tucker's and walked her schnauzer, broken up with Andrew—then stopped for a double dip, eating and crying all the way home to some vintage *NSYNC. But not even a young Justin Timberlake could stop the waterfall of tears and the deluge of snot. But it was a good kind of cry.

Things were not right in my world.

But they were pretty darn close.

Even if Ridley never spoke to me again, breaking up with Andrew had been the right thing to do.

Michael and Cole were playing basketball in the drive when I pulled in. I wiped my eyes, blew my nose, and put on some gloss. A tearstained face might say *I'm a disaster*, but with the addition of lipstick, it at least said *I'm a disaster who still believes in hygiene.*

Lipstick said all was not lost. And I had to believe that was my new theme.

"Mom's been calling you for hours." Cole sank the ball in the bucket. "You're in major trouble."

"You're holding up lunch," Michael said.

"Okay." I just kept walking.

Michael caught a bounce pass and shot. "Dad lost the Mississippi gig."

At that I stopped, walked back to them, not bothering to hide my face.

Michael rebounded his own ball. "Geez, Harper. Are you all right?"

I sniffed. "Tech pulled their offer?"

"Yep," Michael said. "The job offer somehow got leaked to the press. Their coach wasn't even fired yet, so it's a pretty big deal. It's basically a PR disaster for them, and they're out."

"That's awful," I said, uncertain what it all meant for us.

"I guess we're not moving right away," said Cole. "That's a perk."

Michael threw him a pass. "Did you hear Ridley's playing next week?"

"No," I said.

"Charges against him were dropped. Coach called him at home. He plays next Friday."

The first night of state. At least something had worked out.

Cole threw the ball and hit the rim. "You better get in there and tell Mom and Dad you're alive."

I walked away from their game of one on one, only to get halfway to the front door and stop. I took a moment to look at my two brothers. Really take them in, see them as my siblings, my family. They annoyed me to no end. They read my diary, ate my share of the snacks in the pantry, and expelled way too much gas. But they were mine.

"I love you guys," I called.

Michael paused on a shot. "Huh?"

"I said I love you."

The boys exchanged looks. And I just laughed.

Inside I found Mom and Dad in the office.

"Harper, where have you been?" Mom's cheek was dusted with flour, and gravy spotted her blouse.

"The university. With some pit stops."

"Of course." She rolled her gaze heavenward. "I'm sure at least one of those involved a dog."

I looked at my dad right in the eyes, something I had barely been able to do in weeks. "I've come a long way."

"I know you have," he said hesitantly, uncertain where this was heading. "You're a far cry from that broken girl we picked up seven years ago."

"I mean in the last few days. Between breaking up with my first boyfriend and kissing Ridley—"

Dad frowned. "Run that last one by me again—"

"To finally telling Becky Dallas how I felt and how wrong she was, to being reminded what a good man you are by a football player who doesn't know you buy his cleats every quarter."

"Marcus?" Dad ran a hand down my shoulder. "Harper, what exactly are you talking about?"

"You spoke to Becky?" Mom asked. "I'll be calling that

counselor on Monday."

I would have to explain all of that later. After pie. "I think I believed that if Becky Dallas didn't want me, then surely no one else truly would either."

Dad's face softened. "That couldn't be further from the truth."

"But all these years it's like I've walked around with the word *rejected* stamped on my forehead. I guess this was my way of proving to myself I really was enough."

Dad dropped to his knee before me. "That's not what it says. It says loved. Wanted. Adored." He held my hand, and his warmth permeated through my skin, my bones. My heart.

"I hate the abuse Becky put you through," Mom said. "And if I could erase it, I would. But it brought our daughter home, where she belonged. Before you met us, you were looking for your mother's acceptance. But, Harper, we were looking for you."

"I'm so different from you guys though."

"No, you're not." The corners of Dad's mouth lifted as he looked at Mom. "You're so much like your mother. You're smart and beautiful like her. You have her love for the arts and her sassiness. You're both bookworms and travelers. And you can kick my butt at Scrabble."

Mom smiled at her husband. "Sometimes you and your dad are so alike, it's scary. You've been this inseparable two-person team. You both have this laugh that just turns my head. Makes me laugh, even if I have no idea what the joke is. You have your father's sensitivity, his heart for people. You're both helpers, fixers. People are drawn to you because you have an innate gift of making them feel special. You have your dad's way of encouraging." She dabbed at her nose and laughed. "And neither one of you can make a piece of toast without burning it." Mom ran her hand over my hair. "And you're courageous."

"No. I'm not." Though I hoped I was getting there. "I'm afraid of everything."

"Not every girl could survive what you've been through," Dad said.

Mom squeezed my hand. "And come out the incredible girl you are."

"I see bravery in you every day," Dad said. "You were the girl who fought invisible demons, ones we couldn't slay for you."

"I worry they'll never completely disappear."

Dad's blue eyes steadied on mine. "We all have them, Harper."

"Maybe I didn't get a lot of Becky's characteristics, but what I did get from her is fear. This need to stay in my bubble of security. And it's robbed me of so much. You guys, I want to skydive."

Dad frowned. "Let's not get crazy."

"I want to sing karaoke."

"That's more like it."

"Last year I wanted to run for student council, but I didn't. Because who would vote for me? But what if I had ran? I had good ideas. I want to dance and not care who's watching. Tell the jerk behind me in econ that I know he's copying my answers. I don't want to be the girl who plays it so cautiously, who sits and watches the world from the safety of her bedroom window. Girls my age are—they're on a different yard line than me. I'm always on the fifty."

"Is that so bad?" Dad asked.

"Yes."

"But, you're too young for"—Mom searched for a word—

"touchdowns."

"Should it have taken me this long to like my first boy? I'm sixteen!"

Dad patted my hand. "I kind of like this problem."

"Other girls just know what to do. They flirt, they date, they—"

"There's no rush," Mom said. "You just take your time. The right guy's going to understand that."

"And you give me the names of any guys who don't."

"The wrong boy will bore you or annoy you," Mom said. "But the right one? He'll make you laugh, make you feel special."

Dad watched his wife. "And even sometimes make you cry."

"It's like I have all this catching up to do, and it scares me. Six years later and Becky is still controlling my life, making me live in fear."

"It's time to unlock that door and come outside," Mom said. "You've got a whole world waiting for you. And it *will* be scary. You've heard your father sing karaoke." Eyes wide, she shook her head. "Sometimes it will be scary for all of us."

"But for some things you've just got to push through the fear," Dad said. "You don't want to miss out on anything in this life."

"Unless it's your dad's version of 'Paradise City.'"

The three of us laughed, and it felt like old times. Before the affair, before I resurrected the ghosts of my past. Before I screwed up everything with Ridley.

"And what about me?" Dad's tone turned serious. "Do you have a little courage left to believe in me again?"

"I never thought you'd be a risk, Dad." This healing was a process, and it was going to take some time. "You hurt me, and it brought me to a place I didn't want to be."

"I'm sorry, Harper. You can't know how sorry I am."

Time would tell if what he said was more than just pretty words. But for now, he was my dad. The man who had slayed dragons for me, who had been my champion. I hated what he'd done. But I couldn't let it destroy me. And I couldn't let it undo all the good that I knew he was.

"Maybe we could go to the Mainstreet Grill for breakfast Saturday?" I smiled at the man whom I'd missed so much. "Get a double order of hash browns?"

"Hold the bacon," Dad said.

He pulled me to him in a hug, and soon Mom joined in.

"So no more Andrew?" she asked when we finally stepped apart.

"We broke up," I said. "I think I liked him more before I got to know him. Before I realized there wasn't much of a spark."

"You fell for the ideal," Mom said. "But it's not like in the movies, you know. You don't kiss someone and fireworks explode."

"Except at your Aunt Myrtie's Fourth of July picnic our junior year," Dad said. "Remember that, Cristy? I was meeting the family for the first time, and your mom's miniskirt caught on fire. Burned it in very indecent places."

The two of them shared a laugh, a look. And I wished on moonbeams, falling stars, and every penny I'd ever tossed in the downtown fountain there was hope for them yet.

"I just mean it's normal not to feel that Hollywood version of romance with the boy you like," Mom said.

"And maybe you're not ready," Dad said. "But the right guy shouldn't make you avoid his calls and reroute in the halls so you don't have to see him."

"If Andrew doesn't make your heart sing," Mom said, "he's not the right one." She lowered her voice to a conspiratorial whisper. "Is there one who does?"

Dad groaned. "I do not want to know."

"There is one." Ridley's laughing eyes danced in my mind. I saw his arms around his sisters. His arms around me as he taught me to dance. To kiss. "But he's . . . a risk."

Mom sighed. "Sometimes those are the best kind."

My parents loved me. That was really all I needed to know right now. And maybe Becky had totally screwed me up. But little by little, day by day, I could turn that around. I was an O'Malley. And we were champions.

"I'm sorry the Mississippi job didn't work out," I said.

Dad patted my back. "You can support the family on your shelter paycheck."

"What's going to happen?" I asked.

"We don't know." Dad rested one arm on my shoulder. "Right now we have faith, each other, and one very big Thanksgiving dinner. Can you handle that?"

I looked at my mom and my dad, a fractured couple, but 100 percent parents who adored me. I was theirs, and thank God, they were mine. "I think I'm ready to try."

Chapter Thirty-Seven

"HOW DID THE big breakup with Andrew go?" Molly followed me to my car after school Monday. Today she wore a neon pink sweater, an electric blue skirt, and tights that looked like she'd skinned a zebra. She was a sharp contrast to the gray skies above us, a source of her own light. I had filled her in on quite a bit of the last few weeks, leaving out only a few details.

"He took it well." I swung my backpack to the passenger side. "I gave him back his necklace and told him the truth."

"Which was?"

"That I didn't feel for him like I should." I pulled a hat from my purse and settled it over my flyaway hair. "He's a really great guy if you're interested."

"Girlfriend code—never date someone your friend once liked."

"I'm about to break that."

Her frosty pink lips smiled. "Ridley."

"He probably won't have anything to do with me. I've texted him a few times. But so far . . . nothing."

She leaned against my car and crossed her arms. "I guess I can quit Photoshopping his face into our wedding pictures." Molly didn't seem too disappointed. She kept a ready list of crushes, and I knew she would just move on to whatever guy was lucky number two.

"He's pretty mad at me," I said. "And besides, I'm not even his type."

Molly waved at a boy from band. "That's what makes it fun." She pushed off from the car, her side ponytail flapping like a wind sock. "Don't chicken out on this, Harper. If Ridley is what you want, then go after him."

"What if he just wants to be left alone?"

"You keep trying until you know for sure that being left alone is what he wants."

"And how will I know that?"

"For me, it's usually when they throw out the words *restraining order*."

Our laugh was a balm to a hard day, and I pushed away the thoughts of the eventual time when I'd have to pack up and leave my best friend behind.

"You can do this," she said. "If he's worth it, you risk the hurt. You just have to ask yourself if Ridley Estes is really what you want."

Last night I had even gone to Blue Mountain Lodge, then his house. Nobody would let me see him. "He won't talk to me. Won't take my calls. He's completely ignoring me."

"Then"—Molly rubbed her hands together and arched her brow—"we'll just come up with a way to get his attention."

"YOU HAVE A delivery to make." Mavis smacked her nicotine gum and handed me a monogrammed cell phone. "Take this to Angela Smith."

After leaving Molly to her plotting, I reported for duty at the rescue. "The lady who wanted Trudy?"

"Yep."

She tossed a slobbery ball to Larry, a three-year-old lab who was still waiting for his forever home. "Why did she come by?"

"Wanted to discuss why we rejected her adoption. Again. Asked that we consider her for a different dog. Remind me again why you put Mrs. Smith's file in the *no way* pile?"

"I told you, her house was too perfect. She was too put together."

"Uh-huh. So you're looking for something else for one of our strays?" Mavis had the voice of a chain-smoking man. "A crack house perhaps? Maybe the home of a drug cartel?"

"You trust me," I said. "You know my gut for the animals is never wrong."

She slid on her pair of red rhinestone bifocals, watching me over the rims. "And how's your gut with people?"

"At the moment, a little irritable bowel syndrome–ish. But I know these dogs. Didn't I deliver Henrietta Tucker's schnauzer to you last night, as promised?" Yes, it was duplicitous, but Mrs. Tucker was on her way to a posh senior living center in Atlanta, five minutes from her son, and her beloved Mr. Wiggle Bottoms was enjoying homemade dinners from the kitchen of the nearest convent. He had ten nuns spoiling him, and so far, hadn't whined once. Both animal and owner were safer, and I had my *fiancé* partially to thank for that.

"Good work, Agent O'Malley," Mavis said. "But let's move on to the next thing before I choke on all my appreciation. Mrs. Smith visited with me for a bit today, and I'd like you to deliver her phone."

"She could just come and get it."

"She could." Mavis reached for a file on her counter and flipped through it, done with the conversation. "But you'll deliver it to her."

"Fine." I snatched up my keys, not even bothering to turn down the volume on my dramatic huff. "I *do* have stuff to do here. This is a total waste of time."

Mavis winked one wrinkled eyelid. "We'll just see about that."

I RANG THE doorbell three times, praying for a plague of hives to cover Mavis for sticking me with this job. Why couldn't we have just called Mrs. Smith's house and had her pick up her own phone?

My finger reached for one more courtesy ring when the door inched open.

And I took a gigantic step back.

"Yes?" Mrs. Smith smoothed back her hair, no longer in a French twist, but now wrestled into a mess of a ponytail—with lumps, bumps, and, if I wasn't mistaken, a glob of cookie dough. She had exchanged the prim and proper sweater set for a pair of gray sweats with a ripped knee, and a stained T-shirt that declared she was a proud Stanford mom. On her feet were socks, one solid pink, the other adorned with frogs. But it was the eyes that got me. Red-rimmed, swollen. It looked like the remains of yesterday's mascara had attempted an escape, but had died in Gothic streaks beneath her lower lids.

"I'm Harper. I'm from—"

"I remember you *quite* well." Gone was the singsong bird chirping voice.

"You left your phone at the rescue yesterday. Mavis wanted you to have it." I held it out, and Mrs. Smith watched it sit in my hand a moment before finally taking it.

"He never calls anyway." She sniffed and ran her knuckles

beneath her red, runny nose. "It's not like I needed it."

Sometimes you see those land mines and walk around them, saving yourself from all the mess. Other times you know they're there, but step on them anyway, taking one for the team. If Mrs. Smith had been a schnauzer, I would've said she reeked of loneliness and despair. Something I hadn't caught at all on that first visit. And obviously the woman needed a listening ear. "Who doesn't call, ma'am?"

"My son. Went away to college and hasn't looked back. Never mind." She blew her nose on a ratty Kleenex. "I know I'm a fright. Thank you for returning the phone."

"Mrs. Smith?" I sniffed the char-scented air. "Do you have something burning in the oven?"

With a curse that cracked like lightning, Mrs. Smith bolted into the house. "The cookies!"

I wasn't sure what to do with myself. Walking off seemed kind of rude. Stepping inside uninvited was an intrusion. I called to her from the doorway. "Is everything okay in there?"

Any answer she had was muffled by the scream of a fire alarm wailing its angry protest. "Can't . . . get—" The alarm was loud enough to rouse the dead in the next state. "—turned off!"

If flaming cookies were at stake, my help was obviously needed. I walked inside, following the smell of nuked chocolate chips. "Ma'am?"

"In here!"

I found her standing on a chair in the kitchen, banging on the alarm with a rolling pin.

"It won't stop!"

I threw open some windows and turned on her oven vent. Finding a tea towel, I ran it under the faucet, then handed it to her. "Hold this over the alarm."

Nose still dripping, eyes leaking tears, Mrs. Smith obeyed. "Darn thing's connected to our security system."

Three long, loud minutes passed before the house went blissfully silent. Except for the sound of Mrs. Smith's sniffles. She remained on her chair and surveyed her disaster of a kitchen. Mounds of flour covered the floor, and cracked eggs swam in bowls on the granite counter. Five empty chocolate chip bags lay on a pile of dishes that ran from one end of the kitchen to the other. Days of plates, bowls, cups, and silverware stacked in tangled, crusty heaps.

"It's a mess." Mrs. Smith gingerly planted one foot on the floor, then two.

"I could help you clean it up," I offered.

"I meant my life."

It wasn't unusual to have people pour their hearts out to me. People trusted animal lovers. Mavis had a few regulars who came into the rescue not to see the dogs and cats, but to vent and spill their life's secrets to her, their substitute bartender.

Mrs. Smith walked to the stainless steel fridge and pulled out two Cokes. She handed one to me and settled onto a stool. "Cooper's been at Stanford three months, and do you know how many times he's called? Twice. Once he left a message, and the other time he wanted money." She popped the top on her can with nails that had long outgrown their French manicure. "I spent eighteen years being a mom. Twenty-four hours a day, that was my job. When that baby wouldn't sleep for a year because of the colic, did I complain? No, because I got a year of rocking my boy and two a.m. car rides, just the two of us. When he had to be in every sport ever created, and I went to each practice, each game, did I complain? No, I was the mom bringing cookies and brownies to share with the whole team. Wore my Wildcat hat and waved my foam finger like a raving fool. Chicken pox at six, mono at fifteen, his first broken heart last year. And do you know who was there through it all?"

"You."

"You bet I was." Her breath shuddered. "And I loved every minute of being Cooper's mother. I was born for it. I have an MBA I've never even used because he was my job. I was CEO of this home, and now?" Her splotchy throat bobbed as she downed her pop like whiskey. "Now I've got nothing. Just an empty house."

"You still have your husband, right?"

"He doesn't count"

Fair enough.

"I mean, he travels all the time. He's here on the weekends. He's the one who suggested I start volunteering." She picked up the skeleton of a cookie from the nearest pan and took a bite. "Those Ladies of Maple Grove are snots. Every one of them. And yoga? The only thing I'm enjoying about that is having an excuse to wear my fat pants."

"That always gives me a feeling of zen."

"That dog was going to be my new buddy. Oh, sure, I came in for something cute and pedigreed. That's what I thought I wanted, you know? I saw a few who were contenders. But I walked by Trudy, and our eyes met. And it's like I could hear her, you know? Like she was saying, 'I'm yours. I belong to you. Take me home.'"

I did know. It was what I heard in my own head every time I met a cat or dog. Every single one of them told me the same thing. It was why I worked so feverishly to find them homes. And because they all simply wouldn't fit in my bedroom.

"Why didn't you write that on your application? You could

have mentioned this when I did your home visit."

"I felt silly." Black crumbs dotted her upper lip. "Forty-five years old and having my heart stolen by a mutt."

"She prefers the term multicultural."

"I don't know what I'm supposed to do with all my new free time, but I don't want to do it alone. I thought the obedience classes would give us something to do, a way to spend time together. I saw myself walking her in the park, taking her downtown. Driving through the bank so she could get a dog treat in the drive-thru."

"Trudy loves to ride in the car."

"What made you reject my application?"

"It was a number of things. Everything was too perfect. I felt like I was walking through a museum instead of a home. You were a stay-at-home society mom who wore high heels on your day off and filled your every hour with things that wouldn't leave time for Trudy."

Mrs. Smith's chocolate-smeared hands cradled her sweating can of Coke. "That day you came was the first time my house had been clean since my son left. I'd spent the previous week not even getting out of bed."

I stood up, dusting crumbs off my butt, taking in the disheveled woman, the kitchen that looked like a bomb had turned it inside out, the heaps of laundry strewn in the hall, the two empty pizza boxes on the table, the empty donut bag on the floor. And I knew if I tuned in to just the right frequency, I would hear the sounds of a mother's heart breaking.

I loved Trudy. I absolutely adored her. But I didn't *need* her. Animals didn't just need homes where they could be loved; more than that, they needed homes where they could be the missing piece. Just like me and the O'Malleys.

"Mrs. Smith, Walnut Street Animal Rescue has reconsidered."

"You have?"

"Trudy will be waiting for you to pick her up tomorrow after ten."

Her puffy eyes blinked wide. "Really?"

"She's not a perfect dog, and she's not looking for a perfect house."

"I think I can manage a flaw or two." Mrs. Smith flicked a glob of butter from her arm.

"She's learning to play catch. Most times she won't bring it to you. But that's because she wants you to walk to her and get it. She has a weakness for hot dogs and you shouldn't feed her kibbles with chicken. She'll eat it to please you, but she doesn't like it. She snores when she sleeps, and barks when she gets excited. Trudy scares easily, and she just needs love and patience. Because even though she cowers a lot now, there's a good, strong dog in there who just needs a chance. She was treated horribly before. But she's ready to start over and be the dog she was meant to be." I smiled at the woman Mavis knew I'd misread. "I think you're going to make an excellent mom again."

Mrs. Smith's face at that moment was why I did what I did. For all the sad stories I had to endure, all the animal tales that didn't get a happy ending, there were these sweet times.

Trudy wasn't just getting a new home. She was resurrecting a life.

Chapter Thirty-Eight

"THIS IS THE dumbest idea you've ever talked me into."

"Relax and suck it in," Molly snapped. "I'm trying to zip you up."

My best friend and I occupied the largest bathroom stall in the girls' bathroom at the Washington High stadium. Outside were the sounds of cars parking, families walking by.

Inside I was trapped within the confines of a Wildcat mascot uniform that hadn't been washed since Bill Clinton was in office and Molly's clothes were in vogue. "This thing reeks."

"It's all that fur." She attached my right arm, held together by some serious Velcro. "Chaz says it makes him sweat like a sumo wrestler. Time for the kitty-cat head!"

"Give me just a few more minutes."

She held the bobble-like Wildcat head, her eyes droll. "That's what you said two minutes ago."

"I'm afraid of the dark."

"Don't worry." She slid the monstrosity over the top of me. "The stench will probably kill you first."

"I want to reconsider."

"No, I paid Chaz twenty bucks to call in sick tonight."

"It smells like he was sick *in here*."

"Did you say something, Harper? You have to speak through the hole in the Wildcat's belly button."

"I should've tried skywriting."

"Just breathe," Molly said. "Oh, and do that through the—"

"The Wildcat's left boob. I got it."

"Let's review the plan. You just clap and stuff like that with the cheerleaders. Then at halftime, Chaz says it's his job to grab the water bottles and help Sam Musteen bring them to the locker room during the pep talk."

"Since when?"

"Since the other water boy, Jasper Flicks, decided to use his Friday nights to join an all-girls Roller Derby."

"But he's a boy."

"Apparently he's ready to debate that point."

"Am I going to see butts in the locker room?"

"Only if you're lucky."

"Just hand me my paws and let's go."

The stall door creaked as Molly flung it open and gave me a little shove. "This way."

I promptly walked into the towel dispenser.

After snapping a few photos she didn't think I was aware of, Molly led me to the field, parking me right on the cheer line. She leaned into a space near my ear. "I've placed you between Desiree Paulsen and Sierra Towson. They're the worst ones on the squad, so anything you do will look like aces."

The buzzer flared, and the hometown crowd stood to their feet, erupting in cheers. The band threw themselves into the fight song, and I could see Andrew playing his horn. He really was first chair material.

Just not for me.

The team broke from the sidelines, and Ridley ran onto the field. My heart gave a little shimmy at the sight of him. Nobody wore the Washington jersey like him. And nobody played the game of football like him.

The first quarter yawned by. So far I had only received two complaints from the cheerleaders. During the second quarter, I upped my game and even went into the stands, ringing a stupid cowbell and pretending to roar at little kids. Only one of them cried.

With one minute 'til the half, the game was tied, and the crowd was lit like dynamite. Their football star had returned, and so had the Wildcats' chances of winning. The Newton Wombats had the ball, and the clock was blissfully ticking. Our fans got to their feet, anxiously watching for their boys to somehow turn it around. The Wombats stood on the twenty, ready to bring the ball to that sweet spot in the end zone. The play went into motion, and everyone moved. I cursed the blasted fur and one abnormally tall cheerleader for obscuring my sight. Where was Ridley?

The Wombats got closer.

And closer.

Their quarterback speared the ball to their man, who waited with open hands.

And our own number twenty-five, Peyton Billson, intercepted it instead. The stands erupted as the Wildcat offense quickly took the field.

I didn't know if I was woozy from the body-odor scented oxygen or from the game, but with seconds on the board, the quarterback spun and threw a Hail Mary.

Just as Ridley Estes leaped up, a ballet of motion. His body arced, his armed extended.

And angels sang as the ball flew into his hands.

"Go! Go!" I jumped up and down, wobbling just enough to knock into Sierra Towson, but bless her, she quickly got me vertical. "Go, Ridley!"

The announcer in the press box went nuts. "Number twenty-three, Ridley Estes, at the forty, at the thirty, twenty, ten, and . . . *touchdown!*"

I screamed like I had a skirt and pom-poms, doing happy skips with Desiree Paulsen. Fulfilling my duties as mascot, I ran the length of the infield, my hands lifted high toward the crowd.

And that's when I saw Phillip C. Miller.

Offensive coordinator for the USK Eagles.

He held a phone to his ear and scribbled notes on a pad.

But he was smiling.

And so was I.

"Chaz, are you going to help me with the water or not?"

Sam Musteen stomped by me, wheeling a cart with the water system. "Right."

It was go time.

This new desire to take some risks was going to be the end of me.

I grabbed the other cart and pushed my way down the sidelines. Right into the field house.

The locker room didn't smell much better than the inside of this cat getup. The guys drank water like they'd been rescued from a desert, and they grabbed cups from my paws like savages. I filled more cups while I searched for Ridley. My eyes finally locked on him, as he toweled the sweat from his forehead and stood next to his coach. Another player high-fived him, and I had to smile at the unfiltered joy on Ridley's face.

Coach Robbins gave a rousing pep talk, full of words my dad would've been proud of, like *winners, fight, hard work,* and *rip them apart.* The boys were high on win, and when Coach said all hands in, it took everything I could not to join them.

"Who are we?"

"Washington Wildcats!"

"Who's gonna win tonight?"

"Washington Wildcats!"

"Who's going all the way to state?"

"Washington Wildcats!"

They filed out, their cleats clacking like percussion. I pushed my water cart, trailing behind.

But stopped in the doorway.

Where Molly's seven-year-old brother stood, holding out a pen and a ball. "Ridley, gimme your autograph?"

Ridley laughed. "You like football?"

"Sure do." Her brother looked at me as Ridley handed back the newly signed ball. And winked. "Thanks, dude!"

"You bet, kid."

The team had already left him, and Ridley headed in that direction.

Until I called his name.

He turned. Looked at me. Shook his head, then walked out.

"No, wait!" I ran as fast as my bloated fur legs would let me. "Ridley, it's me! Harper!"

He froze. And when he turned around, he no longer wore that euphoric grin.

We stood in the small hall that led outside, and the sounds of the impending second half pressed against the doors. "I want to talk to you."

"What the crap are you wearing?"

"I can explain—my poor taste in tiger wear, the last few weeks. Everything."

"Harper, what is this?"

"I just wanted to talk to you." I lifted the Wildcat head from mine and gave my hair a shake. But it wouldn't budge, clinging to my face in wet chunks. "I've called, texted. I've stopped by your house, your job."

"You said what you had to say last week." His scowl was dark as the sky above the stadium lights. "And you were right—I did need a new tutor."

"No, you don't. You need me." He wouldn't even look at me. "I mean, I need you. I broke up with Andrew."

His head lowered. Was he giving this tidbit serious thought? Or just checking out my giant hairy feet?

"Harper, you made your choice. Now I have to go. As you might have noticed, I'm kind of in the middle of something."

"You still have two minutes. Please talk to me."

"Now's really not good."

"Then when?" My voice was shrill with desperation. "I have so much to tell you."

The eyes that stared back at me said he was done.

It was over.

"I'm all through listening." Ridley put on his helmet. "And you're too late."

Chapter Thirty-Nine

THE WASHINGTON WILDCATS won their game, advancing them to the next round of playoffs. I'd like to think it was because they had the most phenomenal mascot.

But really it was because of Ridley Estes.

The boy who, in the end, did break my heart.

I'd held out the ridiculous fantasy that my pleas had pierced Ridley's heart, and he would pick up his phone and call. Text. Throw a rock through my yonder window.

But none of those happened.

Saturday drifted by.

Sunday meandered after.

By Monday afternoon, I couldn't stand myself, couldn't tolerate my own moping. So I made a call and arranged for myself . . . a date. Mustering my courage, I'd picked the time, the place. And this time I brought the picnic.

At six o'clock, I settled onto a bench and watched the Christmas lights flicker and glow, bringing my beloved downtown to life. There was a nativity scene, Santa's workshop, the tree that stood in the center next to Betsy Callaghan and her horse Blue, the stars of an annual trimming ceremony. Carolers from schools, churches, and various organizations would take turns entertaining the citizens of Maple Grove in the coming weeks, bringing holiday cheer.

I hoped to find some myself by December twenty-fifth.

"I see you saved me a spot."

My date walked down the sidewalk, smiling as bright as the North Star.

I tightened my hold on Jay-Z's and Kanye's leashes and scooted over. "Brought hot chocolate for us. Biscuits for the dogs."

Angela Smith sat beside me, settling Trudy in her lap. "No biscuits for Trudy. We're both on a diet." She hugged her puppy to her. "Cooper has asked me to his fraternity's parent banquet, and I want to look svelte."

She already looked wonderful. Not one person would notice a few extra pounds when she shined like that.

"How's Trudy?" I scratched the dog under her slobbery chin, already knowing the answer.

"She's so great, Harper. And so smart, aren't you? Yes, you are. Oh, yes, you are!"

I poured us each a cup of steaming hot chocolate, then pulled out a can of whipped cream I had in my purse. If my mood didn't improve, I would just keep a constant supply in there. I sprayed some in my drink, then held it over hers. "Are you sure you won't indulge?"

She considered for merely a moment. "Oh, all right. Life's too short for the Maple Grove Ladies League *and* abstaining from whipped cream."

We clinked our Styrofoam cups in a toast, then sipped as we talked. We strolled with our happy dogs through downtown, marveling at the lights, the shop window displays, the coming of Christmas. By the time we ended up back at the bench, I had Angela Smith, society diva, signed up to work with me at the rescue. She talked of visiting her son, sending him more care packages. And making her husband take her and Trudy on a trip.

And I had talked of Ridley. Because Angela Smith knew about broken hearts.

"Good-bye, Harper." She pulled me in a hug, our coats mashing like pillows. "Thank you again for Trudy." She reached down and petted her new baby. "I promise I'll be the best home she could ever have."

"I know," I said. "Animals I understand. But sometimes it just takes me awhile to get a good read on people. See you guys next week?"

"We'll be here!"

The weathermen had talked of the possibility of an early December snow. And as I sat back down on the park bench, I felt the cold seep in, like a blizzard had already started within me.

"There's a game Friday," said a dark, beautiful voice. "And they're looking for a Wildcat."

I blinked once, twice, but my eyes still held the vision of Ridley walking my direction. He wore a black wool peacoat, a USK cap, and one adorable smile.

"Ridley." The dogs jumped as I stood, as if they had missed him too. "Down, boys."

And then Ridley was standing before me, his cheeks pink from the wind, and his eyes luminescent from the fairy lights above us. "Hello, O'Malley."

My gosh, I'd missed that face. "What are you doing here?"

He scratched Kanye behind the ear. "Went to your house, and Cole told me I'd find you here."

Thank God for brothers who butted into my business. "It's, um . . ." My mind filled with flowery adjectives I couldn't use. "Good to see you."

He dropped to one knee, giving the dogs hearty pats. "Faith told me that maybe I needed to hear you out."

"Faith. You mean like God?"

"Like my sister." Ridley stood to his full height, and the dogs watched him in rapt adoration. "It killed me to see you with Levin. I don't know why you thought he'd do it for you, but as long as he's your ideal, I have nothing to offer you."

"That's not true."

"You pretty much confirmed it yourself."

"I'm the daughter of a crazy woman. What do I know?"

"Look, Harper, I'm just here to thank you."

That didn't sound like a promising start to a total declaration of the heart.

"I know it was you who got Dwayne to drop the charges. My mom told me what happened. Said the Eagles went over and . . . talked to him."

"They're very sweet like that."

"So . . . thank you."

"Did you see the USK offensive coordinator was at the game?"

"Yeah, we've talked."

"And?"

"If I can keep a clean record, I'm back in the running. I'll know more in a few months."

I smiled. "Maybe I'll be around to see you play next fall."

He wore a heavy expression, one I couldn't quite read. "You said . . . you said you had something you wanted to talk to me about."

"I did," I sputtered. "I do."

Ridley sat down on the bench, a football king on his throne. "I'm listening."

Now that I had his attention, I didn't even know where to start. "I messed up. Badly. But I was scared."

"Of me?"

I nodded. "A little."

His brows dipped in a frown. "Why?"

"I had such a weird childhood." I was so sick of talking about it. But he had to understand. "My bio-mom liked to say I was afraid of my own shadow. And she was right. People scare me. Because . . . a long time ago they hurt me." I unzipped my coat, tossed it on the bench, and pushed up the sleeves of my sweater.

And for the first time, I showed someone my scars. A puckered canvas that covered both arms.

His curse came hot and fierce. "Harper—"

"I was ten. The courts decided to send me back to Becky. The first week was fine. She stayed home, she paid attention to me. Remembered to buy food. She'd even bought me a puppy. But by the second week, she started fading. I knew she was using again. On a Friday night, she locked me in my room. Promised me she'd be back in a few hours. It was just me and that dog."

"You don't have to do this."

"By Sunday she still wasn't back. I banged on the door, pounded on the windows. But neither would open. And nobody heard me. I still had some food. And my dog never left my side, curled right beside me. That evening a storm came through. Lightning struck the house, set it on fire." I could still smell the smoke, hear my own shrieks of desperation. "I knew nobody was coming for me." Thought Death had come to get me in the licks and hisses of flames. "I finally threw something into the window, broke it enough to crawl through. I had that puppy in my arms, but these ratty curtains ignited, fell on me."

Ridley stood and moved as if to reach for me, but I held up a hand, shook my head.

"I don't remember everything from that night. But when the fire department came, I was hanging out the window, my clothes on fire. They pulled me out. Got me to safety before the roof caved."

Ridley briefly closed his eyes. "I'm sorry, Harper. So sorry."

"I spent the next few weeks in the hospital. And the O'Malleys never left my side. So I finally got my family and a home full of people who loved me. But I have these scars. And though it's stupid, they shame me. I couldn't stand for anyone to see them. Because I hated the story they told. And nobody had the right to that part of me."

"But you're telling me now."

Because I wanted him to have this key. To understand. "I know I'm screwed up. I pray every night to wake up whole. I want so badly to be normal. But I can't ever forget what happened." I held out my battered arms, and my sleeves shimmied back down. "These scars are nothing compared to the ones I carry inside. And I know if anyone can get that, it's you. People hurt us. And we both fight to come out the other side— to be different people."

"You're nothing like your mom," Ridley said.

"But I am what she made me. Andrew was the first guy I'd liked. Do you have any idea what a milestone that was for me? That I felt ready to be in a relationship? I wanted to make that work so bad. He was safe, sweet. There wasn't one scary thing about him—except for how little I felt for him. He should've been perfect. But then I fell for you. What I felt for you . . . it was absolutely frightening."

"I never would've hurt you."

"There's nothing safe about what you do to me. What you make me feel is wild and unpredictable. It's so much bigger than me, and I didn't know what to do with it. These last six years, I've worked so hard to just stay in this protective cocoon I'd built. But I don't want safe anymore, not if it means losing you. You were right. Andrew does bore me. I chose him for all the wrong reasons." I stepped closer to Ridley, looked down into those deep brown eyes. "I chose him because I was afraid of what would happen if I let myself fall for you. You're so out of my league. You're beautiful and popular, and every girl wants to be with you."

"I don't want to be with every girl."

"But I thought eventually you would. You'd see that I'm the girl who sometimes sleeps with a night-light on. I cry when it storms. I'd rather read a book than go to a party. I listen to Bach and boy bands. I'm trumpet section leader. You're the football captain. I'm plain where you're—"

"Stop. Just stop it." He stood then, his hands on the arms that I had just shown him. "You think I don't know you by now? I get you, Harper. Your weird space issues, your compulsive animal smuggling, your difficulty letting people in. And you were the one I wanted. I let you in my life, showed you every piece of me I'd never shared with anyone else. But when I told you how I felt, you walked away."

The bitter wind seeped right through me. "I'm sorry."

"You're not the only one with trust issues here."

"I know I hurt you. And you can walk away. But Ridley Estes, I'm crazy for *you*."

"A few days ago it was Andrew."

"It would've been convenient if I had meant it." I could not let this boy slip away. "You are the one I've fallen for. I can do this relationship. I could be the best girlfriend you've never had. And do you know why?"

He stared, waited.

"Because I've had the very best teacher." Fear fell like snow, but I pushed it away. "Remember lesson number six?"

"No."

"I do. You said to give your guy compliments." I stepped close enough to smell his light cologne. "I love your voice, how it soothes me sometimes and makes my skin tingle at others. I love your hair, the way it's pitch-black until you get in the sun, then I can see the threads of red. Then there's your heart." Dear God, his heart. "The first time I saw you with Emmie, I think I fell a little bit in love. The man you are to your sisters says more about you than any of your stats or championship rings."

"I should probably get home to those sisters."

"Lesson number three. Never reject a girl's compliment. Because I haven't even gotten started on your smile. Did you know I would try to say something shocking just to see the dimples in your cheeks? It was like winning the lottery. I love how gentle you've always been with me, as if you knew how deep my damage was. You never made fun of me, never once laughed at me."

"Harper—"

"You still like me. I know you do."

"It's not that simple."

"You're the boy who braved a man with a shotgun to save my dog. The one who fixed an old lady's toilet so she'd be more likely to give up her schnauzer. The one who taught everything I know about surviving a date." I reached for his scarf, holding the ends in my gloved hands. "The first boy I truly kissed. The only boy I *let* kiss me."

"Part of our deal."

"It was more than that." His eyes were warming, and hope flared in my soul. "Lesson number nine. I believe that one was just be yourself. And that's exactly who I am with you. You'd seen almost all my ugly. And you still stuck with me."

"There's nothing ugly about you." Ridley tossed me my coat. And when I just held it, he plucked it from my hands. "You're beautiful." He lifted my left arm and pulled the sleeve over it. "From the moment you opened your front door to me that first day, I couldn't get you out of my system." He shoved on the other sleeve. "But you were right to run. Because I'm not safe like Andrew." I bit back a smile as he zipped up my coat. "I have no idea what my future looks like. I occasionally throw a punch here and there. I like my music to have words, and I help raise two little girls. You better decide right now if you can deal with that."

Yes. A million times yes. "It's always been you."

"You can walk away now, and I'll leave you alone. But you stay, Harper, and I'm not letting you go."

"I was hoping you'd say that." I framed his face with my hands, looking into the eyes of the boy who was never supposed to steal my heart. "Lesson number fifteen. Sometimes the girl has to take the initiative and kiss the boy."

"I don't recall that one."

"It's new."

"I like it." Smiling, I pulled his face to mine and kissed him with all that I had. And maybe fireworks didn't go off. But carolers did. Somewhere in the distance, an off-tune group sang "O Holy Night."

And indeed it was.

Ridley lifted his head, his eyes soft on mine. "Lesson number twelve. Don't go straight for the lips." He reached for my hand, gently pushing my coat sleeve up just enough to reveal the edge of the old wounds. "Harper . . . you can always trust me with your scars."

And as Ridley kissed the skin the flames had ravaged, I knew the places inside were going to heal. Because of him. Because of the love of the O'Malleys.

And because I had stopped believing the lies Fear had whispered in my ear.

I didn't know for sure what would happen with my parents. Heaven knew I still had some land mines from the past to detonate and dismantle. And I sure didn't know how to be a football star's girlfriend.

But lesson number twenty-one. I was enough. I was worthy.

I was wanted.

And I was right where I belonged.

"Let's go sing Christmas songs, Ridley Estes."

He hugged me tight. "I can't sing."

"Just another way we're perfectly matched."

Dear Reader, if you enjoyed this book, please consider leaving a review at your online retailer. It helps *so* much. Unless this is the worst thing you've ever read. Then . . . forget we had this talk. ;)

About the Author

Award-winning, best-selling author Jenny B. Jones writes YA and women's romance with sass and Southern charm. Since she has very little free time, Jenny believes in spending her spare hours in meaningful, intellectual pursuits, such as eating ice cream, watching puppy videos, and reading celebrity gossip. She lives in the beautiful state of Arkansas and has worked in public education for half of forever. She loves the sound of bluegrass, loves a good laugh, and loves to hear from readers.

For information contact:
Jen@jennybjones.com

Follow Jenny on Facebook:
facebook.com/jennybjones

Follow Jenny on Twitter:
twitter.com/JenBJones

Sign up for Jenny's Book News
www.jennybjones.com/news

Dedicated to Julie Jones

To a funny, sweet, beautiful, smart girl who makes all those around you smile. And you have the awesomest older sister. *wink*

Acknowledgments

To the Boys of Fall, circa 1993, especially the helpful friends who walked down memory lane to help me out with some football information. Thank you Ben Baugh, Erick Harp, and Chris Snow. May you always look on the Concussion Years fondly. They were some of the best days.

Thank you Jason Epps for Epps Sports Consulting Services. You didn't roll your eyes one time at my dumb questions. My people will call your people to get that payment check to you.

Jessica Epps, thank you for answering all my questions. All 100 of them. Okay, 1000. So appreciate your encouragement and friendship.

Christa Allan, thank you for being you. For letting me vent and for always giving me comma advice.

Bentley Fisher, for being one of my nearest and dearest friends, for making me laugh, for Kettle Corn and Dr. Pepper. May you finally find the perfect pair of running shoes. Before you Catch and Release them. Again.

The Real Principal Sparacino, who is a great human being and nothing like his namesake in this book, thank you for being pro-kid, pro-teacher/librarian, and pro-Google.

Rel Mollet, friend and author advocate, thank you for your encouragement, your cheerleading, and for those eagle eyes on my manuscript. Have I told you that you're awesome?

Jocelyn Bailey, thank you for giving me time (um, years) to work out all the story kinks. I so appreciate your friendship, your editing, and all your help. Thanks for making the story better.

We'll always have Lionel.

Thank you to my mom for being my friend and for having the good grace to never come right out and say, "You're my favorite child." Even though we both know I am.

Praise and adoration to my hero, Carol Burnett. This wide-eyed gal met you in a steak house on Staten Island in 2015, and for the first time ever, I was rendered speechless. You will never know the impact you had on that little girl who grew up watching you. I'm so glad we had this time together.

A shout of thanks to God for all things. Except Writer's Butt. Feel free to take *that* blessing back.

Finally, a giant hug to all my readers. Thank you for the privilege of stepping into your world and sharing my little books. You have changed my life.

Other Books by Jenny B. Jones

In Between

On the Loose

The Big Picture

Can't Let You Go

A Sugar Creek Christmas

Wild Heart Summer

A Charmed Life Series

Made in the USA
San Bernardino, CA
08 December 2016